Go Steelers !

Collisions

J. McLain Callahan

Ryan and Heather.
Congratulations on
your daughter. I hope all
is treating you great in Atlanta.
J.M. Callen

This book is dedicated to Katie, McKinley, and Hudson Callahan, the best family a man could ask for.

And to Richard Bagnal, who was a great friend with a giant heart.

ACKNOWLEDGMENTS

I would not have ever been able to complete this book without the help of some very important people in my life. My parents, Rence and Barbara Callahan were extremely helpful throughout the process. Even though Teddy Stille was thousands of miles away in Alaska, he was a huge help as an editor and a good friend, and I am forever indebted to him for his help. My sister, Lawren Desai, spent hour upon hour of her busy schedule helping me with the editing of the book, and I also owe her immensely.

I would like to thank Sabrina Thiel and Emily Elrod for their help with the cover. I would also like to thank Jennifer Handy, Graham Lyles, Tyler Collins, and Joy Van Zandt.

I first heard about the story of Vitaly Kaloyev from the song *Ballad of Vitaly* by one of my favorite bands, Delta Spirit. Everything in this book is completely fictional.

CONTENTS

Blinded by love and the pain of his loss

-Delta Spirit

Posted: April 10, 2009, 9:17 am

Carmen Paul/Williamsburg Daily Express

Williamsburg, VA - A mid-air collision between two aircraft has been reported above the small coastal town of Vitaly, Virginia. Debris from the collision has been reported outside of the wooded area of the closed Campioni Chocolate Factory. Specifics of the crash remain unknown, as does information on survivors.

Calls to airports in Virginia Beach and Richmond remain unanswered. The Vitaly Sheriff's Department and the National Transportation Safety Board (NTSB) released statements that they are investigating matters and will release more specific details as more information becomes available.

Part I – April 09 - 10, 2009

Newton's First Law of Motion:

An object at rest shall stay at rest, unless acted upon.

Chapter 1

Murphy Kearns

"We get to see you tomorrow, Daddy!" Isabella and Patrick loudly shouted into their computer screen. Isabella was wearing a Dora t-shirt, her favorite character that month. The month before it was Barney, and Murph was thrilled that the purple dino's days were over. After about ten minutes with that obnoxiously friendly dinosaur, he felt like pulling his hair out despite the apparent joy it brought Isabella. "I can't wait. I have a surprise for both of you," Murph responded. It was hard to tell who was more excited.

"That's great," Maria quickly added. "I hope you didn't go over the top this time." Murph's constant need to get the kids surprise gifts had always been a bone of contention, one of the few that the couple had. Sometimes when Murph was out, and saw something he thought that either Isabella or Patrick would love, he just got it for them without a thought. All impulse, and the impulses were strong,

Collisions

Murph suspected his condition must be some sort of disease fathers contract when in contact with kids as great as his. Maria managed the checking account for the family; she was a very structured family accountant, putting their money into groups on an Excel sheet. She made a separate group for Murph's sudden toy buying impulses titled "Murphy's Over-the-Top and Ridiculous Gift Fund." He was budgeted twenty-five dollars a month at that point, but this gift would put him way over for the next couple of months.

"Don't worry honey, I got you a great gift this time, too," Murph said. Though she tried to hide it, Murph did catch a little grin from Maria, while the kids clapped on his computer screen.

"I have to run; we have a lot to do today before the kids at school head off for spring break. I'm sure my class is going to be even more wound up than usual," said Maria. It seemed like school systems were taking more and more vacations every year, and Maria's worst days were always those right before a holiday break. It felt like one's pleasure often resulted in another's pain.

"Okay, sounds good. Behave yourselves with Ms. Linker today, kids. I can't wait to see you all tomorrow at the airport," he responded.

Maria and Murph made it a point to Skype once in the morning and once at night before the kids went to bed. That morning the kids were more excited than ever to talk to him.

The flight from Pittsburgh to Norfolk was going to be Isabella and Patrick's first flight. The original plan was to drive, but Maria found a last-minute, cheap flight on some obscure internet site two weeks before spring break began. She went with the lesser of two evils: a trip through the airport for an hour and a half flight as opposed to a seven hour car ride stretched by constant rest stops. Murph offered to fly up and ride down with them, but it would have meant postponing the trip by two days while he finished out the work week. Maria didn't have any luck finding cheaper flights that direction, and they were ready to see each other. Murph felt like a kid on Christmas Eve as he waited for his family.

"Daddy, give Rooney a big kiss for me, and I love you," said Isabella. Murph and Isabella were inseparable when they were together, and his absence had been very trying for her. Part of the reason he went out solo with Kearns Design was to have his own schedule, where he could spend more time with both the kids. So far, that plan had backfired. He hoped that once he got more established he would be able to hire some associates that he could send out on jobs like the one he was working on in Duck. Murph's goal was to be a father who was at every recital and sporting event for his kids, ate lunch with them once a week, and was always there to tuck them in at night. Both Maria and Murph were lucky enough to have dads like that growing up, and setting his own schedule would make that much more plausible.

"I will give him a big, fat, wet smooch right on the lips!" Murph told Isabella.

"EWWWW," she squealed with delight.

"I love you all, and can't wait to see you tomorrow!" Murph said with a huge smile on his face.

"Love you, too!" the three chorused back.

When Murphy Kearns signed on to take the Duck Beach Club Resort job in the Outer Banks of North Carolina, his young family knew that it would be challenging for him to be gone from them for at least three months, the anticipated length of the project. This was something Murph was dreading, but that he knew had to be done. The benefits of this contract for his brand new landscape architecture firm were too great to pass up. Although it was great to set his own work schedule and have free reign over the project, he was trying his hardest to get the job done as fast as possible so he could get back to Pittsburgh, his normal routine, and his family.

Leaving a job with a large and established landscape firm like Collins and Associates in Pittsburgh was a big gamble for his family. His wife wanted him to go for it, but Murph had his reservations. Isabella was just four and Patrick two, they still owed money to the University of Pittsburgh for both Maria's and Murph's undergraduate educations, and they were in debt to the University of Pennsylvania for Murph's graduate school in landscape architecture. Murph wasn't afraid of risk, and Maria's support had always been enabling for him.

When Murph decided to branch out on his own, he knew that Maria would have to go to work. She graduated from Pitt with an elementary education degree, but since the two had Isabella right out of school, Maria stayed at home with her and wasn't able to use her degree. Murph believed that there was no harder job in the world than a stay-at-home mom, but it just happened to also be the most rewarding. This was her first year teaching fourth grade at Carnegie Mellon Elementary in their Squirrel Hill neighborhood. As much as she loved being at home with the kids, Murph knew it was a dream Maria had been itching to start anyway. Other than a few overbearing parents, she had thoroughly enjoyed her first year in the classroom. Murph guessed that they both agreed that there were worse things than parents who care too much. He knew that Maria missed being with their kids all the time, but he also realized that she was meant to teach.

He could see it in her eyes, and her dedication and love of kids was just one of the countless qualities he loved about her.

They worked out a good deal with their neighbor, Ms. Linker. This proved to be better than any nanny or daycare that they could find. Plus Isabella and Patrick got to stay at their own house with Ms. Linker, and Maria still had long holidays and summer vacations with the kids. Isabella would get to go to Carnegie Mellon Elementary the following year, an added benefit since it was hands-down a better school than the school the kids were districted for. That alone made Maria going back to work more than worthwhile.

Even Murph was on his best behavior around Ms. Linker. He wasn't even sure that she had a first name, at least not one he ever heard used. Murph knew that she meant well, and the kids were very attached to her. He thought that if you could take off thirty pounds and shrink Robin Williams to 4'5", then Ms. Doubtfire would pass as a sister to Ms. Linker. Her strict manner was amusing, and she had done a great job helping teach Maria and Murph some key behavior management techniques that they didn't know as relatively new parents. Since Isabella and Patrick couldn't have their mom at home, they should have Ms. Linker.

For a little over two months, Murph had been in Kitty Hawk, a short drive from the job site, in a one bedroom house he rented six houses back from the beach. The one-story house was pretty small, just a little over 600 square feet. It was a typical old-fashioned Outer Banks grey house from the beach house boom of the sixties and seventies. The new, overly expansive and ridiculously big houses that were sprouting up all around Nags Head, Kitty Hawk, and Duck were taking away from the rustic and quaint feel of an area that had been entirely houses like the one Murph rented.

Collisions

Getting away from the big city life of Pittsburgh and being able to breath in the ocean air everyday helped offset some of the stress of being away from his little clan.

Like most construction and landscape projects, it looked like the job would go well over the planned three months, which Maria and Murph anticipated but still hoped against. Pete Mitchell made his millions by creating a website that offered free condoms in the mid to late nineties during the internet boom. He figured out early that what you were selling didn't matter; it was the advertising hits from a novelty site like his that would "bring in the big dough," as Pete would say. Murph was suspicious that Pete was trying to provide a public health service, too, though he'd never admit to it. Pete wanted whoever he hired as the landscape architect for the Duck Beach Club Resort to agree to live in Duck throughout the landscaping phase of the resort. There weren't that many landscaping firms east of Raleigh, so he had to expand his search to the big cities of the Carolinas and eastern Virginia, and beyond, when he was not satisfied with the applicants he had found so far. Murph believed he beat out many more well-known landscape architects for the Duck project when he said he was willing to live in the Outer Banks.

Pete was a very friendly guy in his early fifties. He went out to surf every morning, though Murph was not sure he ever caught any of the Outer Banks so-called heavy waves. He always bought the best boards and wetsuit gear and still wore a pony tail even at his age and even though his hair was graying. Murph believed that Pete single-handedly kept some of the local independent surf shops open with his purchases. Pete was divorced, and Murph met three of his girlfriends at the time who were all at least twenty years Pete's junior. Most of the girls acted like they had smoked a little too much marijuana and Murph was sure some of that had been with

Pete. He was a little too flexible with Coastal North Carolina Construction Company, a local builder, on their timeline for construction of the resort, and he didn't seem too concerned with deadlines. Coastal Construction was probably familiar and happy to abide by Pete's "take her easy" reputation.

Murph was convinced that the resort was as much for Pete as it was for anybody else to enjoy. Pete seemed to have a very big heart though, and Murph could only imagine how much he would appreciate looking out the window of his office down at the people enjoying it. Pete really didn't have to work too hard for all of his money; his fortune was already secure. In his design with the architects, he wanted his office connected to the main building of the resort, but he asked for it to look like a lifeguard stand, so that was what he got. It was the first part of the project scheduled to go up.

Pete was a conference champion tennis player at the University of North Carolina at Wilmington, where he claimed to "major in surfing with a minor in babes." The resort would have ten championship level hard courts, five grass courts, and five clay courts. Murph wasn't sure who would use the courts on a daily basis, but Pete wanted it to be a great location for youth and senior tennis tournaments in the area.

There was also a surf school and an eighteen-hole golf course planned for the resort. The massive outdoor swimming pool would feature an area where small waves were created so beginning surfers could practice the basics. Pete brought in three PGA players to help with the design of the course. They basically just enjoyed the beach, while Murph worked hard on the plans. The golfers would come in at the end of the day and change up a hole location or add a bunker, but really nothing more.

Pete was very good with kids. Murph had seen him down on the beach with the local kids who followed him like he was the Pied Piper. Pete had six grandkids of his own spread out all over the country, and he didn't get to see them more than once or twice a year. When he did have them around, it was all Sweet Pete, all day. He knew what kids would want to spend their time doing at the resort. Pete wanted there to be a miniature amusement park with go-karts, mini-golf, a carousel, and giant water slides. The resort would hold 300 guests at full capacity. In the future, Pete hoped to add a small movie theater, via the early cinemas, and three additional restaurants to the one that was already planned. Maria and Murph were not big resort goers, but the plans for this one were phenomenal, and Murph was sure his family would plan to use it some, especially with the Pete connection. Murph and Maria had tossed around the idea, if they were ever able to earn that kind of money, to buy a small rustic beach house in an older section of the Outer Banks. Pete's would be one of the few resorts in the area, but he was at least doing it the right way, Murph believed.

When Pete hired Murph, he sent him a very simple email. Six words, grammatically incorrect and pure Pete:

Murph,
Your hired, dude.
Sweet Pete

Pete and Murph met two times on interviews. One interview was in person and one was on the phone. Murph felt that at one point in his phone spiel, Pete actually might have drifted off. At the time, Murph worried that he was that boring, but after getting to know Pete, he realized Pete could have cared less what was said in that interview. Pete obviously felt comfortable enough with Murph after their two conversations to call him "dude." Murph was fairly certain that Pete called everybody he liked "dude," and he told Murph a couple times that he had always been a good judge of character. Pete never used the words, but Murph wouldn't have been surprised to hear words like "aura" and "karma" in Pete's description of a good friend or a good employee.

Victor Dancy

Every day Victor Dancy rode to his god-awful job while he sat in god-awful traffic, and he thought about how much his life sucked. He had a wife whom he didn't love and an annoying daughter who nagged the shit out of him. He believed he was a disappointment to his high and almighty father, whom he had never been able to please. He swung between anger at his perceived circumstances and just not giving a shit.

The only enjoyable thing on today's forty-five minute commute from hell was that he hit a squirrel pulling out of the street in front of his house. Two great things about hitting that long-tailed, grey rodent were that he put the sucker out of its miserable life, and it made his five-year-old daughter cry. Maddie gave Victor a headache every morning. He hated how she always needed something. She always wanted Leah or Victor to help with something, anything, everything. It gave him great satisfaction to upset her back. Yes, he could have very easily slowed down. Yes, he could have swerved or stopped to miss the squirrel. And, yes, feeling that little bump under his front-left wheel gave him great pleasure. Then looking in the rear-view mirror and seeing the tears flow from Maddie's eyes, because she knew what happened, intensified that pleasure.

Every Monday through Friday, Victor took Maddie to school, dropped her off in the ever-lasting line in front of the ugly, monotonous brick building with the slow, old lady crossing guard taking her sweet time. The old biddy in her funny hat and piss yellow jacket with the awkward stop sign needed to say good morning and have a brief chat with every car that drove through, while all the other cars sat behind and waited. Murph got a nice scowl from her every time he passed. The scowl was returned with Victor's middle finger. The second day of school that year, they exchanged pleasantries.

Victor pulled up to her, after a particularly long and slow drop-off, rolled down his window and said, "Listen here granny, I know you have nothing better to do than to go sit on your wrinkled ass and read the paper while waiting to do your sorry job again this afternoon. Then you will go home, watch reality television or soap operas and eat some more fat pills with what I can only guess is a piece of shit husband, before you come back and do your sorry job again tomorrow. Important people around here, people like me, have places to go, so hurry the hell up!"

She replied by staring at him with her mouth wide open. Victor could not stand how small and wrinkly it was.

"Spit it out old lady," he said. She remained quiet. "That's right you have nothing to say. Don't worry, there is nothing you can say to anybody about this, so don't try to go to your superiors about me. They will just laugh in your face. What the hell are they going to do for you?"

She had no response, and he drove off. She tried to avoid eye contact with Victor's car, but after that run-in, if she caused drop-off to slow, he made sure to roll down the window and say something after Maddie got out of the car.

• • •

Victor and Leah truly despised each other; it was as simple as that. He screwed up and got her pregnant, and he knew he was stuck with her. There was no way that his Catholic and devout father was going to let him knock a woman up out of wedlock. So he made sure that he rushed to marry her before anybody found out. Victor Dancy Sr., Victor's dad, was a retired General in the Air Force, who went on to have a successful career as a Federal Aviation Administration consultant, where he made an abundant amount of money, and an even larger number of important friends. To Victor, his father was "Colonel" or "Colonel Dancy," even after he had been promoted to General, at first out of respect, then out of awe and fear, and then as a euphemism for something else as he became "Colonel Vic" and then "Colonel Dick" or just "The Colonel" when his dad wasn't around. The Colonel always referred to his son as "son." It was just the way they thought about each other. Victor felt he was a failure in his father's eyes and that he had always been one, but at least The Colonel's money tap was still open.

Victor wished The Colonel would go ahead and die so he could then get a quickie divorce from Leah and use the money for himself. He sure as hell was tired enough seeing his father throw it away on Leah and Maddie on mini-vans, pool and country club memberships, and vacations to California, Disney World, or wherever else he sent them. Victor was sure The Colonel never did anything like that for him, but he must have been trying to make up for it with his grandchild. Of course, the old man and Leah had a great relationship, and he loved his granddaughter.

Pulling into work at the Williamsburg Regional Airport, Victor realized again how much he disliked working there. Work as an air traffic controller was typically supposed to be pretty stressful for most people in the occupation. Victor made sure to never work at an airport in a big city like New York or Boston or even Norfolk once he got the job. They settled close enough to his father, in eastern Virginia, that he could still quickly tap into his fortune, but far enough that they didn't have to see him too often.

Victor was guaranteed to get a job pretty much wherever he wanted to with his father's connections, so they settled in at WRA. They had some flights there for the wealthy businessmen who had their own planes or liked to charter them, and the airport was also a hub for the United States Couriers, a postal service that competed with other courier services behind UPS, DHL, and FedEx. All in all it was a pretty low-key job.

The average salary for an air traffic controller in the United States at the time was over one hundred thousand dollars. Predominately, controllers who received six-digit salaries in his position manned sites in the stressful, big-city towers where flights came and went every minute in large waves. Controllers working in airports like Victor worked in were typically paid at a much lower salary. They didn't have nearly the same volume of flights as bigger airports, and workers at WRA didn't have to worry about overtime. Victor's supervisors were frequently frustrated by performance reports that honestly reflected his lackadaisical attitude and disdain for authority, but were revised after being submitted to reflect The Colonel's influence farther up the chain amongst his FAA cronies. To his coworkers' irritation, Victor's pay grade was an anomaly at the small airport.

The main reason Victor disliked his job was because it was a boring waste of time, and he worked with a bunch of dipshits who smelled funny and talked too much. Victor knew that he always sounded like he was pissed at the world, which was true. He didn't think he was always like that. When Victor was young he had a very good relationship with his grandfather, who was also in the Air Force. His grandfather just wasn't a serious jackass about it like his father was.

George Dancy was a Private in the Army Air Corp in France during World War II and then the Air Force in Korea. He came back and became a small-town car salesman until he retired. He smoked a pack of cigarettes and a quality cigar per day, and Victor knew he was coming into the room by the ashtray odor that encircled him. Every time Victor got to see Papa George, his grandfather made him laugh. He would spend time playing and joking with him, which The Colonel never did.

When Victor was six, he could clearly recollect Papa George calling Victor up to his room to watch his favorite show of all time, *The Pink Panther*. Not the cartoon, but the real one starring David Niven. He remembered his grandfather lying in his bed with his bushy grey eyebrows and his slicked back comb-over of dirty gray hair. The Colonel received the unfortunate eye-brows from Papa George. They looked like a wooly caterpillar sleeping above his eyelids. Victor inherited them as well, but he always made sure to get them trimmed to avoid the embarrassment. Somehow Victor felt the eyebrows looked right on Papa George, though. They were watching the small television from Papa George's king-sized bed, when the Pink Panther jumped on a suspect he was chasing. The next commercial break, Victor jumped on the bed and landed on Papa George's stomach.

"Be careful, sonny!" he exclaimed.

"Why?"

"I was shot four times in my stomach right where you just landed. Take a looksee here." He unbuttoned his pajama

17

shirt and showed Victor four marks under the dark gray hair on his rotund stomach.

"Wow, Papa, how did you get those?"

"Well it was a long, long time ago when I was fighting in France in 1944. I went into an abandoned hotel because I heard yelling after a gruesome battle we had just finished with the Nazis."

"Who are the nat-zees?" Victor responded.

"Those damn Germans who were led by a no-good, dirty scoundrel named Adolph Hitler. Anyways, I was walking up the rickety stairs with my medic bag, when all of a sudden this Nazi came running out of a door and knocked me over, and we both went tumbling back down the stairs. The lucky son of a gun landed on top of me. We both pulled for our weapons; he grabbed his Luger, and I grabbed my knife." The bed squeaked as Victor followed Private Dancy up the stairs and battled the German soldier.

"What's a Luger?"

"It is a gun the Krauts used. Well, we battled some more and that son of a bitch shot me four times real quick in the belly. Pop, pop, pop, pop!" Papa George pantomimed the gun shots and then clutched his belly in bed.

"What's a bitch?"

"Son, you sure do ask a lot of questions. So most people would have keeled over and died right there, but not your Papa George."

"What did you do?"

"That Kraut looked at me with this big grin on his ugly mug. He got up to start leaving because he was thinking he got the best of me. When he turned, I kicked out his feet just like this." Papa George showed Victor his swiping leg action in bed, "I quickly crawled over to him and stabbed him right in the back of his Kraut head."

"No way, Papa!"

"Yes, sir. I even have the knife to prove it to you." Papa George went over to his closet and pulled out a seven-inch military trench knife. It had his initials "G.A.D." carved on the handle, and was made by Ames Sword Company of New London, Ohio. "All of my mates looked in awe at me as I stumbled out of the building with blood everywhere and said I must have a stomach made of iron to survive four bullet wounds. I didn't argue with them." Papa George said as he showed the knife to his grandson. "If you look real close, you can still see some blood marks here."

Many years later, Victor's father, never one for understatement, told him that Papa George's legend was "complete bullshit." The marks Victor saw on his grandfather's stomach were scars from the very bad case of measles he had when he was a child. The Colonel also told him that the Purple Heart that his grandfather gave him was also a fraud. Apparently, Papa George went out and got drunk on French wine when he was still in France after VE Day, in May of 1945. He was stumbling home wasted, and walked out in the middle of the road. A military ambulance struck him and he fell and broke his arm. The Army didn't know what to do, but since Papa George was technically injured by their vehicle, they felt that he deserved the medal.

Once again, Victor's dad ruined something that meant a lot to him. Papa George died of terminal cancer less than a year after he told Victor that story. There was a good chance that he had the cancer that day in his bedroom.

Victor still had the Purple Heart, and he kept the knife along with a pistol with him almost all of the time. He was a proud member of the National Rifle Association and believer in the Second Amendment. Sometimes he wished somebody would just try to jump him in a back alley. Unfortunately, Victor had to leave both of his weapons in the car when he got to work at WRA. He still hated his dad for ruining the legend that Papa George told him, but The Colonel couldn't take the brass attitude or hardware that Papa George had passed on.

Chapter 2

Murphy Kearns

When it was settled that Murph was going to the Outer Banks, the family decided it would be an excellent idea for Rooney to go with Murph as a companion, so he at least had one family member with him. It was actually Isabella's idea, but he had to admit it would be a great link to the family back in Pittsburgh for him to have the big guy along.

A 135 pound, Newfoundland, Rooney, named after the family who owned the Pittsburgh Steelers, was a special kind of beast and not your standard household pet. Newfoundlands were typically classified as working dogs, but Rooney didn't do much work for the most part. His work consisted of shedding, a daily walk, sleeping, shedding, two rather large meals, sleeping, tearing up slippers and remote controls, sleeping, and passing some of the worst-smelling gas in world history. The best part of his constant and death-defying gas was that he always looked around as if to ask "where did that sound and smell come from?" sometimes even in the middle of a nap. He was very loyal to the family though, and he did a pretty good job of barking at strangers when needed. Murph thought that with Rooney's size and daunting bark no intruder would dare try to enter their house.

Newfoundlands, including Rooney, were gentle giants. Isabella and Patrick used Rooney as their personal riding donkey, punching bag, and pillow, and he went right along with all of their antics. The breed was meant for the cold weather, but Rooney didn't seem to mind the beach one bit. Murph really enjoyed Rooney's unique style of swimming, which seemed a lot like the breast-stroke. Murph tried to take him to the beach a couple times a week. For a dog as large as he was, he was amazingly graceful in the water. Watching him swim made Murph think a sumo wrestler might just be able to compete as a synchronized swimmer. Rooney liked Murph to throw a tennis ball up over the waves, which he plowed through like Jerome "The Bus" Bettis, ramming through the defense of the Baltimore Ravens. Then he rode back to Murph with all the style his trip out lacked. For a minute he looked to be under the wave, but then his considerable head popped right through with the ball and his tongue sticking out as he gracefully rode the wave to shore. Even Pete recognized a kindred spirit when he saw one. The first time Sweet Pete witnessed Rooney's skills he stopped and said in awe, "Duuuuude." Inevitably he would come back in and shake off a monsoon on Murph. Going with Rooney to the beach felt to Murph what it might be like to date a celebrity. Everybody came over to see him, ask what his breed was and get a good wet pet in.

Maria and Murph both agreed Rooney was the deal-maker in their courtship. Murph first met Rooney in a very peculiar circumstance. Nothing about Rooney was subtle, and his entrance into their relationship was no exception. Murph and Maria had been dating for two years and riding out a long-distance romance one tank of gas at a time. Murph was in grad school in Philly and commuting almost every weekend on the turnpike for five hours each direction. Maria was finishing up her last semester at Pitt. For a reason Murph could not remember, Murph did not pull out of Philly until after 9:00 pm on the Friday night Rooney landed in their lives.

After two bathroom breaks and a Wendy's grilled chicken run, it was past midnight as Murph drove over the hills just north of the Cumberland Gap. Maria would call every hour to check on him, and he flipped back and forth between whatever talk-radio he could find and a collection of Kings of Leon, the old, good stuff, and Pearl Jam to try to stay awake. Murph was on about his third Diet Coke. After countless trips on a monotonous drive he had almost memorized, any distraction was good.

Sometimes when you drive alone and it's late, you get lost in your thoughts, though still paying attention to the road. The trip becomes an endless blur of those thoughts, and you can't remember much of the driving portions afterwards. Murph's thoughts were on whether Wendy's or McDonald's had better fries. Should he go with the thin and crispy of Mickey D's or the thick and soft of Wendy's? Murph was somewhere between weighing where he wanted to stop to eat, when he began a long ascent up the side of a small mountain. The speed limit was sixty-five, and the cruise control was set at about seventy on the rather empty highway. Just before the climb, Murph passed a tractor-trailer that was carrying bricks and going just about the speed limit.

About a quarter mile up the mountain, he closed in on a large white pick-up truck with extra-large wheels, definitely not street legal. The truck was driving in the left lane and going a little slower than Murph. It did not appear that the driver was going to get over, and he was just going to stay in the left lane and drive at his own leisure. Murph was about to pass in the right lane, when what looked like a bear stuck its head up in the back of the truck-bed.

The rest unfolded very quickly. The bear stood up and did a couple of circles in the back of the truck in what seemed like an effort to get comfortable. Murph swore the bear proceeded to look back at him, stick his head over the bed of the truck, look down at the road, and then back at him to say "Dare me?"

He remembered thinking, "What the hell is that thing going to do?"

The bear stuck its two front legs over the back of the truck, looked down, and in one brief instant leapt over the back. Luckily, it did not roll or land on its head, but it slid on its belly into the right lane in what seemed to be slow motion. All that was missing was the NFL broadcaster breaking down the replay.

Murph quickly swerved into the grass median, and the white pick-up continued on its merry way up the mountain. He put his Jeep into park and jumped out. Quickly coming up the right lane was the tractor trailer he passed a couple miles earlier. Murph booked it across the lane, grabbed the shocked animal by the furry neck and pulled it as fast as a human could pull dead-weight to the side of the highway. Once he got over to the side, just in time to miss the honking truck, he realized that this was no bear but a very bulky and furry dog. The dog was panting and seemed confused. Murph felt under the endless fur on his belly and chest, and there was some blood on his hand when he pulled it back. Other than those scrapes, amazingly the dog didn't seem to be too badly hurt. Instant replay always makes it look worse than it is.

Murph called Maria right away and tried to describe the unlikely incident to her.

"What do you mean a big dog jumped out of a truck?" was all that Maria got from his story.

"I mean," Murph tried to slow his breathing, "I mean that a humongous and hairy dog jumped out of a truck going about seventy, somewhere in the middle of Pennsylvania."

"And it's ok?"

"As far as I can tell, it just seems to be out of it. I'm a little bit worried that it might have some internal injuries though, but I'm no vet."

Maria said, "Well, what are you going to do now?"

"I'm going to wait for the jackass who was driving the truck to get back, and then I am going to punch him in the face for putting a dog in the back of his pickup truck while going seventy on the highway." Maria's voice could only bring so much calm, when Murphy was fired up, which he clearly was.

Unfortunately, Murph never did get the chance to punch that driver in his face. His anger abated with the wonder of having that big goofy dog trying to sit in his lap and lick his face while Murph drove. After waiting for close to an hour for the truck, he texted a simple message to Maria that said, "Make room because I am bringing home a bear."

The next morning they took the dog to a local emergency vet. He gave him a check-up, bandaged his sores, and told them the dog was surprisingly fine after the fall and slide from the speedy truck. The vet estimated that the dog was around two-years-old and was a full-bred Newfoundland.

Collisions

Murph and Maria decided to keep him, even though he really didn't fit in their tiny apartment, and he ate more than a bear.

Within a couple days of coming home with Rooney, Murph read as many books as he could about the breed to see about dietary, grooming, and medical needs. He came across a quote from Henry David Thoreau in *Walden*: "A man is not a good man to me because he will feed me if I should be starving, or warm me if I should be freezing, or pull me out of a ditch if I should ever fall into one. I can find you a Newfoundland dog that will do as much." Six years later, Murph couldn't agree more with Thoreau. The more people Murph came across and was disappointed by, the more he thought the quote was true. He always believed that you can tell a lot about a person's character by how they treat and respond to animals, and both Maria and the kids showed a lot of character in their relationships with Rooney.

Victor Dancy

According to Victor, the only good thing about his wife was that even after having a child, she was still one hot piece of ass. She'd gotten two separate boob jobs. He gave the enhancements to her for Christmas two different years. He also always thought she had a great bubbly butt, and she liked to show it off daily in yoga pants. Whoever invented those pants was a genius.

Victor felt the only good thing about The Colonel was that he hooked Victor up with his job and he was loaded. The Colonel was a fighter pilot in the Air Force and rose to become a Brigadier General and a Wing Commander. He had also been able to help Victor out several times with his sway and his close group of powerful friends. The Colonel was able to wipe Victor's two DUI's away with the help of some powerful lawyers he did business with. He also helped when Victor got kicked out of the Air Force, wiping it from his son's permanent record with a few phone calls to people in high places. "Image management," The Colonel would say. Victor was never clear whose image was being managed, but he didn't really care.

Victor believed that his father had always been good at getting him out of trouble. Victor assumed that The Colonel did it not for his son, but to protect his own name. When Victor was twelve, he was out playing with some school friends when his dad was in charge of Eielsen Air Force Base in Alaska. The boys were standing on an overpass throwing large, icy snowballs at passing cars speeding by underneath them. In the game, if you hit a windshield you got three points, and you got one point for any other part of the passing cars. Victor was ahead by five points when all of a sudden somebody quickly pulled up from behind on the bridge. A man jumped out of his car and sprinted over to them. It all happened so fast that they couldn't run away.

The man just happened to be an off-duty military trooper. He had a thin black moustache and close-cropped black hair, a standard-issue douche bag. They had hit his car with a snowball putting a big dent in the front hood. The trooper figured out where the snowball came from and made his way around to the overpass. Victor guessed that he must have turned off his lights and quietly snuck up on them. The trooper pulled Victor into his car and yelled at Victor's friends to get in beside him.

"You don't know who you're messing with, man," Victor spit out at him.

"Yes, I am messing with a bunch of little brats who are going to owe me big time to fix my car!"

Collisions

"I'm not fixing anything on your piece of shit car." Victor had a grandfather that taught him all of the bad language he needed to know at a very early age.

"We'll see once I get you back to the base and call your parents," the man replied, as most people in the area were affiliated with the local base.

"Ha, I dare you to call my dad. He'll have your badge."

"You are one cocky little son of a gun."

"I can't wait to see what the great General Victor Dancy says when a nobody like you calls him and wastes his time by making him come pick me up. The Colonel will mess you up." As soon as Victor said his father's name, the trooper's whole demeanor changed. Victor's reputation as a troublemaker preceded him to every base his father was ever stationed, and Victor figured that the man had already heard all about him at that point. It was a well-known fact at most bases wherever the Dancy family was stationed that Victor was going to cause trouble, but there was nothing most people could do about it. That was one of the reasons The Colonel eventually had Victor's mother get a house off base.

The kicker was the trooper told Victor to get out, but made his two friends ride with him back to the base. Their dads were both in the Air Force, too, but much further down the food chain than The Colonel. The trooper still wanted to get his car fixed and paid for, and he realized that he could still get the other kids in trouble. Victor heard at school that the two friends each had to pay two hundred and fifty bucks to fix the hood. They never talked to him again. He could have given a shit. When you are an Air Force brat, you learn to make and lose friends very fast.

Chapter 3

Murphy Kearns

When they were a young couple, Maria and Murph both agreed they would each pledge two hours a week to volunteer and help out their community. In Pittsburgh, they distributed their volunteer efforts by helping out at the Western Pennsylvania Humane Society, Allegheny General Hospital, and the Carnegie Mellon Museum. Maria and Murph worked at the humane society because of their love of animals. They had volunteered at the hospital ever since Patrick had ear tubes put in there and the nurses and doctors had been so kind to them. They even volunteered at the Heinz History Center because of their love of all the Pittsburgh professional sport's teams.

Once Murph went down to Kitty Hawk, they agreed that they would both keep up that pledge of weekly volunteering. Murph headed to volunteer before he went to work. Luckily Pete never got out of bed before eleven, and he usually hit the waves, or in his case lay on the board on the waves, before he did anything else. Murph made it a point not

Collisions

to let his exercise or volunteering efforts interfere with his work, but he also never let his work interfere with exercising. He typically would just get up earlier or stay up later to compensate. Murph was always able to get a good run in when he woke up, and he tried to get his volunteering done weekly. Murph got to work on non-volunteering days around eight-thirty after he took a four to five mile run, and around nine-thirty on volunteering days. He usually stayed at work until well past seven. The only reason he didn't stay later was that he wanted to make sure to get home to Skype with Maria and the kids before their bedtime. After the family spent time talking online, Murph usually went out to one of the local spots to grab a bite for dinner. If only the construction company and Pete could have kept up with him, the job would have been done in no time.

Murph went to the Dare County Library to work with the Dare County Literacy Council before work. The DCLC worked on tutoring local adults with either learning English as a second language or to pass their high school equivalency exam.

Murph worked with a man named Johnny Johnson who was in his late sixties. Every session after they finished with their tutoring work, Johnny always told Murph some fascinating stories about his life. Johnny had a long, Santa Claus style beard that was a little less curly and a little dirtier than Old St. Nick's. At close to six-feet tall, Johnny looked like he barely weighed one hundred and twenty pounds, so he had more of an Honest Abe build than jolly old St. Nick. He wore a very similar, if not the same, outfit all three times Murph worked with him at the DCLC: a flannel shirt, a trucker's cap with a fish hook on the end, and some cargo khaki pants.

The two worked for an hour that morning, and Johnny was very focused and driven to learn about line symmetry, angles, and degrees. Johnny and Murph agreed the week before that they would go to breakfast after they finished that week's lesson. Johnny wanted to pass his high school equivalency exam, which was always something that his wife, Lois, wanted him to do, but that he never got to before she passed away. She was sick for a very long time with multiple sclerosis, and Johnny had to work three jobs to pay for her medical bills. He told her on her death bed that his first obligation once she passed was to finish high school. Johnny met Lois accidentally, when he bumped into her car at a stop sign. At least that is what he told her. Truth is he spotted her several streets before and thought she was the prettiest girl he had ever seen and he had to get her attention, so he tapped her bumper. The two had no kids, and either Johnny was not close with the rest of his family or they were all gone.

Johnny left high school when he was sixteen to go to work for his dad on a shrimp boat on the North Carolina coast. His family needed his help, and school was never a top priority, so the likelihood that Johnny would have ever finished high school was slim anyway. He remained on a boat when he joined the Navy for the next twenty years. Typically you are not allowed to get in the Armed Services without a high school diploma, but one of Johnny's cousins was a Navy recruiter and snuck him in. After he was in the Navy, he came back to work on various fishing boats in the Nags Head area. Then he met Lois in his late thirties. Johnny and Lois tried for kids, but it never happened. Once Lois got really sick, he also worked at a nearby restaurant as a dishwasher, and he picked up some work cleaning boats for the wealthy in the Manteo area. Johnny had swabbed decks before, and he wasn't above doing it again if it meant more money to help Lois.

Collisions

Lois used to read Johnny the newspaper every morning, front to back. They would get up at five and make a pot of hot coffee, then they would sit either on the porch in the spring and summer or in front of their fireplace in the fall and winter. Lois had been dead for seven years, and Johnny was finally getting there with his reading, math, and science, but he still had a ways to go. Murph and Johnny were working on geometry, and he was pretty fascinated by Murph's job and how he used geometry to help with angles and shapes in his designs. Johnny let Murph know that it was very rare in the post-World War era for somebody to make it twenty years in the Navy not knowing how to read. Johnny started out working in food services and doing other menial tasks aboard ships. He had a great capacity for memorizing though, and he would make good friends throughout the twenty years that would help him sneak by.

They headed to Sam & Omie's on the beach road around mile marker sixteen; Johnny said they had the best hot cakes in town. The restaurant was right across from the pier and had an authentic feel to it like people had been going there for years, and not much had changed on the inside or out.

The conversation strolled along, as it often did with Johnny. Murph was mid-bite on his second round of hot cakes and a discussion about the best places and times to catch shrimp when Johnny asked about Murph's family. He caught Murph off guard by getting so personal, and Murph really didn't have a great response for his comment. Murph showed Johnny pictures of Isabella and Patrick, and Johnny seemed enamored by the kids.

"The one thing I always wanted was for Lois and me to have kids. I feel like once I go, my Johnson family tree ends," Johnny told Murph while sipping his hot coffee.

"I can tell you that the experience of being there for the births of both my kids are by far the two most spectacular and important moments of my life. Especially for my daughter, Isabella, since she was the first. Isabella actually came two weeks early, when we were at a bed and breakfast in the mountains of West Virginia. It was our anniversary, and for some odd reason I thought it would be a good idea to take a very pregnant wife on a mini-vacation to a remote location. After Isabella was born, Maria admitted that you should never go out of town that close to a due date, because you never know what could happen. Being my loving wife and not wanting to hurt my feelings after I surprised her with my plans, she decided to go along with it. When her water broke at the bed and breakfast, I freaked out and acted like a chicken with its head chopped off. I forgot the keys after I got her to the car and had to run back in. I missed turns from the directions the lady at the bed and breakfast gave us to get to the nearest hospital. I even left Maria sitting in the car by herself when I went frantically running into the emergency room looking for any doctor to deliver my child. It all ended up working out, and even though Maria didn't get to use her regular doctor, the entire birth went perfectly."

"What was it like to be in the room with her?" Johnny asked.

"It was beautiful, a little gross, heart-stopping, and exhilarating all wrapped into one package," Murph responded honestly. "The moment I first held her in my hands and saw her face for the first time was the most beautiful part. Some of the stuff that came out with Bella was the gross part. The whole process was a roller coaster, but my heart-stopped during the twenty or thirty seconds from when her head first started to come out until I cut the cord and the doctor handed her over to me. I swear Bella looked at me with barely opened eyes, and we instantly had a connection. She knew that I was her protector, and I knew from that moment on that I always wanted to be there for her."

"That sounds like something," Johnny said as he stared at his empty plate like he could not decide if he wanted more.

"It really only got better from there. In the last five years, so many fascinating things have happened with Isabella and Patrick. Every day is a treat with them, and there is always something new, whether it is Bella teaching me something new about turtles, or Patrick going headfirst down a slide. I don't know what I would do without either of them around. Being here this long is hard enough, but at least I know that I will get to see them on Skype each morning and night, and this is only a very temporary arrangement. I want to establish my career and my company so that I can give my kids a great life experience and assure I will get to spend the rest of my life not having to be away from them like I am now."

Johnny shook his head the whole time Murph spoke to him, while pulling on his beard, his constant habit. Murph was very surprised that he spoke so much to a man he barely knew, but something about Johnny let Murph know he could trust him and that Johnny was a real good guy. He was just comfortable to Murph.

Johnny took another sip of his coffee, set it down, then asked, "What in the heck is Skype?"

They spent the next ten minutes talking about Skype and the internet, which Johnny had no clue how to use. The only television Johnny apparently had ever watched was the one behind the bar at Sam & Omie's. Murph dropped Johnny back off at the library and headed to work when they finished eating.

J. McLain Callahan

Victor Dancy

Victor never gave a damn about having pictures up of his family at his office; if he could, he would have had the latest Playboy playmate calendar up on the wall. He never felt like telling his coworkers what Maddie wanted for Christmas, what she ate for breakfast, or anything else about her. From the minute he found out that Leah was pregnant with her, Maddie had been nothing but a pain in Victor's ass, just like her mother.

Leah was a constant irritant to Victor when she was pregnant. Her stomach was like a freaking never-ending pit of hunger. Victor would be out getting dinner, and she would call and change her mind about what she wanted. She always wanted the weirdest shit she could possibly come up with to eat. Victor would have to go pick up crazy stuff like Thai food one night and Polish sausage the next night. At the time they were newly married, and he had to pretend like he gave a shit about what she wanted. He would swing by a drive-thru and pick up a hamburger for himself on his way to whatever ethnic food she wanted that night, and just pretend like he was not that hungry when he got home, so he didn't have to share with her. She didn't care that much, because it was just more food for the pit.

The last month of Leah's pregnancy was about as big of a pain in the ass as Victor had ever had. Leah cried all the damn time like a two-year old. One of the first major fights of their relationship came in that last month of the pregnancy. They would have thousands more after.

"My feet hurt so bad, I wish I could get down and rub them," Leah said lying on the couch with her feet propped up on the coffee table.

Collisions

Victor pretended not to hear her, hoping she would just shut-up, kind of like he pretended not to see her swollen feet up on the table, hoping they would just disappear. Victor actually waited until Leah wasn't looking and turned up the television a little louder with the remote.

"This stomach just gets in the way of everything, and my feet are so sore," she said a minute later. She inched her feet closer to him on the couch. Victor knew exactly what she wanted him to do, but Victor only messed with his own feet.

"Maybe you could set up an appointment at one of those pedicure places you go to; they must do massages."

"That sounds okay, but it would be really great if you could just give them a quick rubdown now while we are sitting here," Leah said in an attempt to sound like a little girl begging, while batting her eyes.

Victor didn't go for that nonsense, "I had a really long day at work, and I just want to sit here now and enjoy this game."

"Can't you just do it real fast, while we are sitting here together?" she asked.

"No, I really don't feel like rubbing your feet right now, please stop badgering me about it! Now you'll want me to rub your feet, then you'll want me to rub your back, and then I'll have to go out and get you ice cream or something. I told you I just want to sit here and watch this damn game without you wanting something for once," Victor shouted.

Leah began to cry and said, "Why can't you just be like a normal husband and pay me some attention and act like you love me?"

"Oh for fuck's sake, give me a break. I don't feel like dealing with your shit right now."

Victor got up and headed to Applebee's to watch the game without telling her where he was going. It was only the first of many times that he would leave Leah crying on the couch.

• • •

Maddie was born on the worst possible date and time. Victor kept hoping, as the due date got closer, that she would be born somewhere between nine in the morning and five o'clock so he didn't have to be the one to take Leah to the hospital. He really didn't know what to expect with the birth, since he never went to any of Leah's doctor appointments. Of course, Leah wanted him to go to all of them, but Victor was always able to find a good excuse not to go. He lied to Leah, and told her that all his mother ever talked about was helping deliver her first grandchild. He continuously re-emphasized this to Leah, until she finally got the point and asked his mom to help with her Lamaze classes. Victor always enjoyed his mother's cooking much better than the shit Leah would put in front of him, so it was nice when his mother moved down a couple weeks early to make sure that she was there in time for the birth. Victor's mother also did all of the laundry and cleaning the last couple weeks since Leah was such a fat and wobbly sow, which got Victor off the hook for that as well.

When Leah called and said she was on her way to the hospital, Victor was at a bar throwing back a couple while a very important New York Yankees pennant game was on. The Yankees were one game away from sweeping the series. He had learned by that point that if he really wanted to focus on a game, he needed to make sure to watch it far away from

Collisions

Leah. Victor told Leah that he was stuck at work, but that he would rush out and be there as soon as possible. This was in the third inning. He waited and swigged down one more beer while watching the Yanks at bat in the bottom of the third. Luckily he had satellite radio in his Hummer, so he could listen on the way. When Victor got to the hospital, the Yanks were coming up to bat in the bottom of the fifth, so he had to wait and listen in the car until they had their three outs. They were down by three runs.

It took Victor forever to find the damn room that Leah was in and he was not happy about it, just wasted time when he could be checking the score. His mother told him that Leah was progressing and that the baby could come very soon. She said something about Leah being at some centimeter count, but Victor had no idea what his mom was talking about. Victor went in to see Leah with his mom. Leah was a sweaty mess and wasn't the least bit attractive; it might have been the ugliest he had ever seen her.

He came up with the great idea to say he forgot something in the car and he would run and be right back. Victor went down to a little gift shop he walked by on the way in, and bought the first stuffed animal he saw, which gave him time to watch the bottom of the seventh and the Yanks pull to within one run. When he got back to the room, his mom told him that Leah was well on her way. He made sure to stand behind Leah at the back of the bed for two reasons: one, he could see the game on the television screen out in the waiting area next to Leah's room; and two, Victor really didn't want to have the picture of all that sick shit involved with the birth of a child in his head the next time he was able to get in Leah's pants, whenever the hell that might be. A great thing happened. Not so much Maddie coming out, but the fact that when she did come out, Jeter blasted a three-run bomb to give the Yank's the lead. Victor shouted

"Yes!" and all the idiots in the room thought it was for Maddie. He let his mother do all the cutting and cleaning, and when Victor held Maddie, who he thought looked like nothing more than a blue alien, he really didn't feel a thing.

Chapter 4

Murphy Kearns

Murph was a good two hours into work when Pete stopped by his makeshift office in the basement of their small office building. Pete was sporting a wet ponytail. He liked to just drop by frequently to have conversations with Murph varying from politics to sports. He would never act like or admit to it, but Pete was a very lonely guy.

"What's up, man? How's it hanging?" Pete asked.

"Pretty good, I'm getting excited about the family coming down tomorrow. How about you?"

"It is hanging long and to the right," Pete said cackling.

"Thanks for that unnecessary information; I really did not need to know that at all," Murph said with a laugh.

"When are the wife and kids getting here again?"

"They are flying in tomorrow morning to Norfolk. Do you mind if I come in a little later than normal tomorrow?" Murph asked.

"Shit no, dude. Take the whole day off and enjoy the time with your family," Pete said thoughtfully.

"Thanks a lot, Pete. I have been trying to find some really cool places that the kids will enjoy in the Outer Banks. I know that I definitely want to take them to Jockey's Ridge to fly a kite, to see the wild horses in Corolla, and maybe to a lighthouse. Which one do you think is the best?"

"My favorite is Ocracoke, but you would also do well to check out Bodie. There's also the new aquarium over in Manteo, and they might like to walk on the *Elizabeth II* ship at Roanoke Island," said Pete. "I remember you telling me your daughter likes turtles. They have some awesome turtle exhibits at the aquarium."

"Yeah, they would enjoy all of those, good idea," Murph agreed. Pete seemed lost for a minute to Murph, which sometimes happened. Murph figured it could have been from all of Pete's past marijuana use, but he tended to change course in a conversation regularly. That was just Pete. "Any updates on the draft plans for the Steelers? The Panthers sure have to get better than the shit they are putting on the field now." Pete was a huge Panthers fan; he had box seats in Charlotte. Murph could constantly hear him yelling the roar sound that the Panthers public announcer played when they scored a touchdown. Pete did it whenever he got happy about something, so Murph heard the noise regularly. Pete promised Murph that the next time the Steelers played in Charlotte he would invite Murph and his family to go.

Collisions

"No. The Steelers need their usual upgrades at offensive linemen and a younger defense, so I think that's what they'll focus on."

The Steelers had a huge place in Murph's life, not only because they were his favorite professional sport's team, but because Murph met Maria at a game at Heinz Field right after the stadium opened and the team moved over from Three Rivers Stadium. The two were both in college at the time, but they had never met before. At a school like Pitt with more than 20,000 students, you only ever met a very small percentage of the population.

Murph was at the game with a couple of his friends from school. A couple hours before the game, they took a bus from their Oakland neighborhood rental house to downtown and then walked across the Clemente Bridge over past the new PNC Park baseball stadium towards Heinz Field. Every time Murph walked across the massive yellow bridge, he thought about how much Roberto Clemente did in his short life, which ended early in a plane crash. They didn't have tickets for any game they went to. Murph and his friends always tried to scalp some every couple home games when they had enough money saved up from what Murph believed were noble plasma donations. If they couldn't find a good price for tickets, they would just go check out the game at Mullen's or Clark's Bar near the stadium.

That particular game, the Steelers were playing their archrival the Cleveland Browns, so they knew ticket prices were going to be particularly high. As they were walking across the bridge, Murph told his friends to take everything out of their wallets except for forty dollars. They found what they thought was a shady looking scalper wearing a large gold chain necklace, a Steelers Starter jacket and a white furry Kangol cap on his head. He said he had three tickets for two hundred dollars in nosebleed seats. They played dumb, took out their wallets, combined their money to one hundred and twenty dollars and told the guy that was all the money they had, because they were just poor college students. He looked at them like they were all full of crap, but he probably weighed his options of getting their money or potentially no money at all and gave them the tickets.

They saved eighty dollars from the money they took out of their pockets. Instead of saving it for more sensible things they might have needed at the time, like laundry detergent and a couple bills sitting around their run-down and bug-infested house, they wasted the money on overly expensive Iron City beers and hot dogs in the stadium. The game was a battle between a surprisingly decent and rare Brownies team and the Steelers late in the season, with both teams trying to win their division and make the playoffs. It was freezing cold that day, and snow fell as the two blue-collar teams shredded the turf as the game carried on. The Browns white jerseys fittingly faded to brown as the game wore on. Tommy "The Gun" Maddox led his team at quarterback for the Steelers.

Very occasionally at Steelers games you see some fans of the opposition. The Steelers traveled to games better than any other team in the NFL, and they protected their home field with even more vigor. Typically, Steelers fans didn't interact with other fans and they respected them as passionate supporters of their own teams, although misguided. A couple of young Browns fans a row in front of Murph and his friends were becoming louder and more hostile as the game got closer and they got drunker. Sitting right beside them and apparently attached to the bigger of the two sat a bundled up Steelers fan with brown hair flowing beneath her black and gold Steelers striped toboggan. She was possibly the cutest person Murph had ever seen in a number thirty-six Jerome

Collisions

Bettis jersey. The woman had very girl-next-door dimples, a button nose, and very full lips. She must have been dating one of the rowdy Browns fans since he kept putting his arm around her possessively. As her companions became more boisterous and rude, she got more and more embarrassed.

When the game headed into the fourth quarter and came down to a three point Browns lead, the two Browns fans got out of control. They started cussing, spilling beers, and booing whenever the Steelers did anything good. Eventually the guys behind Murph started to yell at them to sit down or to be quiet. This only led to more raised voices, yelling, and general rowdiness. At one point an usher walked up and asked them to please calm down, which they did for about two minutes, until the usher was back out of sight.

After a rather long rant filled with f-bombs directed at Maddox, a father with two kids turned around and asked them to please respect his family during the game. The two guys told him that he shouldn't bring his kids to a wild place like a professional football game if they couldn't handle being there. The man turned red with anger but calmly turned back around. The girl in the Bettis jersey told the two guys that it might be a good idea if they went ahead and left to beat the traffic, but they ignored her.

With about three minutes and change remaining, the Browns scored on a forty-five yard run. When they crossed the end zone, the two Browns fans jumped up and down, and the bigger one's entire beer tipped over and poured onto the back of the little girl's head. The father immediately told his wife to take the daughter and other kid to the bathroom. As soon as they were out of eyesight of the seats, he turned around and punched the large Browns fan right in the stomach with a strong right hook. The smaller of the two Browns fans, in turn, started throwing fists too. The big guy recovered from the gut punch and joined in with a big haymaker swing, which went high and on his backswing hit the girl in the Bettis jersey right in the face, knocking her back into her seat. As all of this happened in what felt like slow motion, Murph's friends joined the fight along with the two big Steelers fans sitting to the right of them to help the father, which made it about five Steelers fans against the two Browns guys. There was pushing and fists flying every which way, so Murph jumped the hard yellow bench seats to the row in front of him and tried his best to protect the woozy and bleeding girl. Within about twenty seconds, security came in and broke up the fight. They carried the two beat up Brownies to the concourse and made Murph's two friends and the other guys go with them. None of them would return to the game.

Murph's first conversation with his future wife took place as he found some napkins to put on her nose.

"Are you ok? That was a pretty good shot you took," Murph said.

"Yeah, I think I might have a black eye tomorrow, but I should be fine," she said. She had the most unique grayish-brown eyes he had ever seen. "Thanks for making sure I didn't get hit again. I think you got hit in the back of the head there a couple times yourself."

Murph was hit and pushed quite a bit from errant punches, and during the adrenaline rush he really didn't feel any of it, but the back of his head throbbed by that point. Murph thought he surely couldn't show pain to such a gorgeous girl wearing a Bus jersey who just took a shot to the face.

Collisions

"I'm fine too. Do you need to get down there to find your boyfriend? I can help you down the stairs if you need it," Murph said, unable to take his eyes off her.

"For starters, that guy is not my boyfriend. We went on one date, and he told me he had tickets to the game today with his brother and that he had an extra one if I wanted to join them. There was no way I was going to pass up a free ticket to this critical game, so I pretended to like him some for the rest of the date and even let him pop kiss me at the end of the night. He thought he was getting somewhere, but I knew he was only getting me to the game," she said. Murph thought it was pretty cool of her to pull a trick play.

"I guess I couldn't pass up free tickets either to any Steelers game, but I don't think it would be worth it for me to kiss that guy though," he joked.

"He just never informed me that they were Browns fans," she said.

"They weren't just Brownie fans; they were annoying Brownie fans, which is twice as bad," Murph said. He was not sure how to go about talking to her, since he really didn't want to blow it, but she appeared to be enjoying his company.

"Yeah! I wanted to punch him myself about twenty minutes into the game. I'm glad that father protected his daughter the way he did. Fierce loyalty, I respect that!"

"Mr. Dad got a real good one in there, and those guys got it pretty bad, it looked like, during the fight."

Though such a pivotal game was going on in the background for such diehard fans, the two were more focused on their conversation than the game. By that point the game was down to its final minute. They were snapped out of their focus on each other by the loud roar of the Steelers faithful. The offense and Maddox were driving for the win. The woman and Murph gave each other a couple high fives during the final drive. With less than twenty seconds left, Maddox hit Hines Ward on a beautiful lofted and spiraling pass into the corner of the end-zone for the win, clinching a playoff spot. They jumped up and down, high-fived all the fans around them, and turned to each other and gave each other a big bear hug.

After they calmed down from the excitement, she turned to Murph and said, "My name is Maria, and once again, thanks for everything."

"I'm Murphy and anytime."

Since they were both now alone, they left together and decided to walk back to downtown together, and they eventually went over to Market Square to get a sandwich at Primanti Brothers. Murph and Maria figured out that they had a lot in common starting with their love for Primanti sandwiches filled with slaw and fries, and including that they both went to Pitt and actually had a class together. The two surprisingly only lived a couple blocks away from each other in their Oakland neighborhood.

They ended up riding the same bus back to Oakland, and he got her number on the back of his ticket stub, which he carried with him in his wallet from then on. Their first official date ended up being the first-round playoff game for the Steelers. Even on that first meeting between the two of them, Murph knew he had found the perfect girl. Murph never had a doubt: the girl was stunning, a die-hard Steelers fan, and could take a punch and act like it was nothing. He knew then that there was not another girl in the entire world that he wanted to be with besides Maria. That love and desire only intensified throughout their relationship, and Murph was sure Maria felt the exact same way.

Victor Dancy

Victor took two hours for lunch every day, and nobody ever said anything to him about it. He knew it left some of the guys back at the airfield with more work while he was gone, but he thought that if they didn't have the balls to man up and say something to him, he would just keep doing it, and then it would be their problem. He felt like wings, so he drove over to Elroy's Wings and ordered twenty extra-hot wings, some celery and blue cheese, and a pitcher of Bud Light. He knew that he had a tendency to get in trouble when he drank with his history of DUI's, but that never stopped him. Plus, he knew that most people would probably think it was not a great idea to work directing airplanes while drinking, but he really didn't give a damn about that either. He could throw back a case and be fine, so what was a pitcher going to do to him?

The Air Force kicked Victor out for "failure to meet standards," after he was only in basic training for a month. He was not going to listen to some prick shouting at him about what they wanted him to do, so Victor stopped going to mandatory training. Even though Victor could not physically skip the training, he knew he could mentally. Of course, his father was deeply embarrassed, but The Colonel made sure Victor was classified as a "self-initiated elimination."

Victor got his first DUI when he was just out of the Air Force. It was during a phase when he was into dance clubs and house music. He looked completely different back then, when he had enough hair to spike it up and was into bodybuilding. He used to spend a couple hours a day at Gold's Gym lifting weights, and he only ate milkshakes from GNC with a whole lot of Creatine. He had lost a lot of that hair that he used to gel up and the muscles had turned to fat in the form of fifty more pounds. The girls used to love him for both his looks and his money. But when the looks were gone, they still loved him for the money.

He was at the club dancing with all kinds of hoochies wearing next to nothing but skimpy skirts, and tops with their breasts hanging halfway out. Victor was drinking Manhattans and Tom Collins that night. He also had popped a couple pain killers. By three a.m., all Victor could see were the neon lights bouncing to the music. He could have kept going until dawn, but the tramp that he was dancing with was all over him, and really wanted to get out of there and go back to her place. She wasn't so bad to look at, so Victor figured it might be a fun night with her.

Victor and the young girl were in his car, about a mile outside of the club when he noticed a motorcycle cop's lights flashing behind him. For a second, he thought about outracing him and gassed his truck, but the girl started shouting at him, so Victor pulled over. The pig walked up to the car with his flashlight on, and Victor felt he looked just like your stereotypical cop, a little overweight with a wannabe military high and tight haircut. Victor wondered how that doughnut could protect and serve when Victor knew he could drop him with one punch.

"Sir, do you know how fast you were going?" the cop asked.

"Yeah, I was going thirty-five," Victor slurred back to him. The actual speed limit on that road was forty-five, so Victor was not sure why he said thirty-five. The cop smirked at his response. "Sir, you were traveling at about twice that speed. I have you at sixty-eight."

"Ha, sixty-eight my ass, I wasn't going near that speed, you must be confused!" streamed out of his mouth in a boozy breath.

"Sir, I have it right there on my radar; plus you were all over the road."

"Well, if you had a hot broad like this one right here all over you in your car, you'd be all over the road too," Victor blurted out. "But nobody that's as ugly as you would ever have any girl under three-hundred pounds doing anything with you, so I guess you wouldn't know what that's like. Look at this girl next to me! She has this thick butt, but nothing like the flabby asses you're used to!"

The cop turned a little red when that came out. "Sir, you can't speak to me like that. You reek of alcohol, so I am going to need you to step out of the car."

"Nope."

"Yes, you need to step out of the car right now," the cop insisted.

"No, I will not step out of the car."

The girl, who was crying by then, turned to Victor and said, "Please just listen to him and get out of the car!" He could tell that she probably had never been in any trouble with the police, and that she was about to shit herself.

"Shut up, bitch! Nobody's talking to you," he told her.

"That is unnecessary, step out of the car now!" the cop exclaimed.

"She can step out of the car, but I am staying right here," Victor said defiantly.

The girl actually looked at the cop, and he shook his head and said "Ma'am, if you feel like getting out, you can go sit on the other side of the car on the hill and wait for me."

"Yeah, get your ass out of my car," Victor told her as he looked straight ahead and tried to think himself sober.

She looked at Victor in disbelief, rolled her eyes, opened the door, got out and closed it with a slam.

"I am not going to ask you again. Get out of the car now," the officer said in an irritated tone.

"You don't have to ask me again 'cause I'm tired of you asking anyways, you are really starting to get on my nerves. I will move when my lawyer gets here, and I want to use my one phone call."

"Sir you are not under arrest, and you don't need your lawyer.......yet. Stay right here and don't even think about moving."

"Whatever you say, man! What do you like on your pizza?"

"What?"

"I am hungry as shit and I want a goddamn pizza," Victor said, dead serious. He felt so confident that he could get out of anything because The Colonel always came through.

"Sir, just stay here."

51

Collisions

The cop turned around, walked back to his bike and got on his radio. Victor picked up his cell phone and speed-dialed Domino's. They thought he was joking when he tried to order a large pizza and told them to deliver it to "the side of the damned road where there's a green truck pulled over with Officer Chips behind it and a hot piece of ass sitting on the side of the road." Victor's pizza never came, which really pissed him off, and about five minutes later two more cops pulled up. When the other cops came up to the car, he still refused to get out and told them he was mad about his pizza not coming. Victor even asked them if they minded going to pick it up for him. He also went on a rant about the first cop having "the hots" for him and just wanting to feel him up with a pat down.

Victor eventually got out of the car and failed his field sobriety test. His blood alcohol level was tested at 0.20, which was even high by his standards. The cops took him downtown and took the girl home, and Victor never saw or heard from her again. He remembered that he drunk dialed her a couple times later on until she eventually must have blocked his number. He was charged with DUI. Victor had one call and decided to call The Colonel. His father was irate, but not surprised at all by the call. He made Victor stay in the drunk tank for the night as "a lesson," which did a whole lot of nothing for Victor. He passed out as soon as his butt hit the metal bench in the cell. Of course, The Colonel got Victor off to avoid the career implications of having a son with a DUI on his record.

• • •

While Victor sat and munched on his wings at Elroy's, your typical chicken wing joint, Leah called him several times and also texted asking him to please call her as soon as possible. After about the fifth call, he got fed up and finally picked up.

"Leah, I am busy at work, why do you keep calling me?" he lied.

He figured that she probably knew he was full of shit, but she didn't say anything. "Maddie has ballet class this afternoon from five to six o'clock. She was supposed to get a ride home from Stephanie's mom, but she just called and Stephanie is sick, so they are not going. Can you please pick her up on your way home from work?"

"Why can't you do it?" he said.

"I have a haircut appointment at five-thirty that I scheduled two months ago, and I really don't want to have to cancel it," Leah said.

"Just reschedule it. You know that I go to the gym after work." Victor said as he licked the buffalo sauce from his fingers and shifted his attention from the television to the two women sitting behind the bar.

She had to know this was bullshit. If you took one look at Victor, you'd know there was no way he went to the gym every night. He just liked to stop by a bar for a drink or two after work, and he needed an excuse for coming home late. He liked to think of his time at the bar as a time for him to meditate and relax his brain.

"My stylist is very busy, and it will be another month before she can get me in!" Leah exclaimed in frustration.

"There are salons all over the place, just go to another one," Victor said annoyed with the phone call. He contemplated hanging up on her.

Collisions

"I've been using the same stylist for five years, and she knows how I like my hair cut. I can't just go to some other random place."

"It's a fucking haircut. Just go to somebody different," Victor said in a frustrated tone.

"Are you kidding me right now?" she asked. "I ask for one simple favor, and you can't help me out. What a joke! I'll figure it out on my own!"

Victor hung up and slammed the table with his fist. He ordered another beer, and went back to fantasizing about the ladies opposite him at the bar.

He met Leah when she was an escort. He always had a soft spot for escorts, and Leah was one of many who he had enjoyed services from. He later learned that Leah had a very rough upbringing, raised by a single mother who was into booze, heroin, and cocaine. She no longer talked to her mother or really any of her family. He figured that it must be true, though, that once you are raised by someone who likes alcohol, you tend to migrate to others that like it just as much. Leah was a good student in high school, but she had to work thirty hours a week to help pay the bills. She got good enough grades to get into a strong college, but not good enough to get any academic scholarships. She couldn't afford to pay for college on her own, so she tried to work as a waitress, but she wasn't making enough in tips. Leah met another waitress who got her into waitressing at a strip club, which led to stripping, and then to the escort business. She saved more money in a month than she could waitressing for a year.

Even though he had his own place and he could usually score tail easily enough on his own, he liked the thrill of calling an escort and meeting her at some dive motel. He knew you were supposed to take escorts around and feed them and maybe take them with you to a party or two. Victor paid for dirty sex. No more, no less.

The first time they met, at a sleazy motel room, Leah was wearing a tight, red, sparkly dress, with long, black boots that went above her knees and had just the right amount of her breasts showing. She was by far the hottest escort Victor had ever scored. The two had sex that night about ten different times; on the hard motel mattress, in the cramped shower, and on the dirty, old carpet. He thought it was good, very good.

It was so good that he used Leah as an escort several more times over the next year. About a year into the paid-for relationship, Leah said she needed to talk to him.

"You know I really don't like to talk," Victor said as he quickly pulled down his pants when she entered the hotel room.

"I know, but it's important."

"What could it possibly be? Are you quitting on me or moving?" Victor said as he pulled a flask out of his pocket and poured a drink into the cheap motel cup.

"No, I'm pregnant."

"Whoa, so I guess you will be quitting, I'm sorry to hear that. You look fine to me now, so let's go ahead and do this."

"Victor, it is yours," Leah exclaimed.

He let out a thunderous laugh at the statement. "That's bullshit," he said standing up. "You are a fucking hooker; you sleep with all sorts of guys. There is no fucking way you know it's mine."

"I stopped working six months ago, for the most part. I have enough saved for college. I kept seeing you because I like your company."

"So?"

"So, I haven't slept with anybody but you in the past six months. And I'm only three months along."

"Why in the hell should I believe that?"

"Because it's the truth."

"Well then I will pay you to get it taken care of. How much does that cost?"

"I can't do that. I am Catholic, and I have mentally prepared for this baby. I want to have it. If you want, we can get a test to make sure it is yours, but I swear it is."

"You are a fucking escort, and this is complete crap," he said irritated.

"Please stop saying that. I like you, and I want to try to make this work." Victor was confused why she cared for him. He didn't talk to her much. They obviously had a strong physical attraction though, and she did laugh a lot during the times they weren't fucking. Victor had a dry sense of humor that Leah appeared to appreciate. Plus, he knew that he was much better all-around than her other clientele. Victor figured that all of those reasons combined must be why she wanted to make it work. He also knew that The Colonel's money sure helped.

"Make what work?" Victor asked anyway.

"Us."

By that point she knew enough about Victor and who his father was that he was kind of stuck. In the brief times they did talk, he would tell her about his dysfunctional relationship with his dad. He really did enjoy their sex, and the more he thought about it, he thought that a kid might get him some more money from his father. So he introduced Leah to his family. When his father learned she was pregnant, the details of their relationship left vague, The Colonel made them rush the wedding a few weeks later, which Victor was not anticipating at all. He just thought he would have the kid to make The Colonel happy, but he never wanted to get married. He was stuck though. As much as he hated it, Victor knew that he had to do what his father wanted to keep the money flowing into his pockets.

• • •

That was seven years ago. There wasn't shit Leah could do about a divorce; she was jammed just like Victor. He had threatened her several times, both physically and verbally, that he would let his dad know about her past occupation. The Colonel was the only father-figure Leah had ever really had, and, unlike Victor, it would be devastating to her to let her father-in-law down. Victor also made it clear he had no problems letting her new friends know as well. Leah worked very hard to climb up the social ladder in the Williamsburg elite. She was good friends with a large majority of the country club clique and the old-school money. Victor felt that money was money, and Leah would be crushed to lose it. She never made it to college, though she said she wanted to go and mentioned it all the time. There was no way Victor was paying for that shit though.

Collisions

Since she was stuck with him, she had to put up with him, and Victor knew he could be as big a prick to her as he wanted. She got what she wanted by getting to remain in his family and in her social club with her high social status, and he got what he wanted out of it. Leah and Maddie gave the impression of a traditional family that kept The Colonel happy, and Victor got Leah and several others. He still got to screw around as much as he wanted. He got to stay out late or sometimes not come in at all. He also didn't have to do shit for Maddie, and he knew Leah couldn't say a damn thing about it.

Chapter 5

Murphy Kearns

    Murph had been having some issues with Rooney's eating habits since the two made it down to the Outer Banks. Rooney did not like to be away from the normal routine of his house, and he missed Leah and the kids. He was used to playing with Murph and going on walks around their Squirrel Hill neighborhood when they were back home in Pittsburgh, and that had not changed in the Outer Banks. What Rooney missed was the time he spent with Leah and the kids at home while Murph was at work. Rooney was not used to spending eight to nine hours completely alone. Murph couldn't blame the big guy for that. Murph was lonely, too. He tried to rush home as soon as he could after work to get Rooney out and for some company himself. The two were both a little better off for it.

    Rooney usually was waiting for him by the door as soon as he walked in the front door. It always fascinated Murph how dogs have that keen sense of knowing their owners are home way before they get to the door. In

Collisions

Pittsburgh, Leah knew Murph was almost home when he pulled onto their street hundreds of yards from the house because Rooney's massive ears perked up, and he started for the back door.

Since Rooney came down to the Outer Banks, he had been bringing his food in his mouth to the bedroom and eating it on his bed. He would get about thirty pieces of the dry dog food and carry it in, then do the Rooney circle around the bed to find the perfect spot to lie down and chew his food. After he finished he would get up and walk back to the kitchen, where his bowl was, and repeat the same steps over again. Murph tried everything he could think of to get him to eat in the kitchen. He put some chairs in the entry to block his path, but Rooney just stood there with the food in his mouth and whined. Murph put him outside with the food bowl, and he just left it sitting on the concrete stoop uneaten. After trying different strategies and tired of walking around the house with bits of food on his socks, he caved and moved a mat and the bowl into their bedroom. This reduced Rooney's trek from bowl to bed and the time it took him to eat, not to mention the mess.

Murph was meeting Pete later for dinner. He'd wanted to take Murph to one of the local spots where the food was good and the waitresses were nice to look at. Murph wanted to get Rooney out to the beach before he needed to get back and shower to go, so he decided to just feed him after. Out at the beach, he typically could let Rooney off his leash since there weren't too many people in the Outer Banks in early spring. The waves had been rough the previous couple days, but Rooney went right in the water like they were no big deal. While the two were out at the beach they saw a family of five walking back from the pier, Murph couldn't help but get excited for his family to arrive the next day. Of course like most people who saw the big dog, the family stopped and watched Rooney ride waves and chase his ball for a while, and like most others, they asked what kind of dog he was. He ran over to them after he rode a choppy wave in and shook off wet sand all over their kids. When Rooney wobbled water off, it was similar to a sideways downpour that forced a car to the side of the road. His large frame could hold a lot of water, especially with his thick fur. Gallons. Murph talked for a while with the parents. They were staying right up the road for the week, and their two younger kids were right around the same age as Isabella and Patrick. He knew that would give the kids somebody to play with out on the beach if it stayed nice outside. The comforts of being back to normal were already setting in.

Isabella had been obsessed with turtles since she first saw Crush and the other sea turtles in *Finding Nemo,* a little less than a year earlier. Murph could pretty much recite the entire movie, since it was all Isabella wanted to watch on her DVD player in Maria's car. Patrick really liked Jacques, the shrimp, for some reason, and he laughed anytime the character hit the screen. One of Isabella's favorite books for Murph to read to her at night was Dr. Seuss' *Yertle the Turtle*, and she slept with three stuffed turtles every night. She was even a turtle the past Halloween. Patrick wanted to do everything his sister did, so he wanted to be a turtle, too. At that point, Isabella had no problem with Patrick copying her, but Murph knew she would get tired of it soon enough as she grew older. She was very creative for her age, and she did most of the design of the costumes herself. Maria and Isabella found two green kids' Boston Celtics hoodies close to the kids' sizes at Gabriel Brothers. The family used green face paint, newspapers, and felt for the rest of the costume.

Maria had been showing the kids different Outer Banks websites on her Mac for things to do while they were visiting Murph. They came across a site that showed where the best places to see turtles were, and that was the number one activity on Isabella's list of things to do on the trip. Murph had been doing his own research on turtles in the area. It was possible to see them at the local aquarium, but he also imagined that it would be great to see them in their natural habitat. They typically didn't start to lay eggs until May, but since this winter had been particularly mild, he read they could start early. Loggerheads are the most common turtle in the Banks, but they might also be able to see hawksbills and leatherbacks. Murph was planning to start looking for turtles the first night the family was there, and he was going to make sure they kept looking until they were successful.

After exploring most of the marine wildlife holes on the stretch of beach near his rental, Murph took Rooney back to the house and let him go through his strange eating routine. Murph also tried to straighten up and do some laundry. Living as a bachelor, he had not been keeping up with the cleaning or dirty clothes nearly as much as Maria did. He also stopped by Cahoon's Grocery to get some needed supplies like milk, string cheese, and Cheerios for the kids before he met Pete.

• • •

Murph met Pete at Nags Head Grille. Murph had been there once for lunch, and it definitely had some of the best seafood in the area. They were known for the best red drum dishes on the beach. Pete was waiting for him at the bar when Murph arrived. He let Murph know there was going to be a one hour wait, so they went outside and played corn-hole on one of the restaurant's sets while they waited. Pete's status could have gotten them in earlier at most local joints, but Murph knew that Pete was the kind of guy who wanted to be treated like everybody else.

He beat Murph twenty-one to nineteen in their first game, and as they started their second, the conversation took an unexpected turn from their usual sports banter. Out of the blue, Pete brought up his very first serious girlfriend.

"Dude, Shelby and I came here on our first date," Pete said.

If it hadn't been so random, Murph would have come back and said something smart like, "Pete, you know I don't like you that way, so I don't want you to think this is a date." But Murph could tell by Pete's demeanor when he brought it up that there was something different about this conversation.

"Who is Shelby?" Murph asked.

"She was my next door neighbor growing up. We used to play hide and seek and Monopoly together all the time. Then she moved away when we were seven. I didn't see her again for ten years, and then she moved back across the street and a couple houses down. Do you remember Winnie Cooper from *Wonder Years*?"

"Yeah, of course, great show."

"Well, it was a lot like the first episode when Winnie moves in across from Kevin and there is a slow motion scene with kind of a cloudy, dreamy feel. His jaw drops when he first sees her. I can remember it like it just happened. Shelby got out of her parents' Volvo 240 Carolina blue station wagon in the back right seat. She was wearing her "The Police" shirt with Sting holding the microphone and Stewart Copeland ripping it on the drums. She had on white-washed jeans and her all-white, spotless Keds. She had flowing, wavy blonde hair, and looked a lot like Elizabeth Shue in the first *Karate Kid*. Man, I was in love with her right at that moment.

Collisions

It took me six months to talk to her, and another six months to finally ask her out. We dated for the next four years"

Murph could hear the acoustic twang of the "Winnie Song" as he sunk a bean bag for three points and asked, "What happened after that?"

"Dude, she died."

"Whoa," Murph said surprised by Pete's abruptness.

"Yeah, no shit, 'whoa' is right."

"What happened?"

"I was a complete dipshit for one, and Hurricane Gloria happened."

Their buzzer went off for the table, and Pete handed the bean bags off to the two teenage kids who were waiting patiently for them to finish. Pete ordered bourbon on ice, and Murph got a Newcastle. He knew that he was in for a long story, and a beer or two might not be a bad idea. Murph didn't drink too often, maybe a couple beers a month, but never more than two at a time.

"Shelby and I dated throughout college. She went to Duke. She had a lot more brains than me, and I went to UNC-Wilmington. As hard as it is to be in your early twenties with hormones running wild, we both made it through the long distance relationship. She was always worried about all the beach bunnies running around Wilmington. She envisioned girls coming to class in their skimpy bikinis. Truth is I was more worried that she was going to find somebody that was much more intelligent and intellectual than me. She would find somebody that smoked those little cigars and talked about stocks and bonds during his free time. When it all came down to it, we were perfect for each other, and there was no way that I would ever cheat on Shelby or vice versa. She was the girl of my dreams, and I was wild about her. I might have smoked a lot of dope and not been the smartest guy around, but I was smart enough to know not to fuck that relationship up, dude."

"I know what it is like to have 'that girl'," Murph said.

"Yeah, hold onto her tight, because you don't want to lose her. You might never find another one like her or even close, in my case. Shelby and I talked about marriage. I kidded with her that I was going to be a stay at home dad. With her Duke education, she was going to be the bread winner of the family, my sugar momma. Shelby majored in biology, and was accepted into UNC's med school. She deferred enrollment a year though so we could live at home and save some money. We were going to move to Chapel Hill together and get an apartment. She really wanted to work with kids, so her goal was to be a pediatrician. I had never lived away from a beach, and I was really not sure what I would do. I majored in Parks and Recreation, so I was going to look into working at a center for a while. Both of our parents had a lot of money, but Shelby was pretty keen on the fact that we would find our own way through life."

The waitress came and told them the specials. Pete obviously went to the Nags Head Grille frequently because she said, "The usual, Mr. Mitchell?" to him. Murph ordered the red drum plate.

"In mid-September of 1985, my friends and I heard that a strong hurricane was going to hit the Outer Banks. People were saying it was going to be the storm of the century as it made its way towards the Bahamas. Back then the only weather news we got was on the main networks. We couldn't pull up the weather on our phones or look on a computer like everybody does nowadays. The Outer Banks

Collisions

were requesting everybody to evacuate. The people who live in the Outer Banks are typically pretty stubborn, and we like to stay on our little island through anything. My friends and I were excited about catching what promised to be some seriously epic waves caused by an enormous storm swell. Both Shelby's and my parents left town to go stay with relatives. Shelby told her parents that we would come meet them later that day, which was two days before the storm was supposed to hit the Outer Banks."

The waitress brought the food. Pete had a roasted chicken overtop of mashed potatoes. Supposedly, it was the house specialty, and Murph thought it looked great. He guessed when you lived on the beach that fish was something you ate all the time, so it was nice to get something a little different. Murph's special looked fantastic. The fish was sprinkled with salt, pepper, parsley, and dill weed and came with a side of mashed potatoes and cauliflower, but he was starting to lose his appetite in anticipation of the rest of Pete's story. He would need to order another beer to help him get through it and wash down the food.

"With peer pressure pushing me, I begged Shelby to let us stay one more day. She wasn't happy about it but said as long as we left the next morning she would be okay with it. I spent the rest of that day surfing, and came back and spent that night with Shelby at her parents'. I did not tell her, but I made plans to meet my buddies the next morning to get in a couple hours of monster waves before we left. I woke up early and left without even giving her a kiss, thinking I could get back before she woke up. She must have woken up pretty shortly after and turned on the news. The storm was moving a little faster up the Atlantic coast than was originally expected. It was already raining and pretty windy where we were surfing that morning. We actually never even made it into the water. Nobody is positive what happened next, but there was a note at Shelby's parents' house waiting for me. It said:

Pete where are you? We need to get out of here now. I went to your house and you weren't there. I am going to drive up the beach road and see if I can find your car. Wait for me here, if you get here and I am still gone. I don't know where you could be.

Love you, Shelby.

She barely made it a mile up the beach road, when she lost control of the car in the wind and crashed into a telephone pole. She did not have her seat belt on, and she sustained massive head injuries. There were already limited emergency vehicles in the Outer Banks at the time due to the evacuation. I pulled up to the scene about fifteen to twenty minutes after the accident. I had already been home, and we must have just missed each other, so I went back out looking for her. After driving up to the scene, I rushed to Dare County Regional Hospital to be with Shelby during her final hours. She made it one more day before passing on. I didn't even notice the winds and rains outside as the hurricane crashed into the coast. Her parents weren't able to find out about any of it until a day after Gloria passed through. They found the note and never forgave me. They would not speak to me at the funeral, and they ended up moving to New Jersey a couple months later. Hurricane Gloria ended up not even being that bad, since the eye hit during low tide. It lived up to the hype as far as I'm concerned. There were officially eight deaths reported due to Gloria."

Pete looked right into Murph's eyes as he spoke. "When I said earlier to hold onto what you have with that great family of yours, I meant it, dude." Murph was pretty sure some tears welled up, but Pete must not have wanted him to see them as he got up and went to the bathroom without another word.

He came back a couple minutes later and said, "Shit man, how about them Panthers?"

• • •

After he paid for his meal and while Pete was still finishing up his drink, Murph excused himself to step outside. He wanted to Skype with the kids and Maria before they headed to bed for the next day, especially after he heard that story from Pete about Shelby.

Isabella was wearing her favorite Minnie Mouse, red and white spotted pajamas and Patrick was running around in his diaper. He had always been very anti-clothes, and they had a hard time getting him dressed or in his pajamas daily. Maria and Murph decided that they would give him a good twenty minutes each night to run around with just his diaper on, in hopes that he would get his unclothed fix in for the day.

Maria looked tired when she sat down at the computer. She was wearing her Troy Polamalu jersey. Murph felt that Troy had good hair, but that Maria wore the jersey way better. In fact, she looked great in anything she wore. She could put makeup on or go without it, and the same with jewelry. She also could be in sweats or a party dress and he still would find her as gorgeous as ever.

Even though she had some help from her mother and Ms. Linker while he had been gone, Murph could tell just looking at Maria that being alone with the kids had been wearing her out.

"Daddy, we made you a video and Momma is going to email it to you," shouted out an excited Isabella as Patrick ran wild in the background.

"That's great, I can't wait," Murph responded.

"I sent you a video, too, but just make sure to open it when you are back in your room by yourself," Maria said with a wink.

"Wow, I really can't wait to watch that one."

"Daddy, have you seen any turtles yet?"

"No, I made an announcement at the beach for all turtles to wait until Isabella gets here tomorrow to come out of their holes. They are all waiting patiently for you to get here!"

"Wow. Can we go tomorrow, Daddy?"

"That's the plan, Stan. We will come back to the house to put our stuff up, pick up Rooney, and go right to the beach."

"Can you tell us a story?"

"Sure, what do you want this to be about?"

"Hmmm, a rhinoceros that does ballet."

"Patrick, hey Patrick?" Murph said. Patrick was throwing a ball to nobody in particular in the background and having a blast doing it. "Isabella wants me to tell a story about a rhinoceros ballerina. What color do you want it to be?"

"Gween," he shouted.

Collisions

Every night before bed they usually read a couple books, and the kids liked him to make up a story on his own. Isabella typically chose the characters and what they did, but they were working on Patrick's colors, so he tried to incorporate colors into the stories. He spent the next couple minutes telling a story about a green rhinoceros that did ballet.

At the end of the story, Murph said, "I can't wait to see you guys tomorrow!"

"We can't wait either, Daddy! Make sure to tell Rooney that we can't wait to see him too," said Isabella.

"I won't, and I will give him a big, juicy kiss right on the nose for you."

"Ha ha, Daddy!"

The kids and Maria all kissed the computer screen, and Murph kissed his phone screen as they closed the conversation.

Victor Dancy

After Victor finally got off work at 5:30, he headed out to Chili's where he grabbed some endless chips and salsa and a Corona at the bar. There was a rather attractive twenty-something, with gigantic breasts, tending bar. Victor told her that he was a very successful neurosurgeon and he was in town to speak at a convention. The bartender was completely eating up his bullshit, and he was feeling like he had a really great shot at her. Even though he added weight over the years, women still found him attractive. He texted Leah and told her that he was going to be staying late at work and not to wait on him for dinner. She didn't respond back.

Victor felt he had the bartender in the bag. He told her that he was staying at the Hilton in downtown Williamsburg and asked what time she got off. She said since it was slow, she could probably get out of there by nine. She was all about meeting him at another bar for a drink after she left. In the middle of his fish tacos, he excused himself to go to the bathroom. While he was in there, he called the Hilton and made a reservation. Victor figured they could go get wasted together at the bar, and he would take her back to the hotel and be in her pants before she ever noticed that he didn't have any luggage in the room. She was obviously down for a one night stand.

When he got back to the bar, he was shocked to find Leah sitting in his seat, talking to the bartender. Apparently she had come in five minutes earlier and sat down at a table with Maddie. She saw Victor when he walked near their table on his way to the bathroom.

"So how was that extra-long day at work, honey?" she asked sarcastically.

"What are you doing here, Leah?" Victor said, pissed to be caught in the act.

"Well, I am talking to Trisha, the bartender here. Apparently she bought the lie you told her about being a doctor or something ridiculous like that. Trisha, don't worry he's not a doctor, just a wannabe-pilot with a small penis," she said to the red faced bartender.

"What the fuck, Leah?" Victor said as she walked off, and he followed her towards the hostess stand.

"Don't you dare follow me! Maddie has no idea you are here, and I am hoping she doesn't see you. She thinks you are still at work."

Collisions

Leah walked off towards her table. Of all the restaurants in Williamsburg, Victor was livid that his bitch wife had to show up at that one. He headed back to his seat. There was a new bartender behind the bar. He figured Trisha took a quick break, but she never came back out while he was there. Fuck it, he thought. After he finished eating and downed a couple more beers, Victor headed out the side door and luckily did not see Leah and Maddie. He left a one cent tip for the bartenders, and wrote under the signature: "Trisha, you are just a fat cow anyways."

Victor headed to another bar that served hard liquor after leaving Chili's. He wasn't going home after that bullshit stunt that Leah pulled, the whore.

He ended up at a local dive called O'Henry's. Keeping with the Irish theme, he ordered a couple Guinness's and three Irish Car Bombs. The bartender was a fucking dude. There was a Washington Nationals game on the tube, so he watched it to keep occupied as he started to get sloshed. He stayed at the bar until about ten o'clock. Victor still had the reservation for the Hilton, so he decided to just go there for the night and get some sleep. He really did not feel like dealing with Leah.

When he got to the hotel and up to his room, Victor flipped on the TV. Luckily they had Cinemax, so he put it on. As soon as he turned it on, the excellent sex scene with Halle Berry in *Monster's Ball* came on. Two minutes into watching, he was on the phone with Sherri's Escorts. From experience he knew they had an excellent selection. He told the lady on the other end that he was in the mood for some ebony that night after seeing the lustrous Halle Berry. She said that the earliest she could have one to him would be 2:00 am. Victor said that was fine, and he decided that he might as well waste the time by heading down to the bar at the Hilton. While he was down there, he had about ten more beers, Bud Lights to Samuel Adams, whatever.

Laticia got there around 2:30 am. He was used to them never being on time. She was a good six feet and wore a long overcoat and red lingerie underneath. They got down to business very fast with no messing around beforehand. He was worn out by 3:30 am and could have passed out, but Laticia had some blow with her, so he took a couple lines. They went at it a couple more times, and he finally fell asleep at about five o'clock. Two hours later his wakeup call came in. Victor contemplated calling in sick to work, but he had already missed six days, and he really could not afford to miss any more. He left Laticia in bed, crumpled up the two hundred dollars he owed her and dropped them on the floor in front of the door, and headed home to get changed.

Chapter 6

Murphy Kearns

When Murph left Nags Head Grille, he headed back to the rental house. It took him about an hour to put together the presents he got the kids. He had been reading a lot about Plasma Cars, which had just won a national toy award. It looked a lot like a tricycle that you might find in a futuristic movie set in 2075. Murph bought Isabella a pink car with a turtle helmet and Patrick a green car with a shark helmet. He spent about one hundred and fifty dollars at Pirates and Pixies, a small toy store in Nags Head, which he knew Maria would not be happy about. Maria was never one to pamper herself, so Murph bought Maria a day pass to a local spa, and he planned to take the kids for the day and let her have a nice relaxing break. He also lined up a neighbor of Pete's to babysit that same night, so he could take Maria out on a romantic date to The Flying Fish for dinner and then to the Sandbar Bed and Breakfast for the night. When he was done assembling the toys, he took all three presents out to the trunk of the Jeep. He was very excited to surprise his family at the airport with the gifts.

He wanted to get to bed early enough so that he could wake up in plenty of time to get to the airport. It would be satisfying, indulgent even, to wait in the comfort of time for the people who made him happy. Murph let Rooney out and got into bed around eleven o'clock. He read a little bit and dozed off sometime before midnight.

Murph usually didn't dream much, but he decided to take a couple Tylenol PM so he could be sure to get one good night of sleep before the family came. Tylenol PM always tended to make him have very realistic dreams. When he did dream, he had reoccurring dreams in which he went for a run and his feet couldn't touch the ground. He was running on air and no matter how hard he tried, his feet could not touch. Sometime during the middle of that night, he dreamed about his wedding with Maria.

In the dream, Murph and Maria were at their outdoor reception. He spent some time talking to his family, walking around and shaking hands. Murph spotted Maria at different moments doing the same thing with other members of the wedding party. They made eye contact, and she gave him the little shy smile that he was so used to, where her dimples really stood out. She looked gorgeous in her traditional wedding dress. Maria wasn't one for the flashiness of a modern gown. She didn't need it.

Maria's dad got on the microphone and said it was time for the first dance. The crowd encircled the makeshift wooden dance floor. Maria timed the wedding, on a farm outside of Washington, Pennsylvania, so that the couple danced just as the sun was going down. The sun sank in the western sky over top of a brown farm house built in the nineteenth century.

Maria's favorite song by The Avett Brothers was the "Offering." In the dream, Maria and Murph looked each other in the eyes for the entire song, swaying side to side with the music. Maria sang her favorite lines from the song to him during the dance. "Hmm I love you, want to make you my wife someday," and the lyric, "And I dream of children, we can call our own, watch 'em run around in the front yard, from the front porch of our home." The moment was frozen in the haze of the warm summer evening and swooning music.

After the dance was over, Maria gave him a big kiss and said "Murph, I love you more than anything." Then time began to move more quickly, and he felt like he was falling away from Maria, and Murph could not stop the falling. He could see Maria slipping away, like he was looking through a kaleidoscope at her, and she could not reach him as he fell.

Murph shot up from the bed in a cold sweat and the clock in his room said 3:23 a.m. He knew he should have been able to go right back to sleep, but he couldn't after having a dream like that one. He feared falling back into the same dream and was confused whether the pangs he felt were the dreams or his, a fear of losing Maria or the moment, or both. He had this sinking feeling in his gut, and he could not get the feeling of death out of his head.

Twice he had had these premonitions of death, and they ruminated in his head over and over. The first happened when he was a little boy, and he was riding in the backseat of his parent's wood-paneled station wagon, back from a vacation to his grandparents'. He just had a great stay with both his grandparents. While his grandfather was at work, his grandmother took him to Sea World and to the local zoo. The two became very close over that week. As they neared home and Murph watched the passing landscape out of the back window of the station wagon, he had a fear that something really bad was going to happen to his grandmother. He cried for nearly twenty minutes until they got home. His unexpected cries shook his mother, and as soon as they got in the door of the house, Murph's mom called and got his grandmother on the phone to prove that everything was alright. It made him feel better to talk to her, but he still had that nagging feeling that something really bad was going to happen. It circled and circled around in his head. The next morning when Murph got to school, his third grade teacher, Mrs. Davis, looked like she had been crying when he walked into his classroom. She told her students there was going to be a very important announcement on the intercom. When the announcement came out overhead, it was the assistant principal telling the entire school that Mrs. McGee, their beloved principal, had passed away suddenly overnight. Many people, including his parents, always described Mrs. McGee as a grandmother-type figure to the students at her elementary school.

The second time Murph had the feeling was in college. It was in his Introduction to Sociology class, and the professor was talking about the positive and negative effects of affirmative action. Murph was trying his hardest to focus on what the professor was saying, but the feeling again hit him that something bad was going to happen to somebody he was close to. That second time, there was nobody in particular in his premonition, which made it seem even worse. It made him think about potential problems with family members and friends. Murph wasn't able to pay attention for the rest of that class, and the feeling stuck with him for several more hours. Nothing happened that day, but when he woke up the next morning, he had a message from a close friend at home. When Murph called the friend back, he told Murph that another of their good friends was killed the day before while serving in Iraq. The friend left college after his freshman year to join the Army, and had only been in Iraq for two months before he was killed by friendly fire.

Collisions

Murph sat in bed trying to think of anything but death, but he knew better than to ignore feelings like these. After rolling around for an hour, he turned on the television and watched *SportsCenter* twice, but that didn't help either. The main story was about a professional basketball player that killed his wife of twenty years and then killed himself. He got up and tried to do some work on his computer, but nothing helped. At about five in the morning when it was starting to get light outside, he put on his sweats and went for a long run. For the entire hour run, he could not get death out of his head.

Victor Dancy

The drive back home from the Hilton was very painful for Victor. The hangover was starting, and since he didn't sleep much, he was still slightly drunk. It had only been a few hours since he stopped drinking. His head felt like it was going to explode, and his muscles ached. Victor felt like he might throw-up at any minute, but he needed to book it home to change and shower. He could not be late to work. He needed a Bloody Mary, his preferred hangover cure. Victor had to rush to get it all done and be at work by eight-thirty.

Victor really didn't give a damn about where Maddie thought he was the night before, but Leah was waiting when he pulled in. He immediately had second thoughts about coming home. He wished he had just worn the clothes from the night before and gone straight to work from the Hilton.

"Maddie is down in her playroom watching cartoons, and she thinks you just ran out to get milk because we were out of it," Leah told him as soon as he stepped out of the car.

"And?" Victor clutched his head.

"And, I don't want your daughter knowing and asking why you didn't stay at home last night, so please just do this for your daughter, who has no idea yet how much of a creep you are!"

Victor looked away and squinted as he walked past his wife. "I am not in the mood for your shit this morning, Leah. Just get out of my way, and I will do whatever you ask if you just leave me alone."

Victor must have stumbled a bit getting out of the car because Leah said, "You're still drunk, aren't you?"

"I just told you to leave me alone, didn't I?" Victor reiterated.

"You smell horrible; this is disgusting!" she whispered so Maddie couldn't hear.

"Being a hooker is disgusting," Victor said raising his voice because he knew it would tick her off even more. He turned around and walked back to her to get in her face.

"You smell like sex; who were you out screwing last night?" she asked.

"Somebody you might know, she's an escort just like you, but was much better in bed!"

Leah attempted to slap Victor in the face. He might have been drunk, but his response was just quick enough to see it coming and grabbed her wrist and squeezed as hard as he could.

"Stop it," she squirmed. "That really hurts."

Collisions

He started to squeeze harder, and Leah fell to her knees putting her arm in an awkward upside down position. She started whimpering. "Please let go, it hurts, please." Leah limply hit Victor's arm with her other hand to no avail. He started to twist the wrist as he squeezed, knowing that it would cause a burn on her arm.

"Daddy, what are you doing to Mommy?" Maddie was standing in the doorway. He let go of Leah, but first he gave her a smile to let her know that once again he'd won. Her only response was to stare back at Victor. Leah got up quickly and hurried over to Maddie.

"Honey, please go and grab your stuff, and hurry back to the car. I'll take you to Dunkin' Donuts this morning to get a chocolate doughnut," she said patting Maddie on the back as she wiped tears across her own face.

Maddie looked confused and said, "Mommy, why are you crying? What's wrong?"

"Don't worry about it, baby. Please just go get your stuff."

Maddie ran into the other room. Leah turned to Victor and said, "I can't do this anymore." Her mascara was streaked, but her lip was set.

"Oh yes you can, and you will if you want to stay in this house and you want to keep going to the country club. If you want to keep using me and my dad, I will most definitely keep using you!"

"I hate you!" Leah said with more venom than Victor had ever heard from her. Maddie returned, and the two got into Leah's Subaru and drove off. Victor was relieved to see them leave because it meant that he could make a Bloody Mary and get ready for work in peace. He was ticked off that

Leah had just wasted some of his precious time, nothing a second Bloody Mary couldn't cure.

Chapter 7

Murphy Kearns

When Murph got back from his run, he showered and dressed and still had some time to kill before he needed to get in the car to drive to pick up Maria and the kids in Norfolk. Murph decided to eat a good breakfast at Sam & Omie's even though he didn't have much of an appetite. Johnny told him he ate there every single morning since Lois passed away. She used to make Johnny hot cakes when he woke up, and Murph was hoping to run into him so he could have some company and hopefully clear his head.

It was pretty foggy and a little chilly for an April morning on the coast. When he walked into the restaurant, Johnny was sitting at the counter drinking coffee. Murph was very proud to see that Johnny was also reading *To Kill a Mockingbird*, which Murph told him was one of his favorite books. Murph wanted to give him some book choices that were classics that he never got to enjoy, but were not too hard for him to read. Besides, with a little girl of his own now, Murph felt the world would be a little better off with more Scouts around.

"What's good on the menu this morning?" Murph asked as he sat down beside Johnny.

"Heck, man, the hot cakes," Johnny said without looking up from the book.

"That's what I heard from a friend of mine who comes here," Murph said. Johnny finally looked up from the book and noticed Murph.

"Oh it's you, sorry about that. How ya' doing this here morning?" Johnny asked Murph.

"I didn't sleep well last night, but I am excited to pick up the family in a couple hours," Murph said as he gripped Johnny's hand in greeting.

"So this is the morning they arrive, huh? Hopefully you will bring them by here for breakfast; I will buy them cute kids of yours some hot cakes. Hey Cindy, give my man here a big cup of coffee and five cakes on me," Johnny shouted across the bar.

"Sure thing, Johnny," the waitress said.

"How's the book going?" Murph asked.

"Man, I can't put it down. Lois would have loved this book, I tell ya'. That Scout sure is a character. I'm at the part now where Jem and Mrs. Dew-Boss-ee get into an argument."

"I am glad you like it, and it only gets better."

They talked for about ten more minutes about different sections of the book, until Murph's breakfast arrived. He gulped down his third cup, but he still had no appetite for the food. Murph thought his lingering unease had evaporated until he glanced at the television behind the bar that was showing CNN. The anchor broke into coverage of a bad earthquake that happened on April the sixth in Italy, killing over 1,000 Italians. He excused himself from the table and walked outside to call Maria.

She answered after a couple of rings on her cell phone. "Hey, honey, we are getting ready to pull up to the airport. Can I call you once I get checked in?"

"Yeah, I just wanted to make sure you guys were alright," Murph said, with a strong hint of worry in his voice.

"Sure we are, just a little frazzled trying to get these kids ready. Are you sure everything is alright with you? You don't sound too good," Maria said.

"Yeah, I'm fine. I just didn't sleep great last night."

"Probably because you are so excited to see us; only a couple hours left," she replied.

"Yeah," Murph said trying to sound more enthusiastic. "I just want to make sure you want to take the flight. Pete already let me take most of the day. I could probably take tomorrow morning off, too, and drive up and get you."

"No, you don't need to do that. We will be perfectly fine and besides we are already at the airport. Thanks for the thought, but I can't wait to see you in a couple hours. Don't worry; the trip will be fine. I have to go. I'm getting honked at."

"Ok, I love you honey and the kids too!" Murph quickly blurted out.

"You too," she rushed out before hanging up.

Murph went back inside and told Johnny he had to go and that he would make sure to bring the kids in for breakfast so he could meet them in a few days.

Victor Dancy

Once Victor was showered and dressed, he drove to work and walked in surprisingly just forty minutes late. Luckily the day was going to be pretty light since they didn't have many flights taking off or landing during his scheduled shift. There were a couple scheduled charter flights for rich local businessmen who had nothing better to do than fly their multi-million dollar planes on pointless trips. United States Couriers had two outbound flights leaving WRA before lunch and one inbound in the late afternoon. Victor was working with Steve Rodriguez, a robust man in his seventies who had worked at WRA with Victor for the past five years. Victor thought that Steve looked like Cheech or Chong, whichever one was the shorter one with the moustache, if you added about one hundred and fifty pounds. Steve and Victor had a pretty tolerable work-relationship. Steve minded his own business, which was more than Victor could say about a lot of the other dipshits he worked with. Steve did unfortunately have a tendency to talk too much at times, mostly about his family, which bugged Victor.

Steve came back to work five years earlier when his wife, Nancy, was diagnosed with Alzheimer's. She decided back then that she wanted to stay at home and not go into a nursing or assisted living home. Steve worked at Norfolk International until he retired at sixty, but came back to WRA to help pay for their in-home nurse. His wife did pretty well for the first four years on her medications, but she had been going downhill pretty fast that past year, and Steve had been having a lot of problems with her at home. She was getting physical with both Steve and the nurses when she got frustrated, and she had left the house several times without warning. Steve had to hide the keys to her car.

The flight rules at WRA stated that at least two flight controllers and a supervisor should be in the flight room at all times when flights were scheduled to arrive or depart. On dead days like the one scheduled that morning, the supervisors sometimes tried to get in important appointments and forego the rules. There were just a few flights that morning in the airspace, but Michelle called to check in five minutes before Victor got there, which was thirty-five minutes after he was supposed to be at work. Steve lied for Victor and told Michelle that Victor just ran out to use the restroom and that he would be right back.

Michelle Bowen was a tall, lanky, red-headed woman with about a million freckles on her face. Sometimes when she was speaking to Victor, he tried to see how many freckles he could count. It was a great way to look at her and pretend he was paying attention, without wasting his time on whatever drivel was coming out of her mouth. Victor could not figure out why in the world a woman was ever hired into a leadership role. It should never happen, in his opinion, anywhere except maybe at a maid or nanny service. Michelle told Steve she would be in no later than eleven. She was at a parent-teacher conference at her son's middle school. Her son, Dylan, was a pain in the ass, constantly in trouble. Michelle brought Dylan to work, and he would run around knocking things over and causing all sorts of havoc. There had been several times Victor wanted to grab him by his underwear and hang him up on the coatrack so he would settle down. Michelle was into some new age type of punishing with timeouts. If there was one thing that Victor agreed with The Colonel about, it was that there should always be some corporal punishment in the mix. Victor wanted to take Dylan into another room whenever he was at WRA, and give the little brat some good licks with his belt. A good whipping would fix the kid and be alright with Victor. Dylan's latest incident involved sneaking water guns into class and shooting classmates while the teacher was at the chalkboard.

At eight forty-five, Steve got a call from the nurse at his house. He looked frazzled on the phone. "Shit, man, my wife wandered out of the house and our new nurse is freaking out," he said to Victor after he got off the phone. "I better call 911 to have them help look for Nancy. This is the third time she's done this in the past month, and I'm pretty sure the fire department is getting pretty pissed off. She's always going to the house of a friend of ours who moved twenty years ago."

"Can't you just tell the nurse to check there?" Victor asked.

"She doesn't seem like the brightest bulb, and I'm scared to send her out in case Nancy comes back home."

"How long does it take you to get home?" Victor asked.

"About fifteen minutes with no traffic. Why?" Steve responded.

"Man, you covered for me this morning, I owe you one," Victor said as he pulled out the flight chart. "We only have a couple flights going overhead before eleven, and just the one US Courier flight leaving. Just run home and help, but make sure you get your ass back here before Michelle gets back, so we don't both get in trouble."

Collisions

"I don't know about this man, we could get in some serious shit if something happened," Steve said.

"Ha, what in the world is going to happen? I have got this shit covered. What, do you think I can't handle it?" Victor asked in an irritated tone. He did owe Steve, but he was not doing it for him. His head was pounding like a kick drum that somebody kept stomping on, and he figured after he got the US Courier flight on its way, he could rest his eyes for half an hour or so, before Steve and Michelle got back.

"You sure about this?" Steve asked still a bit wary.

"Yeah, get outta here, you're wasting time," Victor said.

"Thanks, man!" Steve said as he quickly grabbed his jacket and rushed out the door.

Victor sat back in his chair relieved to finally have some peace and quiet.

Chapter 8

Murphy Kearns

On Murph's way out of town, he drove by the rolling sand dunes at Jockey's Ridge. He could imagine his kids rolling down the hills in laughter. With its heavy winds, it would be a great place for them to fly kites for the first time, Patrick romping through the sand chasing the brightly colored kite tails.

He'd already checked out Nags Head Kites, and they had a turtle kite he could buy for the kids. These were not the kites that looked like they would break in the wind, but they were intricately designed kites that looked very life-like in the pictures. He wanted to wait for Maria to be in on the purchase so he didn't fall behind any further in his gift account.

Murph had the windows down, buoyed by the breeze and the heavy smell of saltwater. He drove by the barren field where the Wright Brothers took their first flight. Though he was not sure that they would understand the history of the place at their ages, it would be great to take his family to the airstrip where Orville and Wilbur flew. They would appreciate it more after just taking their first flight.

The fog had cleared up some, and there was light traffic. Murph was in such a rush to start the hour and a half trek to Norfolk that his excitement and the fresh air had helped him to forget his feelings of dread. Those feelings came back as Murph crossed the bridge just past Duck on US-158, when he saw a sign for auto collision insurance.

Maria, Isabella, and Patrick should have been mid-flight as he crossed the North Carolina and Virginia border. He talked to them after they boarded the Atlantic Airlines plane for the flight. Maria said that everybody at the airport in Pittsburgh was extremely helpful. It never hurt Maria that she was so striking. Men and women were quick to help her. They offered her a ride through the airport on a cart once she checked in, and she said after she parked, a nice young guy helped her with their luggage. Sometimes Maria and Murph joked about how easy she could have it with her looks, but she typically wouldn't accept help. She must have changed her mind going through an airport with two young children. She needed all the help she could get.

When they talked, the flight was going to be about fifteen minutes late taking off. She said it was a crowded flight and there seemed to be a lot of college kids going on spring break. She overheard some of them talking. They were from Duquesne University and were headed to Virginia Beach for the week. Maria and Murph went on a trip to Costa Rica their senior year at Pitt for spring break. They rented a car and traveled from the Atlantic to the Pacific Ocean through the cloud forests of the Cordillera Central Mountains. They zip-lined through rainforests, had a wild monkey trapped in one of their rooms, and saw their first volcano at Arenal.

"Do you remember our spring break flight?" Maria asked Murph, while she was sitting on the plane and waiting to pull back from the terminal.

"Yeah, the plane was pretty empty so we had a row of seats to ourselves. We also drank a little too much, if I recall," Murph said. Neither of them were huge drinkers, even in college. In Costa Rica, they did enjoy quite a few Guaro's, clear liquor made from sugar cane, and they had their fair share of Imperial beers.

"If it weren't so early in the morning, I am sure some of these Duquesne students would be throwing some back," she said.

"Yeah, it's probably a good thing they are so rowdy, so Isabella and Patrick's noise won't be a problem. How are they doing so far?"

"They are great. Isabella is sitting over by the window reading her Dr. Seuss books. Patrick is in my lap now, eating a bunch of goldfish and spilling more in my lap."

In the background, Murph heard the flight attendant tell everybody to turn off their cellphones and prepare for take-off.

"We have to go honey; we can't wait to see you in a couple hours. I will call as soon as we land."

"I'll have my phone on and can't wait to see you all!" Murph said. Some of his panic before that point had fizzled. "Let me say goodbye to the kids."

"Okay. Patrick say bye to your daddy," Maria told her son.

"Dadd-eee," said Patrick.

Collisions

"Love you buddy, see you soon."

"Here's Isabella," Maria hurriedly said.

"Bella baby, have a great flight and I'll see you at the airport. I can't wait," Murph said to Isabella.

"I love you Daddy, I have on my Alice in Wonderland dress just for you." Isabella loved her Alice in Wonderland dress and black shoes. She would wear them daily if Maria and Murph let her. They told her that it was only for special occasions, in an attempt to keep it from getting ruined, and so they didn't have to constantly wash it. They decided a couple days before that Isabella's first plane ride seemed like a special enough occasion for her to wear it though.

"Love you, too!" Murph said to Isabella as she handed the phone back to her mom.

"Alright, see you soon, and I can't wait to get some alone time with you tonight. I love you very much," Maria declared.

"Me neither. Love you too!" Murph said as they hung up.

Part II – April 10 - 11, 2009

Newton's Second Law of Motion:

If a net force is applied, the constant velocity of an object shall be changed

Chapter 9

Posted: April 10, 2009, 9:58 a.m.

Carmen Paul/Williamsburg Daily Express

Vitaly, VA - More information is becoming available regarding the mid-air collision, where wreckage has been confirmed in the small coastal town of Vitaly, VA. The two flights that collided were Atlantic Airlines Flight 2937 and United States Courier Flight 611.

The Atlantic Airline (AA) flight was an Airbus 320, and it is believed that there were one hundred and forty-one passengers, which includes nine crew members. The AA flight was headed from the Pittsburgh International Airport to the Norfolk International Airport. The US Courier flight had two pilots and was en route from the Williamsburg Regional Airport (WRA) to Chicago, IL. It is unknown at this point if there are any survivors from either flight. It is believed that the US Courier Flight had just taken off from WRA due to the location of the wreckage. Vitaly, where the majority of the wreckage is reported to have landed, is just northwest of Williamsburg. There are no reports of injuries on the ground or damage to structures at the time of this posting.

Vitaly's population is listed at 5,347. The town's population reached over 11,000 in the 1980s when the Campioni Chocolate Factory was still open, but has been steadily decreasing since its close in 1994. The small town, just northwest of Williamsburg, was originally founded by a family from the Caucasus mountain region of Russia, who came to America in the early nineteenth century.

Neither the Federal Aviation Administration (FAA) nor the National Transportation Safety Board (NTSB), both headquartered in Washington, D.C., has yet to release a statement about either flight. Calls to Norfolk and Washington Center, handling approach/departure control and overhead traffic for the region, also yielded no new information.

Jonathan Troop, a resident of Vitaly, was in his car on his way to work when the collision happened. He said that most of the wreckage landed around the closed-down Campioni Chocolate Factory in the surrounding woods. Troop said he saw one plane that appeared to have recently taken off clip the wing of an incoming larger plane.

"It was surreal. I was driving and a plane was headed up just to the right of my car," said Troop. "From what I could see, a larger plane was descending out of the clouds. As the two planes got closer, I kept thinking something seemed strange since they were on a path towards each other. It appeared that at the last minute, the larger plane tried to turn and the smaller one flew right into it. The last time I saw anything like it was when I was watching the news on September 11th, and that second plane flew into the World Trade Center," Troop said.

More information will be released as it is made available.

Murphy Kearns

Murph hit a little traffic, due to road construction, about an hour south of Norfolk that set him back a bit. He was going to get to the airport later than the flight, but since it typically takes a while after landing to taxi and deplane, he wasn't too worried. As he neared Norfolk, his excitement elevated and the fear dissipated with the comfort that he would see his family soon. Murph was finally able to start enjoying himself. "Talk on Indolence" by The Avett Brothers came on a playlist on Murph's IPod, and he sang along and played the drums against the steering wheel as his spirit lifted. It brought him back to a happier time, a favorite memory of him and Maria and a small crowd basking in the band's music in Morgantown, West Virginia.

Murph's cell phone rang, snapping him back to the present. The clock on the dashboard read 9:30, close to the time the flight was supposed to be landing. He was hopeful it was Maria telling him that she landed early. Murph looked at the screen on his Blackberry, and he had a couple text messages in the last couple minutes from Pete. The last text said "CALL ME." Murph disregarded the text and the phone calls thinking that Pete probably just forgot that his family was coming. It was strange for him to call Murph that early. Murph didn't think Pete usually got out of bed before ten, and if so, only to surf.

A minute later, Murph got another chirp signaling another text. He looked at the phone and it was Pete, "CALL ME! IT'S VERY IMPORTANT!"

Collisions

Well punctuated and no "dude," Murph thought and dialed Pete's number immediately.

"Are you at the airport yet?" Pete asked.

"No, I'm about fifteen minutes out. I hit some traffic on the way," Murph responded.

"Are you listening to the radio?" he asked.

"No, I'm listening to my IPod. Why, what's up?"

"I'm not trying to freak you out! Sorry for calling so much and texting, hopefully it's nothing," Pete said. He sounded worried to Murph.

"What's nothing, Pete?" Murph asked feeding on Pete's tension.

"I was getting out of bed, and I left the TV on in my bedroom last night. I looked, and they don't have much information, but there appears to have been a plane accident somewhere near Norfolk."

Murph's stomach dropped and his mouth went completely dry. "Pete, I don't know you so well, but this better not be some kind of joke!"

"Dude, I don't really know what is going on, but this is definitely not a joke," Pete responded in a tone Murph had never heard him use.

With his free hand, Murph started frantically searching the radio for a news station as he hit the gas. Murph found a local NPR affiliate. "Pete, I'm going to listen to the radio and try to call Maria. Text me if you find out anything more!" he said as he hung up and accelerated further.

A mid-air collision between two planes happened above Vitaly, Virginia. Hearing it from Pete was one thing, but hearing it officially on the radio brought his panic to a whole new level. His palms stuck to the wheel, and it felt like the temperature in the car went up twenty degrees. How in the world do two planes collide mid-air in this day and age? He tried to speed dial Maria three times as he continued on to Norfolk since NPR was not giving out many details and Maria's phone was still turned off.

As he pulled within two miles of the Norfolk International Airport the broadcaster reported, "It appears that one of the flights involved in the mid-air collision was a United States Courier delivery flight, and the NTSB has just confirmed that the other flight was a Norfolk bound Atlantic Airlines Flight 2937."

Murph could not believe what was happening. No longer able to concentrate on the road, he pulled off onto the shoulder. Murph remembered that Maria emailed him the flight information so he would know where to pick them up. He looked at the email on his Blackberry and found her message from a couple days earlier. As he opened the email, he closed his eyes. Murph wasn't much into saying prayers, but he said a quick one right then. "Please God, don't let it be their flight." He opened his email and in bold, Maria had typed flight number "Atlantic Airlines 2937."

Murph's body started shaking, and his vision blurred. He tried Maria's phone, and it went directly to voicemail yet again. He sent a text message to Pete asking where the flight crashed. Pete responded very quickly: "Vitaly, Virginia." Murph quickly plugged it into his GPS and gunned his Jeep towards Vitaly in a state of disbelief and shock.

Collisions

Victor Dancy

After Steve left, Victor sat back and rested his eyes for twenty minutes while waiting for the US Courier flight to take off. WRA had been having some maintenance problems with intrafield, direct phone lines, and the VHF radio the past year. They were at the bottom of the priority list for FAA repairs since there was such a limited amount of flights WRA monitored. The airport was scheduled to have somebody come and check their phone system the following week according to Michelle. Victor got a call in the flight control room from the US Courier flight captain asking for a delay from their filed flight plan. Apparently his co-pilot was a little under the weather after eating some bad Thai food the night before, and he needed to sit on the john for a while. Victor told the pilot they could have fifteen minutes, but they had to push off by 9:03.

Victor sipped his coffee and checked out Steve's workstation, enjoying the peace and quiet. He relished some filthy memories of the night before with Laticia. There was a United Airways Flight going overhead at about 30,000 feet headed towards John F. Kennedy International Airport in New York at 8:50. As long as the tightwads at the regional route traffic center in D.C. were doing their jobs, those flights were pretty much transparent and easy to blow off. At 8:55, Victor heard back over VHF radio from the US Courier pilot that they were set to go.

"Tower, this is Courier flight Uniform Charlie 611. My right seat is settled, and we are ready to taxi to runway 31 for departure."

"You better tell him to get some Imodium in his system. There won't be any shitting for him until you guys get up to flight level 360," Victor told them. "You can go ahead and push out to the ol' airstrip, and we are ready for a clean take-off at this very busy terminal," he joked.

"Tower, please confirm departure on runway 31."

"Fucking pilot pricks," Victor mumbled under his breath. "Yeah, yeah, taxi to 31 for departure. You're good to go. Just roll out."

"Roger, Tower. 31," the pilot responded.

Victor watched as the plane pulled away. He got a call on his cell phone at that moment. It was The Colonel. He never called Victor, so he knew something must be up. It was strictly prohibited to use your cell phone in the flight control room at work. Victor's head was still freaking pounding, but he needed to know what The Colonel wanted.

"Yeah, Father, I'm at work," Victor said quickly.

"Then what the hell are you answering the phone for?" The Colonel asked. "You know you can't take a personal call when you are working. Sometimes I don't know what in the world goes through your head."

"Father, we aren't busy at all right now," Victor said. "What do you need?"

"I got a call from Leah; she is very upset about your drinking. She told me you didn't come home last night, and she doesn't know how much more she can take. She told me Maddie is scared of you. How can a little girl be scared of her own dad?"

What in the fuck is going on here? Victor thought. His god-damn wife was talking to his father like the old man was a shrink. What did Leah think she was doing?

Collisions

"Father, I had to be at work late last night, so I just crashed here," Victor said hoping to get off the phone as soon as possible.

"Don't bullshit me, son. She told me about Chili's. She told me everything you've done lately. We need to get together and talk tonight. Leah is much more than you have ever deserved, and I don't know why she stays with you, but I don't think it will last much longer. I told her I wanted to talk to you to set things straight and talk about getting you some help for your alcohol problem."

"Father, I don't have an alcohol problem. Talk about bullshit," Victor said aloud. That fucking whore wife of his was going behind his back. She fucked up big time; it was time to tell his dad about his wife's not so clean past. His religious views and conservative-ass beliefs would never accept what she used to do. Victor wasn't sure what he was saying out loud and what was only in his head, which was pounding again. "There is something you need to know about Leah, Father."

Victor was getting a couple calls at Steve's console position that he ignored, and the VHF buzzed in his headset earpiece that now hung around his neck. The US Courier flight was ready to take off. "Hold on!" he told the Colonel.

"Take her up," Victor told the crew of the Courier flight without raising his headset, instead holding the mic to his mouth.

"Roger, Tower, cleared for takeoff runway 31. Will contact departure control, one-one-niner-point-four-five." The pilot didn't know Victor by name, but he knew his voice and anticipated which blanks he'd need to fill in for the tower.

Victor watched as they started their ascent cleanly. "Okay, Dad, I'm back. There is something I need to tell you about Leah. She was an escort when I met her," he said as he scooted his rolling chair over to Steve's radar. "What the fuck?" out loud or under his breath. There was a flight on the radar that was not supposed to be there.

"Son, what in the hell are you talking about? Don't get pissed off at Leah for your mistakes," The Colonel demanded.

"I gotta go," he told his dad as he hung up. Where the hell did that flight come from? It was on a direct course for UC 611's heading.

He jammed the headset back on his head. "This is WRA, change your course of direction immediately," Victor shouted in the blind over the airfield's VHF channel to the flight that was circling above. The errant flight was flying at roughly 135 degrees, nearly due south. He turned to the screen at his desk and watched the departing vector of the US Courier flight, and hastily changed frequencies.

"Turn right! There is another flight heading directly towards you!" Murph screamed over departure control's channel.

"Our TCAS popped as soon as we were wheels up telling us to climb because another plane is in our range," the pilot yelled back. "What is going on, Tower? Why weren't you answering on your channel? What should we do? Williamsburg? Norfolk??" Victor had two other phones ringing in the control room. Where in the hell was this flight coming from?

"Turn left immediately," he yelled, making a horrible mistake when he should have told them to turn right. The two flights were right on top of each other. Norfolk Departure Control was dumbstruck with confusion. The Courier flight was late and had barely switched to the departure frequency, let alone checked in.

"Williamsburg, return to your channel. Uniform Charlie Six-One-One, traffic alert, advise turn right, heading zero-four-zero and climb to…"

"What the fuck," the pilot yelled as Victor heard a loud noise and looked out toward the sky. "No, this can't be happening to me," Victor thought. His radar screen showed two overlapping vector sticks.

"We hit it, man. We hit it. Mayday, mayday, mayday! Uniform Charlie Six-One-One, going down," the pilot said. The co-pilot must have had an open mic because the last thing Victor heard before he passed out was the co-pilot screaming in the background that he didn't want to die, the phones in the office ringing off the hook, and the captain of the flight saying, "Tell my family I love them."

Steve had forgotten to tell Victor that a dramatic shift in wind patterns around Norfolk had forced a change by Norfolk International for the Atlantic Airline flight into a holding pattern above WRA. Norfolk made the change knowing that WRA had very little traffic and could hold departures until the AA flight was cleared for landing in Norfolk or they diverted. Steve made a mistake by forgetting to report this information to Victor. Victor made the mistake of telling the pilots of the US Courier flight to turn left.

Chapter 10

Posted: April 10, 2009, 10:39 a.m.

Carmen Paul/Williamsburg Daily Express

Vitaly, VA-More information is becoming available in the mid-air collision of Atlantic Airline 2937 and the US Courier flight in the skies above Vitaly. Preliminary reports claim the US Courier flight had just taken off when it struck the left wing of the Atlantic Airline plane. There is still no word on survivors from either flight, but a witness did say that a significant portion of the larger plane was still intact.

The most recent, major, mid-air collision between two airplanes occurred in Brazil just above the Brazilian state of Mato Grosso in 2006. A Boeing aircraft operated by Gol Transportes collided with an Embraer Legacy business jet. The 154 passengers on the Gol Transportes flight died when the plane split in half. All seven passengers on the Embraer Legacy survived.

The last mid-air collision in the United States happened in Cerritos, CA in 1986. A small plane owned by a California family collided with an Aeromexico plane that was headed to Los Angeles from Mexico City. All three passengers on the small plane were killed along with all sixty-four passengers on the Aeromexico flight. There were also fifteen bystanders on the ground killed in a Cerritos residential neighborhood.

There is a press conference planned by both the Vitaly Sherriff's Department and the National Transportation Safety Board, but an exact time has not been announced for either.

Murphy Kearns

Everything on Murph's drive from Norfolk to Vitaly was a complete blur. He must have been going at least thirty miles over the speed limit. Once he pulled off the highway, he ran several stoplights and stop signs hoping to get to his destination as quickly as possible. About ten miles outside of Vitaly, his empty light, on for close to thirty miles by then, finally got his attention. He knew he better stop for gas and not run the risk of running out, which would only delay him more. Murph stopped at a vintage looking gas station. It was the type of place that you would expect an attendant wearing a white jump suit and black bow tie to come ask if you wanted full or unleaded, and if he could wipe your windshield off, hoping for a small tip. Murph ran inside as soon as he started the pump since there was nowhere to pay outside with a credit card. An old man sat behind the counter on a wooden stool in an otherwise empty station that felt like it had been on pause since the 1950s.

"I need to put thirty dollars in my Jeep," Murph told the man. He was watching an old, beat-up television that Murph was surprised to see wasn't in black and white. The old man was watching the local news. Murph stopped and looked shell-shocked at the screen. The reporters had just arrived on the scene, not long after the police, ambulances, and fire department. The old man, fixated on the screen, still had not looked Murph's way. "Sir, I need the gas now, my family might have been on one of those planes."

The old man looked towards Murph, and his face turned red very fast. "Are ya' headed that way, son?" he asked in a concerned tone.

"Yes, do you know where the crash site is once I get in town?"

"The town is so small it won't be too hard to find. I am sure you will see some emergency vehicles, but why don't I ride with ya' to show you just in case. I know a short cut."

"That would be great." Murph said, thankful for the navigator. "Here's my money."

"Keep it!" he said. "Go out and fill up your tank quickly while I lock up in here."

Murph ran outside, and a minute later they were on the road.

Victor Dancy

When Victor awoke it took a couple minutes for the grogginess to wear off and for him to regain his bearings. All he could think was that he must have fallen asleep and that he had dreamed of a plane crash. The phones were ringing off the hook in the flight control office. He answered the one at his desk.

"What the fuck just happened?" said an angry male voice on the other line.

Collisions

"Who is this?" Victor stuttered.

"It's ORF. What in the fuck did you just do?" Victor's stomach dropped, and it all came crashing back to him. He was definitely not dreaming. Victor puked all over the floor. "What the fuck?" the man from Norfolk kept yelling. Victor hung the phone up.

"Holy shit, I am so fucked." he said to himself. He rushed to clean up the vomit, knowing that the flight control center at WRA was about to be swamped with who knew what authorities at any minute. While he cleaned the area, he picked up his cell phone and called his dad.

"Why did you hang up on me earlier?" his father said immediately after he answered.

"Dad, I screwed up bad!" Victor said as the tears started to flow. He told him what happened.

"You are a stupid son of a bitch," he yelled at Victor. His father quickly became The Colonel again, thinking about what this could potentially do to him. He told Victor a couple things to do before anybody got there. "I'm on my way," the Colonel said. Victor didn't know if even The Colonel could clean up this royal screw-up, though.

As his head began to clear, Victor vaguely remembered a conversation with the pilots aboard the US Courier flight. He was unsure whether or not they listened to his instructions immediately before the accident or if they followed the TCAS. Everything was hazy, but he quickly realized that he needed to start building a story.

The TCAS, or traffic collision avoidance system, was designed for the purpose of avoiding collisions between aircraft. Victor spent several training sessions at WRA learning about the TCAS on planes. The International Civil

Aviation Organization required that all planes have them in their cockpits to monitor the airspace around an aircraft to avoid conflict with other flights. It was deemed the last line of safety. Victor began to worry about whether his advice contradicted TCAS and whether Norfolk was monitoring the radio traffic, too.

He knew that there were going to be serious questions asked about where Michelle and Steve were at the time of the accident. There was no gray area there. Their absence from the tower put them in the wrong, and Victor knew he needed to place all of the blame on them. With his dad's connections it might just be possible.

Chapter 11

Posted: April 10, 2009, 10:58 a.m.

Carmen Paul/Williamsburg Daily Express

Vitaly, VA-A press conference is scheduled for 11:30 a.m. today with the Vitaly Sheriff's Department. The NTSB has yet to announce a time for their press conference. It is being reported that the two pilots on the US Courier flight were both killed. There has been no official report, but there is word that there could be possible survivors on the Atlantic Airline Flight.

Emergency responders are showing up from Williamsburg, Virginia Beach and Norfolk at the crash scene to assist with the recovery. The Campioni Chocolate Factory reportedly also avoided major damage based on several eye-witness reports.

Both Atlantic Airlines and US Couriers have confirmed that it was their two flights involved in the collision. The Atlantic Airlines flight had one hundred and forty-one passengers, including nine crew members aboard.

J. McLain Callahan

Murphy Kearns

The old man from the gas station told Murph his name was Milo as they rushed to Vitaly. Milo didn't give Murph any personal information nor ask for any. He could tell Murph just wanted to get there as fast as possible. Milo stayed quiet, only shouting out occasional directions when necessary. He got Murph to Vitaly in less than eight minutes.

As soon as the two pulled into town, they could hear sirens all around them. Murph spotted a yellow fire truck and started to follow it. Nobody was going to stop his Jeep for speeding; they were all going to the same place. The town of Vitaly was basically a one-way street with a Subway, a small pizza parlor, a closed down gas station, a small furniture store, and another restaurant named Apple Alice's on the main road. There were several other run-down and unoccupied buildings. The James River and a railroad track ran alongside the edge of town.

The yellow fire truck flew through the main street and turned right across an old, beat-down bridge crossing the river. There were several craftsmen style houses right off the main road that all looked like they could use a paint job and some work on their roofs. Surprisingly though, all of the lawns were immaculate. Murph could start to see smoke in the distance as they rounded some turns. Once again, his stomach sank as he began to comprehend just how much smoke there was, dark clouds tarnishing the otherwise clear blue morning sky. It seemed as if a bomb had been dropped on eastern Virginia.

Murph followed the fire truck as far as he could until a deputy stopped the Jeep at a roadblock that looked like it was recently put together. There was not much traffic in the small town. Murph was sure that they were preparing the best way a small town like Vitaly could for the impending swarm of media likely on its way, let alone what would certainly be a massive rescue and recovery effort.

"Nobody allowed past here," the bearded deputy said as Murph rolled down his window.

"My family might have been on one of those planes!" Murph shouted at him.

The deputy's demeanor changed from serious to astounded, but he said, "I'm sorry, but I just can't let you past. We can't have anybody that is not emergency personnel near the wreckage."

"Son, get the sheriff on your walkie-talkie for me," Milo said across Murph.

"Oh, hey Milo, I didn't see you in there," the deputy said. "I will try Oscar, but there is a good chance he won't respond."

The deputy called into the sheriff and they whispered back and forth for a minute. He quickly handed Milo the walkie-talkie. "Oscar, I am here with the husband and father of some of the victims of one of those flights. Let us come in and help with the search. Let this man look for his family."

"Tell Deputy Hegarty to let you in. Drive up here and park on Jamestown Road as close as you can get to the chocolate factory. I will have Deputy Silva meet you there with some directions and a clearance badge. We have emergency help from all over. Tell him that it is not pretty down here," Murph overheard on the walkie-talkie.

"Alright, go on in, you know where to go, right Milo?" the deputy asked as he motioned the Jeep through the barricade.

"Sure do, thanks, son," Milo said. Murph stepped on the gas and drove around the barricade.

"How did you get us in here?" Murph asked.

Milo responded "Sheriff Baker is my nephew. I helped raise him, so I thought when you were at my station that I might be able to help you in more ways than just getting ya' here."

They took a couple turns and parked across the street from what appeared to be the backside of the long and worn-down brick chocolate factory. Deputy Silva was waiting for them where they parked.

Victor Dancy

Within about thirty minutes of the accident there were members of the NTSB and local authorities swarming into WRA and overtaking the small flight control deck. Victor had been escorted to an empty office on the first floor. As he was heading to the elevator, he walked past Michelle. She was talking to the head of WRA, Sam Sheets, in his office, along with a couple other suits Victor didn't recognize. Michelle saw Victor through the window and they exchanged glances and the room felt cool to Victor. When they got to the first floor, Steve was rushing in the front door. He was out of breath and mouthed to Victor, "What happened? What did you do?"

Victor continued to walk on ignoring Steve. He went in and sat down in a hard metal chair with a worn-out cushion. WRA was built in the seventies, and not much had been updated including the furniture. Everything just looked worn and felt old. All of the furniture was uncomfortable and smelled a bit like a mixture of Victor's grandmother's house and mildew. He sat back still trying to collect his thoughts and rehearse what he was going to say once he started getting questioned. He knew consistency was key, so he better get it right the first time. Victor also had a couple pennies that he was swishing around in his mouth to help hide his alcohol breath. He was glad he got to shower that morning. After Victor cleaned up his puke, he went into the bathroom and sprayed some of the Lysol air freshener all over himself just in case. It made him gag a couple times, but he figured it would help cover the alcoholic odor that was surely seeping out of his pores.

Victor sat in the room for what must have been at least one hour thinking about the account he was going to give. He figured that whoever came in to talk to him must have been working hard to gather some facts before running through the litany of questions standard to a civilian accident investigation. Luckily for Victor, this time was also giving The Colonel a window of opportunity to make calls to all his high-up friends in the FAA. Victor still had no clue about the fate of either plane.

Surprised that no one had confiscated his cell phone, he decided he better use it before they did. There was no way there could be anybody listening. It was not like he was in an interrogation room, so he called Leah. She answered a couple rings into the fourth call. Victor knew that he needed to talk to her and talk fast. He had never done this before, but he was sure that kissing Leah's ass would not taste great. As bitter as it was to admit, he needed Leah. There was a lot of wind in the background when she answered in a cold tone.

"What?" she said obviously irritated by Victor's incessant calls.

"You haven't heard?" Victor asked.

"Heard what? Is Maddie okay?" she asked panicking.

"Who? Listen," he answered, "something really, really bad has happened here today. I am going to be under a lot of scrutiny, I think. My father is on his way down now."

"I am out walking around the outskirts of Jamestown and the cell signal isn't so good." Leah had been on a huge walking kick the past year. She would go on ten to fifteen mile walks. She said it was for exercise, but Victor figured it was more of a stress reliever and yet another way for them to not have to spend time together. "What happened, Victor? Did you do something?"

"Two planes collided mid-air, and I'm getting ready to be questioned about it. It was Michelle and Steve from WRA's fault," he said very loudly, in case anybody was listening to the conversation on the other side of the wall.

She hesitated for a few seconds and said, "Oh, no. Are the passengers on the plane okay?"

"I'm not sure about any of that. There are a lot of people teeming around here, so my gut feeling is that it is bad, really bad. It might be a couple long days, but I want to make sure that you know that it was not my fault. Nobody was here at work to help me, and they left me all on my own to handle the flight control deck. I was really busy, and I am not sure what happened."

"I just pray that everybody on those flights was okay," Leah said starting to sound worried.

"I don't think so, babe, it doesn't look good." Victor never called her babe, but what the hell. He was already beginning to feel like he was getting things under control. As they talked he realized that the suit who walked him down to the office had left him alone before a urine sample was taken.

He wasn't even sure who the guy worked for, but Victor figured he'd better cooperate with what must be standard protocol. That being said, Victor had been down this road enough times that he knew a break in custody was an easy target for a defense lawyer, if it should come up. He needed Leah on his side now; she was the only one who could say that he was drunk that morning.

"I really hope you had nothing to do with this; it sounds awful."

"I promise, I didn't," Victor answered, trying his hardest to sound sympathetic.

Somebody knocked on the door and came in. "Honey, I have to go now. There are some people here to talk to me. There was nothing more I could do. We will get through this together," he said, putting on his best concerned act for everybody walking into the room.

"Sure," she said sarcastically on the other end.

Chapter 12

Posted: April 10, 2009, 11:46 a.m.

Carmen Paul/Williamsburg Daily Express

Vitaly, VA - Vitaly Sheriff Oscar Baker stated there are a small number of survivors from Atlantic Airline Flight 2937, but he did not give an exact number. He also confirmed that both pilots on US Courier Flight 611 were killed in the accident. The sheriff verified that survivors have been taken to a local hospital, but he did not specify if it was in Williamsburg or Norfolk, nor the severity of their injuries. The fire departments from the surrounding areas were able to extinguish a couple small fires in the local woods that resulted from the crash. Baker said he will be giving another press conference this afternoon. The NTSB has still not announced a time for their press conference, and it is believed that it now might not be for some time. Through an email release to the media, they did confirm the flight numbers and that there is an open investigation.

Collisions

Eyewitness Megan English was outside working on her garden just a couple hundred yards from where the Atlantic Airline plane crashed. "There was a loud noise in the sky, and a large white plane made its way towards the ground. At first, I thought it was going to be able to land, but then I noticed that its right wing appeared to be fractured. The plane landed more on its right side, and must have skidded for several hundred yards, before it stopped just outside of the chocolate factory. A small fire began towards the front of the plane, and debris flew off as it skidded across the ground. A large piece of the back of the plane also detached from the rest of the plane during the crash landing," said English.

The Daily Express is currently trying to speak to more witnesses, local emergency services personnel, and to local hospitals where the survivors might have been taken.

Murphy Kearns

On their drive in, Murph and Milo drove past a few local media vans, the first of the hordes that Murph was sure would quickly multiply over the next several hours and days. There were also two helicopters flying overhead, circling the scene like hawks searching for prey. One appeared to be a police helicopter and the other was from a local news organization.

"You can follow me towards the wreckage, sir," Deputy Silva told Murph after he got out of the Jeep. She was a short, Hispanic lady, with raven black hair coming out from under her hat.

"Go ahead, son," said Milo. "I'll just slow you down."

Murph turned to him hastily and said, "I don't know how I can thank you," as Deputy Silva and he started on a jog away from the Jeep.

Milo yelled from behind, "Good luck, son." His heart thumping in time with his footfalls, time stretched as Murph became aware of details that should have been a distraction. Murph and the deputy jogged up a small hill and past an older playground that had a spiraled slide, see-saw, and sandbox in a wooded area of what must have been a community park. Patrick could spend five hours a day at the playground up the street from their Pittsburgh house. He loved the slide and went up and down, up and down. It reminded Murph how Rooney would chase his tennis ball and bring it back, over and over again. Joy is joy, no matter how it is expressed. Patrick would love the twisty slide on this playground. These were his favorite kind. The equipment was old, but the space in the trees formed a natural sanctuary that Murph couldn't help but notice as he and Deputy Silva ran through. Rays from the mid-day sun passed through the dust and smoke, filling the vaulted space under the canopy.

After they passed the playground and entered denser trees, the two ran by several eastern white pines that covered the landscape. They entered a clearing, and it was as if they ran into what Murph would imagine a Civil War battlefield at Gettysburg, Chancellorsville, or Petersburg to be like in the aftermath. He had never been in a war. But at that moment he felt like he had entered a battlefield - the wreckage of a plane, the debris, the smoke. The smaller plane, or what was left of it, was still smoldering from where the fire trucks had recently extinguished its fire. A foamy fire retardant was hanging all over the place to keep the flames from spreading into the woods. There was a horrid and unfamiliar smell. It was a mix of smoke, jet fuel, burned metal and grass, and what he was hoping were not burned bodies. It was confusing to stand in the midst. His senses all vied for his attention. It was all so incongruous.

Breathing heavily after a good eight hundred meter run, Deputy Silva said, "Do you know what area of the plane your family was in?"

Running alongside her he said, "I know they definitely were not in first class." Thinking a little more as they ran he did remember Maria telling him that they got to board early since she had two young kids, and she was glad because they had to walk way back in the plane past the wings.

Murph told Deputy Silva, and she got on her walkie-talkie. After a minute of talking, she said, "Sir, follow me this way. The back of the plane was separated from the rest of the plane." She veered to her right, and he followed her. He was amazed that she was running as fast as she was for her size, but his look of determination must have inspired a second wind.

The two ran through some more trees, and Murph spotted what he thought was the back of the plane in the middle of the white pines. Time sped up as he got to the wreckage. The right stabilizer was tilting up and the remnants of the left stabilizer were against the ground. The rudder was at a forty-five degree angle. The last forty feet of the plane had been completely severed from the rest. There were two dozen emergency workers running around the area. Murph knew it would be impossible to get any ambulances back into the trees, even with a lot of them burned or knocked over from the crash. There were a few gurneys arriving, but there were not many being rushed back out.

He would later learn that most of the passengers in the back section were thrown from the plane on impact with the ground. Bodies were spread all over the woods.

Emergency personnel were not in any hurry once they got back into the woods, which worried him. It seemed more like recovery than search and rescue. Deputy Silva called a fireman to come over. "How many people are you looking for?" he asked Murph.

"My wife, who has long brunette hair, my four-year-old daughter, and my two-year-old son," Murph told him.

He thought for a second, and then in a very solemn tone, the fireman told Murph to follow him. Time slowed again on the hundred yard walk. Murph could hear the sound of the crunching, sandy soil and pine needles under his feet and see the faces of the men and women walking around him. Everybody looked like they were in a state of disbelief. He imagined none of the workers in this small town had ever seen anything as devastating as this either. The fireman suddenly stopped and pointed to what looked like the back of a dislodged row of seats that was about twenty yards from the back of the plane. "That way, sir." He raised his hand as if to warn Murph, but let the husband and father pass thinking of his own family and knowing he would want the same.

Murph could not see who was in the seats from the back, but the row of seats was clearly pretty beat up from its trip out of the back of the plane. The remnants of the row were surprisingly sitting upright on the ground, like it was meant to be a bench for people walking through the woods to rest on. Murph hurried around the back of the seats, and he knew immediately that Maria was there. She was leaning over from her seat, which she was buckled into. A lot of her clothes were burned off, but she was unmistakably leaning on top of something.

He looked under Maria, and it was Patrick. Murph could tell just from looking at both of them that neither was breathing. Maria had tried to protect Patrick until the end.

Collisions

Her face in death was as beautiful as it was in life. Her eyes were open, and her arms were wrapped around Patrick. Murph desperately tried not to look at all of the blood and bruises covering their bodies. He wanted to remember it as if Patrick was just sleeping in his mother's arms. Murph could only hope that his son slept through the whole nightmare. In a fit of sorrow, he jumped on top of both of them, and cradled them in his arms. Murph didn't even have the time to think about where Isabella was at that moment. He silently rocked his two loved ones in his arms for what felt like eternity.

There had been talking and yelling all around Murph the whole time. His world shrunk to Maria and Patrick. Eventually a conversation behind him between two women in all black clothes penetrated his fragile shell as soon as he heard them mention a little girl.

"They found a little girl flung from the main portion of the plane, and they say she is alive," Murph caught one lady saying.

"She's alive? How is anybody alive after this?" the other one said.

"She might not be the only one alive; apparently part of the plane was not badly burned and remained intact after the impact. They say she is barely alive. They are getting ready to take her to the hospital. She is in critical condition but still breathing. They found her just outside of the cockpit. Evidently she was dressed like a princess or a fairy tale character. Amazing."

Murph's head shot up and he noticed they were EMTs, "Did you just say the little girl was wearing a fairy tale costume?"

One of the ladies jumped back startled. They clearly didn't know he was there. After she collected herself she said, "That's what I'm hearing."

"Can you please find out if it was Alice in Wonderland?" Murph asked still holding onto Maria.

The EMT had a quizzical look on her face, but made a call. She shook her head a couple times and with her ear still up to her emergency radio she said, "Yes, it was an Alice costume, how on Earth did you know?"

"That's my daughter!"

Victor Dancy

Three people walked into the room to question Victor. One was the head of WRA, Sam Sheets. He had been at WRA forever and was an old buddy of The Colonel. Sam was part of the reason that Victor got his job and the promotions that came with it. Victor didn't know the other two. The woman introduced herself as Catherine Douglas from the FAA. The other was Clarence Conner who was from NTSB. They were both sharply-dressed. Sam looked as rough as Victor, probably not from partying though. Victor was never good at sympathy, but he knew that he needed to conjure up some right about now. He knew this initial meeting and interview would play a significant role in how his overall responsibility in the incident was judged.

Conner did most of the talking during the meeting. It seemed that Sam and the Douglas lady were there more as witnesses and to collect information than to ask questions. Conner rubbed the goatee of his well-groomed beard during the entire interview and said, "I see" about everything Victor said. Victor wanted to reach across the table and choke the annoying little man, but knew he needed to keep up the sympathy act if he wanted to get this group on his side.

Victor took drama for four years during high school. He didn't take drama because he had any interest in the art, but to piss off his very manly father, who expected him to be in the ROTC, not in theatre. Besides, there was never any shortage of girls in those classes. Victor had paid attention to the teachers, though, and found he was able to use some of the acting techniques he learned from class while netting women and dodging responsibility through the years.

Victor still had no idea what happened between the two flights that collided, so it really wasn't that hard to feign a sense of disbelief and shock. Before they had a chance to ask any questions, he blurted out, "Is everybody okay? Please tell me everybody is okay!"

"There are a lot of people dead now, Mr. Dancy," Conner answered.

Victor's mouth dropped open. "This can't be happening," he said as he put his hands on the back of his head and started to shake it front and back in a slow motion. "Are the two pilots from the US Courier flight okay?"

"No, they are both deceased. Please refrain from asking any more questions. We have a lot to get through right now to figure out just what happened," said Conner.

"Yes, sir." Murph hated to use sir and really never did, a relic of the days he lived under The Colonel's roof. So as soon as he moved out of the house, he stopped ever using those phrases.

The hour or so between the time of the collision and the meeting with the three authority figures gave Victor time to strategize. He was definitely going to throw Michelle and

Steve directly and completely under the bus. They had to be his scapegoats. At the same time, Victor needed to keep Sam Sheets on his side. Victor knew that Sam could use his authority to help him. Victor wanted to make sure he came across as shocked, but not nervous. It was going to be his word against Michelle and Steve. He was lucky his communications with the US Courier flight were limited, which meant there would be little on the black box. Maybe they would even be able to find fault or place blame on the equipment in the two airplanes as well. The Safety Board weenies were all about "prevention of future accidents or incidents." They rarely went after an individual.

Most of Conner's questions to Victor in the initial meeting were to draft a timeline. He knew they were recording the interview. Victor had to remember everything he said and keep the same timeline in case anybody tried to stump him later. Victor told Conner that he had arrived to work on time, and at the time he was not surprised that it was just Steve there. He told them that Michelle commonly stepped out of work or left for a while, especially if they weren't busy. He said this behavior had been going on for a while, and that he always felt uncomfortable not having his supervisor present when she was supposed to be. Victor emphasized the job was highly stressful, and anytime somebody stepped out of the tower the stress level doubled.

Victor made sure to mention that when Michelle called and Steve answered, he was in the bathroom. He knew that this would come up in both of their interviews with Michelle and Steve and with the investigation of the incoming and outgoing phone calls that morning in the flight control center. When asked why he never reported his concerns to anybody about Michelle skipping out on work, Victor went on a rant that his military father taught him to never overstep a supervisor, no matter what the scenario.

Collisions

When they got to the part about Steve, Victor felt a tiny bit of guilt, but it quickly faded. Steve was caught in several bad spots. He was supposed to be there. Victor said he was at work on time that morning. If Steve tried to say he was late, Steve would catch himself in a lie. Steve told Michelle that Victor was in the bathroom. If he admitted to lying about that, he would undermine his own credibility.

Victor also didn't say he told Steve to leave to go check on his wife. Victor said that Steve received a call and that he told Victor that he had to leave. Victor told the three interviewers that he urged Steve that it was a bad idea to leave him alone to work all the stations, but that Steve frantically said he "had to go."

Victor thought he did a good job of depicting Michelle as somebody who would leave work often when they weren't busy. He characterized her as an employee whose job came second. Even though it was a common practice at WRA among supervisors, Sam would never be able to admit it, nor would other supervisors when asked. This would only illustrate WRA mismanagement. Victor's role in the collision would seem smaller and smaller. Everyone looked out for himself. It had been that way in the wake of all of Victor's disasters, at least. This was a role he knew well.

They took a break after about an hour of the interview, right before they got to the questions that would be about the actual collision and what actually happened in the flight control room. The break would give Victor some more time to conceive a plan. He felt like he passed his first part, but he still was going to have to talk about the actual crash, why he did not answer the phones, or respond on the radio, and what he was doing to help prevent the two planes from colliding. This would be a command performance that would include a little improv.

Chapter 13

Posted: April 10, 2009, 1:41 p.m.

Carmen Paul/Williamsburg Daily Express

Vitaly, VA - The exact number of deaths and survivors on the Atlantic Airline flight is still yet to be announced. There has been one confirmed passenger from the Atlantic Airline flight who survived the plane collision outside of Williamsburg.

Fire Captain Clint Howard, from Williamsburg Fire Department #3, stated, "Members of my fire department found flight attendant Sandy Hatch from Atlantic Airlines near the cockpit section, buckled into her seat. She seemed to be in shock, and the EMT said she suffered a major concussion and several broken bones. She was rushed to the Williamsburg Regional Hospital, but she did not appear to be in a life-threatening condition."

Captain Howard said he believed that there could be other survivors based on initial reports from the scene, but the flight attendant was the only survivor he personally saw rescued. Howard said, "Our crew spent a lot of the time putting out fires in the woods. There were several small fires in areas where different parts of the Atlantic Airline flight crashed."

Murphy Kearns

The two EMTs looked at Murph stunned. At that point he was getting used to the looks from the concerned first responders. He had to find Isabella immediately. Murph said a final goodbye to Patrick and Maria in the place they died. He leaned over and wrapped both of his arms around them and embraced them one more time. They looked so gentle and at peace there sitting on the seats together, like they would both wake up and Patrick would be raring to go. Murph gave them both a kiss on the lips, having to move under Maria to get to Patrick, and he turned to the two women who were crying behind him.

"Can you take me to my daughter?" Murph asked.

After a second to compose themselves, the taller of the two ladies said, "I can get you there." He got up and looked at his wife and son one more time, and then he headed off with the emergency worker.

As they ran past, Murph turned around and said, "Please make sure they stay together," to the other EMT that stayed behind. She nodded her head in agreement.

Still in a daze, Murph followed the woman as she corresponded with somebody on her phone. She picked up her pace, turned to him and said, "They need to get your daughter to the hospital as soon as possible. I asked them to wait a few seconds for you, but they said to hurry."

Collisions

"Let's go faster then," he yelled, and they took off at a blistering pace. Murph's body had completely forgotten that he had already gone for a long run that morning. It felt like days ago to him.

In a couple minutes, the two got to the ambulance where Isabella was being treated. Murph's daughter looked so small on the gurney. She was strapped down, and had an I.V. plugged into her arm. Part of the Alice dress was ripped, and Isabella had a pretty big gash on the left side of her forehead near her temple. The look on Murph's face was apparently enough to identify him as "Dad." The guy in the back of the ambulance said, "We need to go now! Are you coming?"

"Yeah," Murph said. As the backdoor of the ambulance was closed, Murph looked out and saw the most horrific scene of his life for the last time.

They decided to take her to the closest hospital, Sentara Williamsburg Regional Medical Center. There was the chance she could be airlifted to another hospital later if they felt she needed different care, but they wanted to get her completely stabilized in Williamsburg first.

Along with the driver, there were two EMTs in the ambulance with Isabella and Murph. One was tracking her condition while Murph spoke to the other. "It appears that she has sustained some brain trauma, and she might have some broken bones. She was flung from the plane, luckily not near any trees, and she landed in a meadow of wildflowers. Luckily it has rained a lot lately, and the ground was pretty soft."

"Can you be more specific on what exactly is wrong with her?" Murph questioned.

"Sir, we will need to get to the hospital and get her the care she needs. A doctor is going to be able to give you a lot more information. I don't want to tell you anything that is premature."

"She will make it through this, right?" Murph asked. The man took a second to respond, and he said he thought so with an uncertain tone. Murph wasn't sure if the man was telling him this because he thought it was true or for Murph's well-being.

They sat quietly as Murph held Isabella's hand for the rest of the ride. He did not let go until the hospital staff asked him to step out so they could start to work on her.

Victor Dancy

During his break from the interrogation, Victor walked outside for a cigarette. He usually only smoked when he was drinking at the bars after work. Now that the public smoking restrictions were so ridiculous, he had to cutback even more. He wasn't exactly stressed, but smoking helped him think, and he knew that he had to get his thoughts in order before he stepped back inside to talk about what happened during the exact moments of the crash.

Victor had a voicemail on his phone from The Colonel. He had called while Victor was in the interview. The message said, "I will be there in a couple hours. I have talked to a couple people at the FAA, and the NTSB is going to need to take some time to check into what happened today in order to reconstruct events. I am sure you are already talking to people. Just tell them the truth son." The Colonel was in full stride, thought Victor. He knew what his father really meant. He didn't care if Victor told the truth; The Colonel always taught Victor that sometimes the truth was not the best course of action to get you to where you needed to go. It didn't matter to The Colonel how the job got done, as long as it resulted in the desired outcome; "Effects based operations," the cocky old fighter pilot called it. The desired result for Victor and The Colonel was a clean record; it didn't matter if they got there with truth or fiction.

The Colonel was also probably worried that at some point Victor's phone could be seized as evidence. He undoubtedly figured that somebody already had it when he left the message.

When Victor walked back towards the makeshift interview room, two men stopped him and finally asked for him to turn over his cell phone. He hadn't noticed these two men before. The man who took the phone identified himself as an agent from the FBI and the other had a paper, which he held up. Victor assumed it was a warrant, but was trying his hardest to keep his cool and play the part of "cooperative." The natural Victor would have laughed in the man's face and said, "Search Warrant? My lawyer first." He most likely would have thrown in an "asshole," too.

Victor was surprised to see his wife in the window of a room that he walked past. Leah looked very nervous as she chatted with two men. Hopefully she was playing her part well. Victor was sure his father had already briefed her about what to say. They made brief eye contact, and Victor grinned to try to ease her nervousness, which she returned with a scowl.

Victor walked back into the room. Sam was already in there waiting. He must have rushed back to beat NTSB Agent Conner and Catherine Douglas. Victor was grateful because he learned a lot from Sam about what his counterparts were saying in their interviews.

"Rough fucking day," Victor said to him. Sam was about The Colonel's age, but he usually dressed in a way that made him seem younger. Sam was an avid golfer who spent the entire weekend playing eighteen to thirty-six holes to the chagrin of his wife. Sitting at the table now Sam looked ten years older, Victor thought.

"You bet your ass," he said. "I can't believe this happened! How did something like this happen?" He had his hands on the back of his head. Victor was not sure if Sam was asking him that question or if he was asking himself, so he didn't respond.

"Steve said that his wife got out of the house and you told him it was okay to go home," Sam told him.

"Not true," Victor said continuing his lies. "He did get a call. He told me he was leaving no matter what, but that he would get back as soon as possible. With Michelle already gone, I didn't think leaving me alone to man the whole station was smart. I wanted to call and get Michelle to come back in before Steve left, but he said that wasn't a good idea. He did *not* want Michelle to find out he was leaving. We walked in together a couple minutes before eight-thirty, and I wasn't surprised to see that Michelle wasn't here," Victor said testing to see if Steve had told his interviewers that Victor was twenty minutes late that morning. Sam didn't respond, so Victor figured he was in the clear and that Steve made no mention about Victor's late arrival.

"I was in the bathroom when Michelle called Steve, but I am used to her taking off from work frequently. I've always thought that was unacceptable from a supervisor. What is she saying in her interview?"

"She's too distraught to talk right now," Sam told him. "They can't get much out of her, but she admits to not being here, and she keeps saying how sorry she is for everybody on the two planes. That will all change if the FBI or the District Attorney decides to press the issue. You know they've got people at the crash site now, too, right? They won't play nice like the NTSB guys. They'll be looking for fault, not for some discussion about, 'Gee, guys, how do we avoid this from happening next time?'" Victor immediately felt a surge of confidence. No matter what they felt he did wrong, it was now very possible to make Michelle the scapegoat. Hell, once Steve saw the writing on the wall, maybe he would wise up and put the blame on her to save his ass, too.

Victor didn't want to risk anything, so he made sure to go after both of them. He was sure The Colonel would agree that was the best course of action. Victor wasn't positive about what was admissible in court and what wasn't, but he knew there was tension between the NTSB and the criminal investigators in similar, past situations. He also knew he hadn't been read a Miranda yet by anybody. If nothing else, while Conner built a timeline and looked for a fucking "safety lesson" to talk about while all these agencies held hands and drank coffee with doughnuts, Victor would at least have already laid the groundwork for the DA or the FBI if they decided to play hardball with him. Victor leaned back in his chair.

Conner and Catherine Douglas walked back in. Conner didn't seem too happy to see Sam in there with Victor. "What are you two talking about?" he asked, irritated.

"Just how shocked we are," Victor said. "We aren't talking about anything that happened." He already knew that he had Sam in his pocket. Sam wouldn't have shared any of the information about Michelle and Steve if he weren't on his side. Sam stood to lose a lot too, so Victor knew that Sam was counting on him to put Michelle and Steve squarely to blame.

"I hope not," Conner said. He proceeded to ask Victor some more questions about what led up to that morning, and how WRA workers typically went through a day in their station. Then he got to the questions that enabled Victor to start pointing fingers at Michelle and Steve, all text book, incident reconstruction questions. The NTSB probably had a checklist with the same questions for any kind of accident. Victor reiterated to the two in the interview room what he had just told Sam. He made painfully clear that he really thought it was a bad idea for Steve to leave him working alone at the station, and that Michelle made it commonplace to leave whenever she felt like it. He couldn't get a good read on Conner, but Douglas from the FAA didn't appear impressed by his story up to that point. Victor wondered if The Colonel knew Douglas. It really didn't matter though, because the FAA didn't have any teeth here, and The Colonel could control what they did. He needed to worry about the NTSB, and what account would be passed along to the suits in the hallway with his cell phone.

Thirty minutes into the second round of questioning, they started to cover what happened when he was alone, after Steve left, and up until the collision. Victor told them that he was in constant communication with the US Courier Flight, which in fact was true and they would easily find out during their investigation. Victor also covered the base of his phone conversation with The Colonel. He knew that they would be able to trace the fact that Victor and The Colonel were on a call together right before the collision.

Victor had thought about this a lot already, and he came up with what he believed to be a very clever story. Victor told them that since he'd retired, his father got bored very easily. The Colonel missed the action of his years in the Air Force and working as a consultant for the FAA. He liked for Victor to put his phone on speaker and set it down while he was working. He knew Victor had to focus on his work, so there was no way he could talk. He just enjoyed listening to the constant commotion, dialogue, and frenzy of a day in the flight control center. Victor planned to use his father's phone call to his advantage as opposed to a potential distraction and rule violation. As a witness to the incident, they'd surely question The Colonel as well. Victor would make sure that his dad made it clear how concerned he was at the beginning of their phone conversation before the collision that Victor was working alone. Steve and Michelle were gone, so Victor was at a disadvantage to begin with.

Next, Victor had to implicate the WRA facility as an entity. These investigators loved to identify "organizational deficiencies," which was really just an impotent way to avoid finding fault in a person. That meant Sam would look bad, too, but not enough to make Sam mad. Victor knew that most of the facility's equipment was outdated, but since there weren't a lot of flights in and out, WRA was not a funding priority for the FAA. Blame the budget; everyone can get behind that. Victor made it clear that a lot of their equipment malfunctioned on occasion, and they had several instances where they had to differ from standard protocol due to the faulty equipment. Some of it was even documented in the FAA's read files that noted things like occasional bird activity or radio interference.

Best of all was that it was true; WRA did have problems with equipment. Last year, there was an entire week the console communications system was out of service, and the airport had to cancel several flights. There had always been heavy interference on the VHF radio frequencies that were channeled through the communication suite and into the tower. There was persistent static on both ends, and Victor heard once that there were problems with the ringers not going off as a result, something about a constant tone that the tower consoles couldn't differentiate from actual radio traffic. They had all learned to work around it by always keeping one position tuned to VHF traffic from aircrews and using the other position as a multi-communications switch. It was an easy target for Victor. When Conner asked why Victor didn't answer the line at Steve's position, he simply said that their equipment had major problems. He lied stating simply that neither the calls from Norfolk nor the US Courier flight rang through. He didn't even know he had missed calls from Norfolk, but that might explain why the hell another aircraft was in the Courier flight's departure path. He still couldn't quite piece that together, but he thought he better be indignant about it. Sam rubbed his forehead during this part of the interview, but Victor tried to make him feel better by stating that there was no way Sam would have ever tolerated supervisors leaving during their shift. When in truth, Sam not only tolerated them leaving if it was slow, he did it himself. There was no way in hell he was going to bring up his own deficiencies though. Victor thought he might have talked his way out of that shit-storm after all with his "A+" performance. Victor felt his confidence growing.

Chapter 14

Posted: April 10, 2009, 2:41 p.m.

Carmen Paul/Williamsburg Daily Express

Vitaly, VA - The White House held a press conference on the tragic plane collision between United States Courier Flight 611 and Atlantic Airlines Flight 2937 as more details about the passengers on both flights, as well as new information on survivors became available.

White House Press Secretary Phillip North announced President Jackson Reeves will make a statement later this afternoon, "As the day proceeds, we will provide as much information on our end about the collision as is available. We are currently collecting data on the collision and offering support to the search and rescue attempts. The National Transportation Safety Board is the lead investigative agency at this time. The FBI is supporting state and local law enforcement. As the day proceeds, the President will continue to be regularly briefed concerning the situation." No specific time was given for the President's statement.

Earlier Fire Chief Howard, of Williamsburg FD, stated that Atlantic Airlines employee Sandy Hatch survived the crash, and that information has been confirmed to the Associated Press. We are also investigating another survivor who was transported to a local hospital, but the status of both remains unclear.

Atlantic Airlines has confirmed that Flight 2937, originating from Pittsburgh, had one hundred and forty-one passengers, including nine crew members. Duquesne University has verified that sixty-one of its students were on Flight 2937. This upcoming week is listed as spring break at the university, and it is expected that the students were headed to the Virginia Beach area. The Duquesne statement did not present any information on possible survivors.

Murphy Kearns

They rushed Isabella into surgery upon her arrival at the emergency room. The hospital had its entire trauma staff on site to treat survivors, but the expected throng of survivors never materialized. Murph couldn't sit still. He paced back and forth along the shiny, polished floors of the emergency room waiting area. He felt numb. His thoughts went flying back and forth between mourning the loss of Patrick and Maria, and hope for the survival of the only remaining member of his family. Murph didn't know a lot about brain injuries. He was worried that if she did survive, would she still be the same Isabella? Would she remember everything? Would she remember anything? Would she have brain damage?

He talked to the doctor and to the nurses more than a few times. They simply restated that it was way too early to make a prognosis. The team made clear that, no matter what,

Collisions

Isabella was going to have a long recovery if she survived. Murph called his parents and then Pete, who he asked to take care of Rooney. An NTSB agent came and talked to Murph and said they would need to talk to him at some point about his family. He would also need to make a positive identification of Patrick and Maria with the county coroner.

About two hours into Isabella's surgery, the NTSB agent came back to talk to Murph. She said that the flight attendant who apparently helped save Isabella's life wanted to talk to him. Murph felt compelled to stay as close to Isabella's room as possible, but the flight attendant was only down one floor. The nurse promised Murph that she would come get him immediately if there were any new developments. Murph walked down with the NTSB agent, anxious to learn about the last moments of his wife and son's lives and what happened to Isabella.

Sandy Hatch looked surprisingly good given her ordeal. Murph wasn't sure, but he guessed that Sandy might have been in her late forties. She was sitting up in her room, her curly reddish-brown hair pulled back behind her ears and a blanket wrapped around her hospital gown. She had some minor scratches on her face and a busted lip. One leg was propped high above the bed and the other had a small cast. A man, who Murph later learned was Sandy's husband, stood up when Murph entered. He shook Murph's hand before walking out in silence. Murph looked at Sandy and said, "You asked to see me?"

"How is she?"

"We don't know," Murph responded.

Tears began to well up in Sandy's eyes. "You look just like her. I am so sorry." She burst into tears, and Murph began to console her, a woman he'd just met. It took Sandy about ten minutes to compose herself. She looked at Murph and again told him how sorry she was. She couldn't stop crying. When Sandy finally collected herself, she reached for the glass of water on the bedside table. She took slow sips and began to recount the flight.

Sandy helped Maria and the kids board the plane early. She told Murph how cute she thought the kids were and how good a job Maria was doing keeping them occupied while waiting for the plane to take off.

"Most of the time, you see parents putting a video player in front of their kids to keep them occupied, but your wife was playing games like Simon Says and I-Spy with your kids," she said.

"Maria's a teacher and she has always been creative both with her kids at school and at home. They do watch their share of television, I won't lie, but we also spend as much time outdoors and playing games with them as we can," Murph responded. It was hard for him to not talk about Maria and Patrick in the present tense.

"That's wonderful," she said.

"Do you have kids?" Murph asked. He felt compelled to just keep talking.

"Yes, I have two in college. They're both on their way here now. They are a true blessing, and I couldn't live without them," Sandy said. As soon as the words came out, Murph unwittingly bowed his head towards the floor, and Sandy immediately caught her mistake. "I'm so sorry I just said that," and she began to cry again. Murph started to choke up, but took a deep breath and composed himself. He needed to stay strong for Isabella.

Collisions

Sandy carried on with her story once she had collected herself again. She said that during the flight she continued to check in with the kids and Maria. She was stationed in the front of the plane, but would make her way back towards their seats whenever possible. She gave them extra snacks, something she rarely did for customers.

With only a little time left in the flight, Isabella complained about having to go to the bathroom. Sandy noticed and offered to walk her up to the front even though the pilot had already asked for everybody to remain seated and belted until the plane landed. She rushed with Isabella up to the bathroom. Maria was embarrassed about Isabella having to go and tried to get her to hold it, but the trip to the bathroom ended up saving Isabella's life.

"I stood there and waited for her while she was in the bathroom," Sandy said. "As soon as she came out, the plane suddenly made a hard bank and then there was a huge jolt, the lights flickered, and the plane immediately began to descend faster. I grabbed Isabella and held her as I buckled into the flight attendant seat near the cockpit. Everything else happened so fast," she said. "When we hit the ground I tried so hard to hold onto your daughter. I tried so hard. All I can think about is that I should have buckled her in, but at that split second I was sure I could hold her. I didn't even know what happened, everybody was yelling and crying before we hit, and then there was a big whoosh of air. And that's all I can remember," Sandy paused to catch her breath.

"I can tell you that as I took Isabella to the bathroom, her mother told her she loved her, and Isabella gave her a kiss as she squeezed out of the row."

"Thank you so much for trying to protect my daughter," Murph said. "Without your help, she might be gone now, too."

Victor Dancy

When Victor's interview was over, he was allowed to leave. The Colonel was waiting at the house with Leah. He had arrived in Williamsburg at some point during Victor's interview process, but he didn't show his face at WRA. The Colonel's friends were not there, so he made all of his calls by telephone to friends in the FAA. Leah sent Maddie to stay with a neighbor. Victor was sure Leah asked her to make sure that the television never came on. When he called her to say he was on his way home, Leah told him that almost everyone was dead on both flights. He decided to drop by a grocery store on the way and grab a quick six-pack. He really just wanted to get some drinks in him before he got double-teamed by Leah and his father.

Victor chugged a can before he even pulled out of the grocery store parking lot. He drank three more on the way home. He had a quick swish of mouthwash from a little airplane bottle he kept stashed in his glove compartment, and he immediately went inside to see the last two people on Earth he wanted to talk to at that moment. Just as Victor suspected, they both attacked him for his stupidity. The Colonel shook his head in disgust most of the time while Leah cried. Victor sat through the barrage of insults and daydreamed about sitting up in a tree hunting a buck, alone. Hunting had always been an escape for Victor, a way to get away from everyone. He typically hunted deer, even though he wasn't a big fan of venison. Victor once killed a black bear. He wanted to go to Alaska to hunt grizzlies. Victor believed animals were put on this earth for humans to hunt and eat. Finally, Leah quickly got sick of him not saying anything. She stormed out, probably to go cry some more in their bedroom, and Victor slipped out of his reveries about sighting a deer. Victor got down to real business with The Colonel.

The Colonel cheated on Victor's mother for years; it was common knowledge with his siblings and probably with just about everyone else. He never did a good job of hiding his infidelity. Victor assumed his mom knew even though she never said anything. Like Leah, she was set and happy with her place in life and didn't dare rock the boat by leaving his father. It was expected they live on base, given his rank and position, but The Colonel always made sure the family lived off base where he was stationed. He kept their base housing, but moved the family into a place off-base. His excuse was that he might stay at work real late and just crash on base for a couple hours instead of driving home, and that way they could keep Victor in the right schools. The Colonel told his family that he wanted them to try to have a normal life off-base, and not to always be stuck living the military life. A real normal life it was with their father always absent. They'd move every couple years. Victor didn't know why he just didn't pick one location for the family to stay where he could occasionally visit them; it really wouldn't have been that big of a difference from the time he spent with them. At least he always let Victor's mom pick the houses they bought and lived in.

The Colonel couldn't really give Victor a hard time about his obsession with escorts, when he had countless mistresses throughout his own life. He did a great job of hiding all of their identities. During their conversation at the house, Victor and The Colonel agreed that they would have to have a meeting with Laticia, the escort, very soon. The Colonel wanted Victor to set it up with her for that evening. He wanted Victor to call from a phone at the hotel and to use cash. None of this was new to his father. The Colonel was on the job.

The two discussed everything about the crash. The Colonel wanted a step by step account of what actually happened versus what Victor told the investigators. Just as Victor anticipated he thought the best idea was to go after Michelle and Steve, making them the scapegoats. The Colonel would deal with the FAA for Victor and try to extend that pressure to the NTSB. He said he wasn't too worried about the FBI. The Colonel also wanted him to see a psychiatrist and pretend that Victor was in a deep depression over the accident. Victor always thought taking Xanax made for an easy buzz, so he had no problem with that suggestion. It would show that Victor was truly upset by everything that happened, and remorseful for the dead. It's always harder to pin a guy who is sympathetic. The Colonel wanted to push Sam Sheets to give Victor several months of mental health leave, paid of course.

"You need to get out of here, too," The Colonel said at the end of their conversation. "There is no way your dumbass can fuck up again. I am going to find you a cabin on some remote lake in the middle of nowhere to keep you away from society so you don't screw up anymore."

"Leah doesn't have to come does she?" Victor asked.

"I don't think she wants to have anything to do with you. The last thing you can afford is to get divorced though. I have convinced Leah to bring Maddie and live near your mother and me. You will need to make trips home occasionally, just in case anybody is watching. The media can be vultures. I can handle the FAA and NTSB, but I'm worried some reporter is going to dig up information that he or she doesn't need to know. The FBI and DA will poke around a bit, but unless they have cause, they won't dig too deeply. Besides, they always end up tripping over each other and the NTSB in cases like this. NTSB would rather not have them around. To them criminal investigations jeopardize building lessons learned. This will all blow over eventually, but we need to be careful. Can you not fuck up for a while?"

"Yes, sir." Victor mumbled.

"One last thing," he told Victor before he walked out, probably more to comfort Leah, who was still crying in the other room. Victor was almost certain his father had some sort of crush on Leah, so he just wanted to have her close to him so he could see her more. It was pretty sick to Victor. "You absolutely disgust me, and I am ashamed to call you my son."

"Well fuck you too, Colonel," Victor thought. He couldn't give a shit if his father was ashamed of him. Victor caused two planes to crash into each other, and now it looked like he was going to get paid to take a vacation away from Leah and Maddie. He would be free to do whatever he wanted. Victor was sorry people died, but this was some of the best news he had heard in a long time.

• • •

The two met Laticia at a Best Western late that night. The Colonel didn't want Victor anywhere near Chili's or the Hilton, so people didn't have a second chance to place him. Victor was a little disappointed he wasn't alone with Laticia. He could use a stress-relief screw.

"Whoa, I don't do threesomes," Laticia said when she saw the two of them sitting in the room.

Victor couldn't help but laugh. The Colonel sternly told Laticia to "sit her ass down." He actually went over and grabbed her by the middle of the throat as soon as she sat down, in some sort of aggressive military move, which even surprised Victor a little bit.

"Do you see this man over here?" The Colonel asked Laticia.

Laticia was shaking from the surprise of the attack, and from struggling to breathe. "Yes, I see him," she gasped.

"No, you don't fucking see him," he let go and slapped her with his massive left hand. She fell back against the bed and covered her face. "You don't see him and you have never seen him before. People like you fucking disgust me. You are the scum of the Earth," he spit out.

"Who are you, and what did I do?" Laticia begged.

"You didn't do anything with this man. Do you understand me?"

"Yes, I do."

This was much more natural for The Colonel than Victor would have guessed. Victor had seen him pissed off plenty of times, but nothing like this. The Colonel even scared Victor with his beet-red face and veins popping out of his neck. He calmed some, leaning up against the small, wooden, hotel desk.

"You will forget we had this meeting. Do you understand?"

Laticia recovered; she must have been knocked around before. Victor guessed as an escort, it was part of the job. "Who the fuck do you think you are? I've got friends, too. They'll find your old, white ass and fuck you up good," she yelled. She was mistaken. Victor saw his father's face twist as she spoke.

Collisions

With the speed of a dog, The Colonel shot up from the desk and was on top of Laticia. He pinned her down with his left forearm on her throat so she could not move or speak, and Victor swore that The Colonel dug his right fingers just outside of her left ear as hard as he could on what must have been a pressure point. She was gasping and trying to scream. She looked like she was in some serious pain. Victor stood back, surprised at his father's aggression.

"You will never threaten me again, you dirty whore," he said looking right in her eyes. "I will go after you and your son Derrick." He let up, and she whimpered. How did he know she had a son? He must have already done his research; it always shocked Victor how many connections the old man had.

She began shaking and balled up into a fetal position. "Please don't hurt my son. I'll do whatever you want," she cried.

"Don't talk anymore. You may be approached by some authorities asking who you were with last night. You will tell them that you did not work at all. They might bring up a phone call you received, and you will tell them it was a wrong number. Here is ten-thousand dollars," he said as he dropped a large roll of cash by her feet. She sat up and looked at the money and at The Colonel in shock. "If you are a good girl, I will get you another ten-thousand dollars a year from today. Remember, say anything to anybody, I will find out. Every time you look at Derrick, think about what I could do to him. Take the money and make sure he doesn't live as dirty of a life as you do. Do you understand?"

"Yes," she answered.

"Good, now get out, and don't ever forget what I said tonight. We were never here. The rest of the money will be delivered to you next year."

Laticia rushed out of the room. The Colonel got up, and followed her. Victor wasn't sure if he was supposed to go with his father, but he decided just to crash at the Best Western for the night. It had been a long day. Based on The Colonel's intensity and the amount of money offered, Victor felt very confident the plan so far would work. He sat back and had a drink, and contemplated calling in another escort, since he already had the room.

Chapter 15

Posted: April 10, 2009, 7:45 p.m.

Carmen Paul/Williamsburg Daily Express

Vitaly, VA - Vitaly's Sheriff, Oscar Baker, revealed the death toll from this morning's mid-air collision to be one hundred and forty one people. The two pilots on US Courier Flight 611, Collin Bridger and Shawn Baldwin, were both killed. On Atlantic Airline Flight 2937 there were one hundred and thirty-nine confirmed deaths, including sixty-one Duquesne University students, but only two survivors. Of the two survivors, Sandy Hatch, an Atlantic Airline flight attendant, is expected to fully recover, while the other unnamed survivor is in critical condition.

President Christopher Holden of Duquesne released the following statement: "We at Duquesne University express our sincere condolences to all of the victims and their families of today's terrible accident, but especially to the families of the Duquesne students onboard Atlantic Airlines Flight 2937. Our immediate concern is for our entire student population at Duquesne and the families of our victims, whose lives are now forever changed."

The NTSB held a brief news conference. No questions were taken. Colleen Garcia, the NTSB spokeswoman, stated, "The National Transport Safety Board is the lead agency in this investigation. We are currently working with the Federal Bureau of Investigation to find out the cause of today's unfortunate and tragic plane collision in eastern Virginia. We will conduct a thorough investigation to determine the cause of the accident. We will not stop until we are satisfied with the outcome of the investigation. On behalf of the FAA, the NTSB wishes to express our deepest condolences to all of those affected by today's events."

The White House announced that President Jackson Reeves will visit the site of the crash tonight, and he will give a brief speech from the site later this evening.

Murphy Kearns

After Murph left Sandy's room, he headed back to the surgical waiting room. His parents and his brother had arrived to give him some much needed emotional support. After Murph spoke with them on the phone earlier, they rushed to Williamsburg to be with Isabella. Murph wasn't ready to talk. They just sat with him quietly, saving the questions for another day. Their company ended up being very comforting.

Ms. Linker showed up a couple hours after Murph's parents, which gave him some reassurance that Isabella would get to hear a voice that was as regular to her as his and Maria's. After remaining in the waiting room for about an hour, the doctor came and talked to Murph. Middle-aged, white haired, glasses and the smell of coffee on his breath, this same doctor was in a thousand emergency rooms across the country at that moment. He sat Murph down with a very serious tone in his voice, crossing his leg, with his hand on his chin.

He said, "Mr. Kearns, I completely understand that it has been a tough day for you. I am very sorry to hear about your wife and son. I wish I had some better news for you about Isabella, but right now we really don't know what will happen. It is all up to how she battles through. We are going to keep her in a coma until the brain swelling goes down. During that time, her broken bones should be able to begin to heal. She suffered no permanent damage in her legs, which is a good thing."

"Will she suffer permanent brain damage?" Murph asked.

"Right now there is just no way to know. If she makes it through this, we will know more," he said.

The thought of losing all of his family was too much for Murph to handle. He continued to feel disoriented.

"How long until we know something?"

The doctor said "We really don't know right now. We are just going to need to take this day to day."

"Okay. Can I see her now?"

"Yes, we are currently taking her to one of our larger rooms where you will be able to stay in the room with her," he said. Murph and the doctor shook hands. Murph felt like he was a character in one of those TV hospital dramas.

When Murph walked into the room and saw Isabella hooked up to all of those machines, all of the weight from the day finally settled in on him. Seeing his only daughter with all of those tubes connected to her as she lay in her hospital bed was too much to bear. He gently held her and cried for her, for Maria, and for Patrick. He didn't know how long he rested there with her. Although Murph normally didn't pray, in those hours he prayed to God, Jesus, Buddha, and anybody else he could think of. He needed Isabella to make it because he couldn't contemplate a life with all three gone. There would be no point.

After a couple hours, Murph walked out and asked his family to find a bookstore. He gave them a list of books that were some of Isabella's favorites for him to read to her. His parents tried to get him to eat something, but he had no appetite. Once his brother got back from the bookstore, Murph spent the night reading and re-reading *The Giving Tree*, *Where the Wild Things Are*, and *Go, Dog, Go!* to his motionless daughter, hoping that she could hear him wherever she was. The last time he saw the clock on the wall it was well past 3:00 a.m.

The only interruptions in his reading came when the nurses came to check on Isabella. Murph took a break from reading in the uncomfortable hospital chair next to Isabella at about 3:15 a.m., so he could watch the videos they sent him the night before that he still had not watched. Maria narrated her video in a very attractive, skimpy t-shirt and promised to wear it for him as soon as the kids went to sleep the night they arrived. The kid's video was of them doing the Cupid Shuffle. Isabella, dressed in her favorite pink and purple striped dress, had all of the hand and feet movements down pat, and Patrick, in his diaper, had absolutely none of them, but he tried to keep up with her. The only part that Isabella was getting confused about was when she would go to the right when it said to the left and vice versa. It all seemed so innocent then. At some point Murph leaned his head on top of Isabella's stomach and fell asleep.

Collisions

During that short slumber next to Isabella in the hospital bed, he dreamed that he was lost. Murph didn't know how old he was in the dream. He was in a wooded area near the house he grew up in, where he spent countless hours with neighborhood friends playing hide and go seek, capture the flag, and any number of other childhood games. Murph was looking for something in those woods, but he ran through the dead needles and cones from the fir and spruce trees over and over. No matter where he ran, he always ended up back in a shiny, open area where the grass in the meadow was high, but nobody was waiting for him.

When he awoke from the dream, the hole in his chest doubled in size and left him feeling empty. It was his job to protect his family, but in their moment of need he was nowhere to be found.

Part III – April 11, 2009 and on…

Newton's Third Law of Motion:

For every action, an equal and opposite reaction

Chapter 16

Murphy Kearns

Nothing had changed with Isabella over the past several days. She was still in a coma, and there were no positive signs of recovery. He didn't want to leave Isabella, but Maria's family wanted to have a funeral. Murph's mother stayed behind at the hospital to be with Isabella. She would call Murph if anything happened. He told her he didn't care where he was. He would head back to Williamsburg immediately if anything changed.

Murph wouldn't fly out of Norfolk, the airport where he should have picked up his family safely a week and a half before, even though it was the closest airport that flew into Pittsburgh. The drive to Raleigh would only take a few hours. Murph had not watched any news or read articles about the collision. The NTSB had briefly questioned Murph about the flight. "Any contact with your wife before or during the flight? Any information from her that might be of concern in hindsight?" and the like. Pretty innocuous stuff, but Murph knew they were just doing their job. He was aware that the FBI was around, but they had not contacted him.

Murph also talked a lot to Sandy Hatch, whom he had kept up with since their first meeting. She was released from the hospital five days earlier, and went back home to upstate New York. She called Murph daily to find out if Isabella had shown any improvements. Sandy had become a media darling over the previous week. She had been on the Today Show, CNN, MSNBC, and just about every talk show imaginable according to Murph's mom. His mom had been keeping an eye on the news. Murph was not ready to find out the cause of the collision. He was sure one day he would need to know who played a part in the disaster that killed his wife and son, but not yet.

He hadn't slept more than thirty minutes at a time since the accident, and he couldn't eat. He tried to force himself; it felt like there was a brick permanently lodged in his stomach and there was no room for anything else. Isabella's doctors had one of the hospital psychiatrists come by. He prescribed Murph an anti-depressant and sleep aid. He picked up the prescription from the hospital pharmacy, but he hadn't taken a single one. He didn't feel he deserved any relief from his pain while Isabella was still in a coma.

Isabella had been in the intensive care unit since they brought her out of the emergency room. She was intubated and on a ventilator. She was engulfed in a web of intravenous tubes in her arms. He hated to see her just lying there in that hospital bed. There were three possible outcomes: death, life in a vegetative state, or recovery. Murph knew the odds. The first two were the most probable, unfortunately. He felt guilty leaving Isabella for the funeral service, but there was no alternative.

His plans were to head to Nags Head to grab a bag, check in on Rooney, and give Pete keys to his rental house. With Johnny's help, Pete was going to move Murph's stuff out so he didn't have to keep paying rent. He didn't have a ton of clothes, and the rental was already furnished, so Pete was going to keep everything at his house where he had some extra room.

Pete was also going to do Murph a big favor and continue to watch Rooney. Murph didn't know how he would ever be able to thank Pete enough. Murph was flying out of Raleigh late that night, and he would return to Williamsburg two days later. He had convinced Maria's parents to just do a small graveside service, and to wait to do a memorial service until either Isabella could be there in person or she joined them. Murph was starting to have trouble keeping the possibility that it could be a memorial for her as well.

Pete was going to keep Murph on for the landscape job. "Just keep on keepin' on for now," Pete said. Murph couldn't see himself ever going back to work though, especially if the worst happened to Isabella.

Murph had become more and more depressed over the past twelve days. He couldn't stop seeing these images of Isabella in her coma and Maria and Patrick sitting dead together in their airplane seats. The dread that Isabella might not be with him any longer was just too overwhelming. All he did was stare out the window on the ride with his dad from Williamsburg to the Outer Banks. His dad tried to engage Murph in conversation, but Murph had no capacity to talk to anybody. He didn't feel shock or disbelief; he just didn't feel at all.

When they got to the rental house, Murph asked his dad to let him go inside on his own for a while since the flight wasn't scheduled to leave Raleigh for eight more hours. His dad agreed and headed out to get some coffee. When Murph walked in the door, Rooney ran up to him, and for a second Murph forgot all about the tragedy. When he was done rubbing Rooney's stomach, he looked up, and he saw all of the grocery shopping he had done for the kids and Maria's stay. It took him right back. Both Isabella and Patrick loved when Murph made blanket tents for them to sleep in. They were going to share the double bed in the spare room. It would have been the first time that Patrick and Isabella had ever shared a bed, one of the main reasons was that it would give Maria and Murph some time to themselves at night. To ease the transition from sleeping alone, Murph made one of the best designed blanket tents ever. It took him hours the week before they came to build and perfect it, and he was sure at the time that the kids were going to be ecstatic about sleeping in a bed together as long as they were in the tent he made. Murph had to use every spare blanket, sheet, and beach towel he could find, but he managed to cover the whole room with the tent. As soon as he saw it, he hurried over and pulled it down in one strong jerk. Murph fell down on the mound of blankets he just created and wept. He let it all go for the first time since the collision. He felt like he had nothing left emotionally or physically. He must have cried for a good hour, Rooney lying right at his feet, panting and slobbering on the floor, but otherwise quiet.

As Murph lay there, intertwined in the blankets, all he could think about was the impossibility of a life without Maria and the kids. Murph couldn't stand to be in the house any longer. He walked out the front door in a tired stupor. He tried to leave Rooney behind, but the dog was not going to let Murph out of his sight. He darted out the door before Murph could close it. They walked around the back of the rental, which backed up to the sound. Since being in the Outer Banks, he had taken Rooney with him to fish on a little boat that the owners kept tied up behind the house. He decided the best way to get away from the house was to go out on the skiff for a while. The skiff looked like it was hand-made, possibly by the owner. Rooney jumped in, and Murph pushed out on the surprisingly chilly and windy April day.

Normally most people enjoy their days in the sand on the beach in the Outer Banks, but every now and then some people choose the sound side. That day the sound was empty, but for small white caps and a few birds. Rooney liked to hang his big paws over the side of the boat to look down into the water as Murph paddled. Knowing his past tendencies to jump out of moving means of transportation, Murph made sure to keep a foot draped over top of him. He was not overly worried about the big guy's swimming capabilities if he did decide to jump in.

When they were about two hundred yards from shore, Murph put the paddles down and leaned his head back against the side of the boat. The boat drifted. Rooney came over and licked Murph a couple times before he headed back to scout for fish. The rigid side of the boat that he was lying against normally wouldn't have been comfortable, but by then he felt little at all. Murph knew that he was no longer going to be able to hold Patrick, or play catch, or go to a Steelers game together. He would never be able to sleep next to Maria and grow old surrounded by her warmth. He believed that people were like puzzle pieces and had but one connecting piece in the world. There was potential for others to be close fits, but there could only be one perfect fit, and Murph's was gone. The boat drifted.

Murph couldn't really explain what happened to him next. He looked at Rooney, and scratched him behind his ears.

Collisions

Then he turned to the side and just rolled out of the small skiff like he rolled out of bed in the morning. Murph barely made a splash as his body passed through the surface. He had been through enough agony over the past week and a half. Momentum instead of logic told him that Isabella wasn't going to make it, maybe she was already gone. He couldn't imagine living anymore without his family. Murph briefly floated near the surface looking straight down at the abyss beneath him waiting for it to suck him in, taking him to Patrick and Maria, and to where Isabella would soon join them. He didn't try to stay afloat, but his body's natural instinct to swim kept him up for a brief moment. Then he was sucked in and began to sink. In that moment, he saw Maria and Patrick waiting for him at the bottom, but something stronger pulled him back to the surface. He liked to think the force was Isabella grabbing hold of him and telling him not to give up on her. He was, of course, not alone.

Typically, when Murph got in the water at the beach with Rooney, the dog swam over to him and wrapped his monstrous legs and paws around Murph, clinging to him like he was a baby that couldn't swim. He would almost pull them both under when he grasped onto Murph. As Murph began descending into the depths of the sound beneath him, there was a powerful pull on the collar of his shirt that dragged him back to the surface. The big guy had jumped in as soon as he saw Murph begin to fall below the top of the water. Rooney grabbed a hold of Murph like an adult dog grabs the nape of a puppy, and thousands of years of genetic selection for swimming and automatic loyalty to a human saved Murph from himself.

After catching his breath in the boat and helping Rooney get back in, Murph realized three important things. The first was that he was being self-absorbed and outrageous for doing what he just about did. Second, he was going to use this new opportunity to live the rest of his life doing the best that he could, since he would now be living not just for himself, but also for Patrick and Maria. And third, he was going to do whatever it took to make sure something as horrible as the collision that took their lives never happened again and to get an apology for everybody affected by whomever was responsible. He paddled back into shore with his trusty sidekick, muzzle draped over the side of the boat like nothing just happened, with a new lease on life, a new goal in mind, and a realization that it should all be about Isabella.

Victor Dancy

Once all of his interviewing was done, Victor did what The Colonel told him to do and found a place in a remote area close enough to visit Leah and Maddie to avoid suspicion, but far enough away from everybody else to keep him off the radar. He settled on Lake Anna, a quick, seventy mile drive to the D.C. area.

The reservoir lake that was formed by the North Anna River was a popular weekend vacation spot for people from Richmond, Charlottesville, and D.C. It was a destination for water sports aficionados, which meant young babes in skimpy bikinis. It would be a great fit for his recovery. During his first day there, he rented a kayak and paddled himself out on the river until he found some young co-eds sun bathing on the shore a couple hundred yards from where he pushed off. He stayed a little ways out and laid back to pretend like he was taking a nap with his shades on. He was close enough for a good view of the young women, but far enough so they couldn't tell what he was doing.

Collisions

Victor rented a lakefront home with plenty of trees for shade and privacy and about three quarters of an acre of land. The home was built in the early 2000s, so everything was virtually new. There was a hot tub, which he planned to use a lot, especially once he got the lay of the land in terms of the ladies. There was a covered dock that led to a dredged canal in the lake, so it was not too loud and far enough away from everybody. Leah and Maddie came when he moved in, but Leah was so disgusted with him that they spent virtually the whole day shopping in the nearby town of Louisa. The Colonel had obviously advised the visit, but couldn't dictate all of the terms.

Just like The Colonel anticipated, no charges were expected to be filed against Victor. Steve caved in with some pressure from the FBI, and also placed most of the blame on Michelle and her absence, which probably helped Victor's cause. Steve was fired by the FAA immediately and lost his pension. Michelle was fired and was probably going to face some criminal charges once the NTSB wrapped up their investigation and handed things over to the FBI. Victor was given an eight-week unpaid suspension, which he readily agreed to, while he would recover from his feigned mental breakdown. Everybody believed that he was in the Lake Anna area to get his head screwed back on straight from such a horrific experience, or at least that was what they were telling people. Victor was seeing a well-respected shrink once a week in Alexandria, Virginia. The head doc just happened to be a golfing buddy of The Colonel.

It would take several more weeks for both the NTSB and the FBI to completely wrap up their investigations. Victor spent the first five days interviewing and telling his story to everybody and their mother in the two organizations, and he thought he did an excellent job retelling the same story over and over. The Colonel had some insider information as well to give him a heads up about whom he would be talking to next and what to expect. The NTSB would just be building "lessons learned" from the interviews, and Victor figured that the FBI still might be keeping an eye on him. The media still had no idea where he was. On the third day after the collision, the media got a hold of their names, and they swarmed the houses of everybody involved at WRA. Victor left immediately for his father's house in a gated community with strong security. They snuck out in the middle of the night in one of his dad's friend's cars when they came to Lake Anna. Victor enjoyed watching Steve and Michelle try to dodge the media with their jackets pulled over their heads. It made them look completely culpable. The media talked about Victor some, but they never found much, which fortunately kept his well-hidden dismissal from the Air Force and his DUIs out of the public eye. The Colonel did a great job of covering everything up, and Victor appreciated that the old bastard was good for something.

A number of factors were being blamed for the collision. The investigators were focused on the malfunctioning communication system at WRA. The FAA was taking plenty of media heat for letting an airport operate with old and faulty equipment. Norfolk International was taking some blame for diverting the Atlantic Airlines flight so close to another airport without properly clearing it with WRA personnel (which, of course, they had tried to do). The entire traffic collision avoidance system installed in airplanes was under scrutiny, and every plane allowed to fly by the FAA would be updated, all costing billions of dollars. Of course, Atlantic Airlines and US Couriers were accusing the other plane's pilots for not following instructions on the TCAS to try to escape any responsibility. In all, it was a big jumbled mess, but the bigger the mess, the better it was for Victor.

Collisions

There would most likely be civil lawsuits by families of the crash victims, and there was a strong possibility that Victor would be included as a defendant in some of them. The Colonel and his lawyers agreed that there was really nothing Victor could do to avoid those charges, and he would probably eventually have to pay some compensation to the victims. Fortunately, he was such a small fish in a big sea in terms of culpability that he wouldn't have to pay too much. It would be delayed in the legal system for so long that the lawyers might eventually be able to find a way out for Victor. Or the FAA might just cave in and settle early. The twenty-four hour news channels had been all over the collision from all angles, but eventually something else would happen in the world and this would be relegated to a thirty-second update. Victor was hoping for a new war, celebrity murder, or act of terrorism to occur to move everyone's attention to something else.

Chapter 17

Murphy Kearns

People spend all of their lives either wanting life to speed up and looking forward or wanting it to slow down and always looking back. When you are a young child you want time to speed up to get to your next birthday or to Christmas. Everything seems to move at a snail's pace. When you are in school, you can't wait for the next party or for summer break and you count down the days. Then you get older, and you want time to slow down. The days, months, and years fly by much faster. Murph was at a point before the collision when he was starting to wish time would slow down. After the crash, he just wanted it to fly by. He couldn't wait for the funeral to be over, to find out what was going to happen with Isabella, and have the question of who was responsible for the collision answered. He wanted to demand an apology from them.

After his lapse on the skiff, Murph headed back to the house with Rooney and never told his family or anybody else what happened. He was embarrassed. At the time he was thinking solely of himself. He forgot that his parents had lost a daughter-in-law and a grandson. Murph showered and then his dad picked him up, and they headed to the airport in Raleigh. Rooney, on the other hand, was not happy for him to leave again. The big guy saved his life, and in return Murph left him.

Murph got his best sleep since the collision on the short flight back to Pittsburgh. The airport and the flight were pretty crowded. The media reported that airlines were only suffering a short falloff from passengers after the accident. After all, people in America tend to have a short memory, especially if they have places to go. He really didn't have time to be anxious about flying with everything going on. Murph took heed of what the doctors told him and swallowed the anti-anxiety and anti-depressant medications they prescribed. They made the whole trip home much easier. In fact, as soon as he took a seat and buckled in, he was passed out until the plane touched down.

Maria's car was waiting at the airport for her and the kids to come back from visiting Murph. It took some time to find it in the long-term lot. As soon as he opened the door to her Accord, a wave of nostalgia washed over Murph and stuck with him for the rest of his drive home. Since it was the city where most of their story unfolded, everything reminded him of something to do with Maria.

The dent in the hood of their Accord reminded him of the time that Maria hit a man in an attempt to stop a robbery. They were at a small Giant Eagle grocery store pretty shortly after they moved into their new house in Squirrel Hill. Maria was three months pregnant with Isabella, and it was their first trip to that particular store. It was well past eleven o'clock at night, and she was craving some rocky road ice cream. She pulled into the fire lane right in front so Murph could run in real fast. Maria sat in the driver's seat and kept the motor on. After he checked out, as he was walking out into the dark through the automatic doors, he heard a yell a little ways up the street.

"Stop! Stop, he has my purse. Stop him!" the voice of a terrified lady screamed.

Murph looked up and saw a guy with bushy blonde hair running away from a hysterical older woman whom the man had obviously just robbed right outside of her parked car. Murph quickly turned to look at Maria as she mouthed the word "go" to him and pointed the way the thief was headed. The guy had a good two hundred yard head-start on Murph as he was already crossing Darlington Road and the Manor Theatre, but Murph was a sub five-minute miler in high school, and he always kept in pretty good shape. Murph threw the ice cream into the Accord's open window and took off after the delinquent not quite sure what his plan would be once he caught the guy. Murph tore after him and started to catch him after crossing Forbes Avenue, just past Carnegie Mellon Library. Murph had never been in a rundown before and was not sure what to do, so he just started to yell, "Drop the purse, man, just drop it!"

The guy cut over on a little back alley towards Shady Avenue, and Murph caught him just as he crossed Shady. The crook fit the part on Shady Ave. He looked like he might have been smoking meth every minute of every day for the past five years with his sunken cheeks and eyes, pale face, and dozens of scabs.

"Listen, man, just give me the purse so I can return it to that poor lady back there," Murph gasped at the guy.

The guy laughed at Murph and said in a crackly voice, "Fuck you. I am keepin' dis purse and now give me your wallet."

Collisions

Murph felt a little badly for the guy who must have weighed one hundred and ten pounds. "I won't get the police involved if you give me the purse. I'll even get you some groceries. You look hungry."

He seemed to have no feelings, and he laughed again, "I said give me your wallet!" He reached into his dirty gray hoodie and pulled out a steel pipe that must have been about a foot long. He swung it at Murph twice. The first time he was way off, but the second swing Murph could feel the breeze from the pipe as he jumped back and it just missed him. In a flash, a dark green vehicle flew in front of Murph hitting the guy with its front bumper, sending him up on its hood, across the front and back to the ground. Frantically driving the Squirrel Hill streets looking for them, Maria had tracked Murph and the man down.

"That was crazy," was the first thing Murph said to Maria after the police dragged the guy off. Apparently he had been robbing women in the area for the past week, and they were already on the lookout for him.

Maria said, "There was no way I was going to let him hurt my hubby. Plus, I really wanted my rocky road, and that guy was dragging things out for me."

"Yeah, but you could've hit me when you pulled up on the curb to stop him! Where did you learn that move, anyways?" Murph asked.

"I watched a lot of *21 Jump Street* when I was a kid," she responded. And with that she was already digging into the carton of ice cream with a plastic spoon from the glove compartment. They decided not to get the dent fixed, even though both the cops and the woman whose purse was stolen offered to fix it in gratitude. Murph and Maria kept it as a badge of honor for them to look at every time they drove the Accord.

• • •

As Murph pulled into their hilly street, he was reminded of another reason he loved Maria so much, her stubbornness. Maria fell in love with their house across the street from Frick Park the first time she laid eyes on it. They had been driving all around Pittsburgh on a house hunting expedition. The two had already agreed on the maximum price they were willing to pay for a house. The Frick Park home was just a tiny bit over that budget, so they decided to take a look. The brick house was built in the early twentieth century and sat on a quarter of an acre, which was a huge slab of land for that part of Pittsburgh. The school district was good enough, and the more they looked at it the more she fell in love. Murph had to admit he really liked it, too. The kitchen was newly renovated, there were hardwood floors throughout, and it had all the bedrooms on one floor, which Maria really hoped for in their new house.

They were not using a realtor, and that was the first house they really went all out for. Maria was set in stone in two areas. First, she wasn't going to go a penny over their budget. Second, she wasn't going to let the sellers and their realtor say no. Murph just sat back entertained by her exchanges with the seller's agent. She sealed the deal on the third round of negotiations.

"I will not leave your office today until we sign some papers for our house," she told him immediately when they walked in his office.

"Have you decided to come up some on your offer?" the increasingly perturbed agent said as soon as he saw who it was. "No. We are sticking with our original offer. But like I said, I want that house, and we are not leaving here until we sign papers," and she plopped down in a seat in the corner of his office and patted the seat beside it, Murph's cue to take it. "Just please get the sellers on the phone and re-emphasize how much we want it."

The agent stepped out of his office on his cell phone, and within thirty minutes the sellers were there. They were an older couple in their late seventies, and they had been in the home for over forty years. Their children and grandchildren had renovated the kitchen for their mother's seventieth birthday as a way to say "thank you" for a lifetime of great meals. Maria won the couple over to the astonishment of the agent, who was fuming by that point as he calculated how much commission he would lose on the lower offer. Though good looks can be an intimidating quality in some women, people always immediately felt comfortable with Maria and trusted her right off the bat. Maria listened to the couple talk about their experience in the house and then asked a lot of questions in turn. She always told Murph that older people had a lot of great stories to tell, you just had to ask them. Then she talked about how much she loved the house and how she wanted to live in it with her family for the next forty years just like they did. She wanted her future children to have the same experience their kids did. The older couple ate it up, and they closed on the house two months later.

• • •

Murph was reminded of Maria and the kids wherever he went during his stay in Pittsburgh. When he walked through the house, the half-eaten bag of potato chips reminded him of their New Year's resolution to stop eating chips for a year. Murph caught Maria sneaking a small bag of barbecue chips only two weeks into January, but that was okay because he had a bag two days earlier. The Lucky Charms box reminded Murph of how much Patrick liked to dump the whole box out and separate out the marshmallows one by one into a pile that he would eat later. The hand-me-down cheval mirror in the hall upstairs brought back memories of when Isabella had to get eleven stitches because they were playing tag and she slipped and fell against it, hitting the back of her head on the bottom corner.

Since they were only doing a private burial and the public memorial would come later, there were only a few people in attendance. Maria's close family was there, Ms. Linker, two of Maria's closest friends, and her favorite professor, who she kept up with over weekly cups of coffee. It was a gorgeous day, seventy degrees with a slight breeze. There were a few clouds in the sky, but Murph was thankful because they helped distract him during the service.

A month before he left to go to the Outer Banks, Murph's grandmother passed away. They kept Patrick with a babysitter, but Isabella went to the funeral with them because she had spent a lot of time with Nana. While his family was sitting in the cold and hard metal chairs waiting for the service to begin, Isabella became fascinated with what would happen to Nana after she'd died and left the earth. When Murph was young, Nana's husband, Gramps, passed away of a heart attack. Murph asked Nana some of the same questions that Isabella was asking him now. He found himself giving Isabella many of the same answers.

"When someone dies, their Spirit rides on a cloud to Heaven," Murph told Isabella.

"How do they get to the cloud?" she asked.

"Well, Spirits are invisible, but as soon as the funeral begins they float up through the ground and the sky to a cloud way up high. The clouds go by so slowly because once the Spirit gets there, it wants to watch down over all of its family at the funeral and wait until they leave before the Spirit continues on its way to heaven."

"How do we know which cloud Nana is on?" Isabella asked.

"I'm sure if you look closely at the sky you can find the right cloud." Isabella craned her head back in her seat and looked around at the slow-moving clouds.

"I think she is on the low one there that looks like a crocodile," Isabella said pointing at a stratus cloud.

"You must be right then," Murph responded. After the funeral, when they got to their car, Isabella blew a kiss up towards that cloud that was still up in the sky and said, "Bye, Nana. Have fun in Heaven."

Murph only had three objectives for the service. He wanted Maria and Patrick buried together in the same casket. They died together, and Murph thought it was best that they be buried together. He figured that would be the way Maria would want it. He also did not want to focus too much on the casket or the burial, so it was not the last memory he had of the two. Lastly, Maria was always fascinated with Khalil Gibran, the Lebanese poet. Neither of them was very religious, but Maria kept a copy of *The Prophet* next to her bed and read a poem of his pretty regularly. As the casket was being lowered, Murph read Gibran's poem on death:

Only when you drink from the river of silence shall you indeed sing.
And when you have reached the mountain top,
then you shall begin to climb.
And when the earth shall claim your limbs,
then shall you truly dance.

As he finished reading the end of the passage, he heard the sound of the casket reaching its final resting place on the Earth's bed. The Earth was receiving two of his three most sacred gifts for eternity.

Murph silently cried during the reading, with slow and steady tears rolling down his cheeks onto his suit jacket. On his walk back to the car after the service was over, he looked up and found a stratus cloud just like Nana's cloud up in the sky. He thought Isabella would agree that it looked like a turtle shell. He wanted to picture Maria and Patrick on their way to Heaven together. Murph blew the cloud a kiss and said, "Love you."

Victor Dancy

It had been a little over a week and a half since Victor got to Lake Anna, and he was starting to go a little stir crazy. He had not been properly screwed since the plane collision. The lake house was cool, but he was getting tired of being so isolated. He tried as hard as he could just to sit around the lake house and drink himself into a stupor, but internet porn could only get you so far. Victor did a few internet searches for escort services, but there were none within fifty miles of his place. He even tried to sleep with Leah a couple days earlier when he went to visit her and Maddie, but she was having none of it. The Colonel wanted him to avoid as many public places as possible for the next several months, but he had had enough of sitting around. He decided to go to a local dive bar in Louisa called The Rusted Spoon; while he was there he met the girl of his dreams.

He had driven by The Rusted Spoon a couple times, and though he'd had the bug to stop in, he always kept on driving. After a six-pack at the lake house, he decided to just go in for a couple liquor drinks and then head back home. The bar was on the corner next to some antique shops in an old strip on the main road. There were no windows and just a little plain white sign hanging above the door. It was supposed to be a membership-only club so they could sell liquor, but you just had to pay a dollar to join. When Victor entered the bar, there were two or three dart boards on his right and a couple of small round tables to the left, then the long bar and a couple pool tables in the back near the restrooms. The place couldn't have been more than five hundred square feet. The ventilation was almost nonexistent. It was one big cigarette. It really didn't matter if you smoked or not because if you spent a couple years working in that place, you were a shoe-in for lung cancer.

When Victor walked in, he saw some older locals sitting up near the dart board. A couple manly looking women were behind the bar serving the drinks, and there were four or five men and women sitting at the bar throwing back tallboy beers and whiskey. Nobody was in the back of the place. As soon as he sat down, he saw her. She had to be ten to fifteen years older than Victor, but he knew he wanted to go home with her the minute he saw her. Even though she was the only single woman in the bar that didn't look like Roseanne Barr, Victor was sure he still would have picked her out of a bar that had a thousand women in it. She looked like a blonde-haired, country western version of Susan Sarandon from her early acting days of *Bull Durham* and *Thelma & Louise*. She was smoking a Virginia Slim cigarette and drinking what looked like a Cosmopolitan. She had thick, curly, blonde-hair that looked like it came straight off the cover of an old Dolly Parton record.

Victor parked himself next to her and worked his magic. He didn't know where the lies he told her came from, but he pulled a sob story and told her that he had two family members killed in the recent plane collision in Vitaly. He'd work the angle for a little tail, but truthfully Victor was sick and tired of watching the sappy stories that they kept airing and airing on the twenty-four hour news networks about the families of the people killed in the two planes. He couldn't wait for those people's fifteen seconds of fame to run out. For some reason the media had been really fixated on this one family, and they were treating them like they were royalty. The guy lost his wife and his son, and the young daughter was barely hanging on. Blah, blah, blah. Victor saw the media's angle, but it was getting old, fast. The guy, Murphy something or other, wasn't doing any interviews, which was only making the media hounds want to interview him even more. They did show pictures of him, and he looked like a guy Victor wouldn't mind hitting over the head with a beer bottle. If Victor were him, he'd be eating that shit up and writing a book to make some bank in the process. But, Victor wasn't Murphy Something-or-Other, and, damn, he was sick of it on the TV all the time. The Colonel was right; "effects based operations" applied to a wide variety of situations, and he wasn't afraid to employ whatever it took to sack this girl.

"Yeah, I'm trying to just get away for a while. My brother and his wife were on the Atlantic Airlines flight. We were really tight growing up, and we tried to visit each other every couple months. We had a fishing trip planned for the weekend. They had two sons and a daughter that I am also really close to, and I am going to have to be their father figure now. My brother was especially helpful to me when my wife left me four years ago," Victor told the sympathetic woman as he continued to pour it on. She was looking at Victor like he was a saint.

"You poor soul," she said. "My husband, Ricky, was killed in a motorcycle wreck three years ago, so I know what it feels like to be in your shoes," as she put her hand on top of Victor's forearm. They had just met and though he didn't know her name yet, he knew he was in there already.

They walked back to play pool after a couple drinks. He finally found out her name, Gretchen Sanders. Gretchen moved to Louisa after her husband was killed so she could be near her elderly mother. She grew up outside Louisa, but moved to Nashville after college to pursue a singing career. She recorded one album in the nineties, but it never did much. She did some modeling for Levi's to make ends meet, and that was where she met her husband. He was in the rodeo on the Professional Rodeo Cowboys Association circuit. Gretchen did some back-up singing for Shania Twain and toured around the country with her. Since they traveled so much, Gretchen and her husband were never able to settle down enough to have kids. Her husband died in 2005, and Gretchen moved back to Louisa shortly after during the next year. She was living in a house that was on farmland owned by her parents. The house was on the forty-five acre farm where Gretchen grew up, but on the opposite side of the land from where her mom lived, so she could have some space.

"So do you like it back here?" Victor asked as he tried to sink the ten-ball in the corner pocket.

"It has been great to be back with my family, and I have taken back up horse-back riding," she responded. "But I miss traveling around the country, either on a tour bus, or on the back of Ricky's chopper."

He couldn't help gazing down her flannel shirt every time she bent over to take a shot like he was in middle school looking down Senorita Gonzalez's shirt as she bent over to ask him a Spanish question. Gretchen must have been at least a size D. She was also quite a pool shark because she tore Victor apart every game they played. The longer they talked, the more he couldn't wait to get her in bed. "I love traveling around the country as well. It has always been a goal of mine to get to all fifty states. Right now, I am at forty-seven states with just Alaska, New Mexico, and Arizona left," Victor lied.

"I have been to every state, most of them a couple times, but I wouldn't mind going back to those three again," she said with a wink.

They played a number of games and each had several drinks over the next few hours. They talked a little about each other, politics, and their gun collections. The more they talked, the more intrigued Victor became with Gretchen. She had a lot of the characteristics that Leah was missing, and she seemed like a no bull-shit type of gal.

Victor was surprised how easily they'd connected and he was positive that he was going to go back home with her that night. She shocked him when they walked outside and she headed to her car without extending an invitation to him. She did give Victor a kiss on the cheek and asked for him to come back to the bar again to do it all over three nights later. He was not used to having to work for women, especially since he paid for most of them, but Victor couldn't stop thinking about Gretchen and their time together, and he was definitely intrigued to find out more.

Chapter 18

Murphy Kearns

After the funeral, Murph went back to the hospital and didn't leave Isabella's side for the next three days. His parents and brother had been such a massive help that he wanted them to be able to go home and get a break. Murph found a really cheap, tiny apartment a couple blocks away from the hospital to keep some clothes in and go to shower. Isabella and Murph had visits from Johnny Johnson, Sherriff Baker, Deputy Silva, and Milo, which all raised Murph's spirits. Pete visited almost daily.

He knew he would spend most of his time at the hospital and it would not be fair for Rooney to stay cramped up in an apartment that literally was not big enough for him, but Pete did bring him up to visit one day. The hospital was kind enough to let Murph bring Rooney up to see Isabella for a little bit. Rooney went right over to her and rested his massive head right on her stomach. Murph swore that he saw Isabella's mouth slightly move upward into what looked like a grin, but it was most likely just his hopeful imagination.

It was not the easiest thing to do when they transitioned Isabella into a big girl, full-sized bed and out of her crib. She was very attached to the crib, and though Maria and Murph talked it up for a couple months, Isabella was not budging. There was actually a time that they had to put both the crib and the bed in her little, pink room at the same time, leaving barely enough space to scoot through the room. They tried everything they could think of to get her in the bed, but each night Murph would read in the big bed and immediately after the book was done, Isabella would want to go to the crib. A couple nights they tried to leave Isabella in the bed crying, but they would find her later sleeping on the floor right beside the crib. Once again, Rooney came to save the day. Typically, he would lie outside of her room in the hall as Maria and Murph told Isabella a goodnight story, waiting for Murph to take him out for a walk. On that particular night Rooney came in and jumped on the bed for some odd reason. He was too big to get on most of their furniture, so he never even tried. When Rooney got on the bed that night, virtually knocking Murph out, Isabella's eyes lit up like when she saw Christmas lights or a carousel from a distance. She asked if Rooney could sleep with her, and Maria said as long as she stayed in the big girl bed, which Isabella quickly agreed to. Rooney spent the next several months lying in the bed with her until she fell asleep. Murph would go in later and get him out of the room for his walk. Maria and Murph joked that if Rooney could talk, he would say, "Do I have to teach you two everything about raising a kid?"

Rooney sat there with his head on Isabella in her hospital bed for close to an hour, and it was hard not to be touched seeing it. Murph was pretty sure that both the nurse and the doctor who came in left with tears in their eyes. There had been a couple other young kids in and out of the hospital on Isabella's floor. The nurses let Murph and Rooney walk around the floor to meet some of those sick or injured children. Murph had seen a little boy who regularly did laps around the floor pulling around his I.V., with his hospital gown hanging to the floor, and always wearing an Ironman mask. He had talked to the small super hero's parents some at the vending machines or when he would go out to get some exercise. The boy's name was Trevin, and he was a five-year-old with leukemia. He got an infection a couple weeks earlier, and he couldn't seem to get rid of it. Murph would talk to Trevin about different action heroes, and he had Pete pick up some comic books when he brought Rooney. Trevin was ecstatic when Murph brought Rooney in and gave him the comic books. Later that day, Trevin came by Isabella's room to say thank you again for the comics.

"Mr. Kearns, I wanna thank you for the comics you gave me! My daddy read them to me!" he said in his very serious and deep voice. The boy sounded a lot like Webster from the eighties television show. Murph didn't know if he was mimicking a super hero he saw on television when he talked like he did.

"Hey, man, you're welcome. Anybody who likes Ironman as much as you is cool in my book," Murph said as they pounded fists.

"Is that your daughter?" he asked as he walked over closer to her bed.

"Yeah, her name is Isabella."

"She is beautiful! I bet her momma is real pretty, too."

"Yes, she sure is." Murph didn't know how much, if anything, Trevin's parents had told him about the crash. Trevin was standing right next to Isabella and staring at her intently. All of a sudden he put his hand out and on top of

Isabella's hand and stood there for a couple minutes like that. It was fascinating to see that little boy with his mask on his hairless head standing there and holding Isabella's hand. Only a kid who knew pain as well as Trevin knew could connect with Isabella's anguish.

Trevin turned to Murph and said, "Mr. Kearns, Isabella is gonna be just fine," and then he walked out of the room. Astonished at the interaction, Murph didn't say anything to him. For the first time he really started to feel some hope. Besides, who was he to argue with Ironman?

• • •

Murph had been getting calls on his cell phone, emails, and messages on his work answering machine asking for interviews. He asked his brother, who had a public relations background, to return the calls denying the requests. It seemed that every newspaper and news television show wanted to interview Murph. There were calls from The Today Show, Diane Sawyer, Larry King, and many more.

There had been a photograph of Isabella playing in wildflowers released after she was identified, and it had continued to command interest. She had become the face of the tragedy. Like the photo of the "Napalm Girl" in Vietnam, people felt extremely sympathetic to a little girl that was unjustly hurt. Murph noticed every now and then when he looked outside or went on a walk that there were prayer vigils for Isabella. There was also a makeshift memorial of letters, pictures, and stuffed animals on a wall next to the hospital. Late at night when Murph knew there wasn't anybody out there, he liked to walk out and read the letters. They varied from letters by young children written in crayons to people in nursing homes writing to say they were thinking about and praying for Isabella. Somebody left a stuffed turtle, which

Collisions

Murph brought up to Isabella's room where it remained on her bed next to her.

After several weeks of not watching any coverage, Murph spent a couple hours watching the news to get caught up on the investigation into the cause of the collision. He decided it was time to give an interview. He had always been a big fan of Tom Brokaw, so his brother contacted NBC and said he would only do one interview if Tom Brokaw was willing to do it. Brokaw had been officially retired from broadcasting the nightly news for over five years, but Murph knew he still did special correspondence pieces and some political punditry. The producers jumped right on it, and the interview was scheduled to take place at the hospital and air on NBC Nightly News. They wanted to have the interview at the crash site, but his brother informed them that Murph was not comfortable with the idea. He wanted to stay close to Isabella.

The hospital closed off a large meeting room for the interview. When Murph walked in he was shocked at all the lighting required. The nerves hit his stomach pretty quickly. Murph had never been a big public speaker. When he was in high school and college and he had to do presentations, his hands would constantly shake, and sometimes he would get water in his eyes. Murph had gotten a little better as he aged, but it was still not something he was comfortable with. He talked to some producers, and they gave him a rundown of how the interview would go and informed Murph that if he needed a break or stumbled through an answer that they could always edit it out, which made him feel a little more at ease. Plus, he knew that NBC was not going to make him look bad in the interview. His brother told him that a poll had been done on CNN and he was the most sought after subject in the country at the moment. People across the country were obsessed with news about the collision like they had been about the O.J. Simpson trial, September 11th, and Hurricane Katrina. Murph realized that the interview was his stage to demand apologies and begin a public campaign to prevent a similar tragedy in the future. Murph needed the public perception of him to remain positive so that he had leverage in case he ever needed it in his quest for answers.

Murph only met Tom Brokaw very briefly right before they sat down. Though he spoke in his deep voice, wearing his designer frames and suit, he was very affable and right away he made Murph feel at ease. He reiterated that if Murph needed a break or if he needed to restart a question to let him know. The interview was recorded, so they didn't have to worry about slips on live television. Brokaw also let Murph know how devastated he had been to hear about the collision, and that he was thinking about Isabella.

The interview started with just a few basic questions to find out a little bit about Murph's personal background, and then he talked a little bit about Maria, Isabella, and Patrick. Murph surprisingly held himself together until Brokaw got into the topical portion of his interview questions.

Brokaw: What were your first impressions when you walked up to the crash site?

Murph: Well, I really didn't walk, I sprinted alongside Deputy Silva. Utter devastation was my only thought, but I was really just focused on finding my family.

Brokaw: What do you mean by "utter devastation"?

Murph: It was what you would imagine the end of the world would look like. There were fires spread out across the woods and meadow, emergency personnel running around everywhere. It was complete chaos and thinking about those minutes, I have to take this opportunity to thank everybody who helped me that day from Milo Baker at the gas station to Sherriff Baker and Deputy Silva. There was also a female EMT who was very helpful, but I never caught her name. I will always remember those people (he patted his chest in gratitude), and be thankful to them and my family and friends for all of their help the past couple weeks.

Brokaw: I know this will be tough, but can you explain to everyone how you came across your family and your reaction to seeing them?

Murph: You never in a million years expect to find yourself in my situation that day. It is just nothing that you can prepare for, and I would never wish it upon anyone. Nobody should ever have to see it (his voice quivered). I walked up to the airplane row, uhh, a row of seats that had been thrown, that Patrick and Maria were in, and I knew immediately that they were gone. I had the best wife and son that anybody could ever ask for, and they were taken away from me. Most people probably would not want those to be last images of their loved ones, but I take solace in knowing that they were together and holding each other. Maria was a tremendous mother, and she would be proud to know she did everything she could until the very end to protect Patrick and that they died together. That's why I decided to have them buried together in the same casket.

Brokaw: You mean Patrick and Maria are buried together? Did you know right away that they were not alive?

Murph: Yes, unfortunately it was pretty obvious.

Brokaw: How did you find out about Isabella?

Murph: I was saying my goodbyes to Maria and Patrick, and I heard two emergency responders conversing behind me. I was in such a state of disbelief at that point that I am not really sure that I truly understood what they were saying. The mixture of despair and hope was too much to take in. I honestly don't know how my heart kept beating and my body continued to function. One of those women and I ran to the portion of the plane where Isabella was located. They held the ambulance until I arrived, and by that point she was already on a gurney. Seeing her like that brought more jumbled feelings, and to this day all I can really hold onto is the hope that she will pull through this.

Brokaw: What were those first couple days like in the hospital with Isabella?

Murph: I really have not been able to truly grieve Maria and Patrick, even at their funeral. I think that time will have to come later. All of my thoughts and efforts have been devoted to Isabella since the accident. I know I will never find another woman like Maria, and I will never have another first son. But I know that all of my attention must be focused on Isabella and trying to get her better. I can't sit here and feel sorry for myself because she is counting on me.

Brokaw: What would you like to say to those responsible for the accident?

Murph: How could this have happened? How in this day and age, with all of the technology, can two planes collide in the middle of the sky? I can understand, and I can live with mechanical failure, but if human negligence is determined to be the cause then I want a meeting with those that are responsible. I want them to sit across from me and tell me what was more important to them than doing their jobs, because someone was not paying attention that day! I want them to sit there and apologize to me because most of my family is lost to me now!

Collisions

Brokaw: So you think it was human negligence?

Murph: Well it was a beautiful sunny day, not a cloud in the sky. I have yet to hear anybody mention that something was wrong with either plane.

Brokaw: How is Isabella doing? Any updates on her status?

Murph: She is hanging in there. She is incredibly resilient just like her mom was, so she is fighting. We really don't know what will happen. It's just a wait and see game, but I can't be anything but optimistic that she will come back to me.

Brokaw asked Murph some more questions about Isabella's medical status and wrapped the interview. What the public wanted was a chance to see Murph. The interview aired that night, and clips of it re-aired all over the press the next day on the other networks.

Victor Dancy

As Victor saw the first of Murphy Kearns on the news, he muttered "asshole" and marveled at what a freaking joke the guy was. To Victor the guy looked like a major dork in his geeky clothes. Victor guaranteed every dime Murphy Kearns received for donations would go right into his pocket. Victor did hope his daughter pulled through for her sake, but not for Kearns's. He seemed like a real pain in Victor's ass.

The guy was hunting for an apology. Victor was not apologizing to him or anybody else for two reasons. First, he didn't want anybody to think that he had anything to do with this, so the last thing he wanted to do was send out an apology looking like he was guilty of something. The Colonel agreed with Victor there. Second, he wouldn't bow down to anybody. The investigation was still going in his favor, and he was keeping it that way. Heck, Victor felt like he might just ask for an apology from the Kearns guy for asking for an apology from everybody that was working at WRA on the day of the crash. He was trying to place guilt on everybody involved, and even though Victor really was involved, nobody knew that, especially Kearns.

Still no sex for Victor, but he was slowly making headways with Gretchen. He couldn't stop thinking about her, especially her ass, and he had plenty of time to think, sitting in the middle of nowhere six days a week. He met her at The Rusted Spoon four times, and every time he thought he was finally going to go home with her, and every time he was disappointed to just get a kiss on the cheek. It drove him crazy. She was playing an excellent game of cat and mouse with Victor. Gretchen finally agreed to go to dinner with Victor and took him to a local Italian restaurant called Montecatini's Fine Dining.

Before Leah, Victor just hooked up with girls and never really dated. During his college years and his partying years, he preferred to just sleep with really wasted sorority girls, even some who he might have slipped pills to make things a lot easier. Victor never really had to take Leah out to dinner given the circumstances of her being an escort, getting pregnant, and having a shotgun wedding. Gretchen was really the first woman Victor wanted to spend time around. He hoped she was not turning him soft, before dinner he even thought about buying her flowers. Looking back on it, the idea of the flowers might have been more to try to get her in bed. He still thought about it though, which was a first for Victor.

Collisions

Gretchen wanted to meet at the restaurant, and she was late. He actually sat and worried that she would stand him up, which never happened. Victor was not a worrier, it wasn't in his blood. She showed up fifteen minutes late, but when she walked in he realized it was more than worth the wait. She had her thick, curly hair down, and it hung to her mid-back. She had on a polka-dot dress that showed just enough cleavage to make Victor want to rip it off. The cowboy boots were a nice touch too.

"I'm so sorry I am late. Momma locked herself out of the house and called me from the neighbors' just when I was about to leave," Gretchen told him.

"That's perfectly fine," Victor said standing up to give her an awkward hug. "I'm really close to my mother, and I completely understand," another lie.

"I'm so glad you are such a family man. My late husband was too, and we liked to spend as much time with our families as we could, even though we both traveled quite a bit."

"I make sure to call my mother to check on her every night at around nine o'clock, her bedtime. She lives alone now with my dad gone, and I just want to make sure that she is not having any problems getting to bed. If she did, I would be up there in a heartbeat." She pulled her chair around closer to Victor, which made him grin.

"Aww, you are a momma's boy. That's sweet," she said. He was just thinking that he would be any type of boy she wanted him to be, as long as it ended up with the two of them under the sheets.

"Did you see Murphy Kearns interviewed last night?" she asked.

"I'm not sure who that is," Victor replied.

"He was interviewed by Tom Brokaw. He had family on the Atlantic Airlines flight just like you."

"Oh, yeah, I saw clips of that interview on Fox News, but not the whole thing." There was no way Victor would sit and watch that prick being interviewed.

"I figured it would have really struck close to home for you with your family members on that flight too. I feel so bad for that man. His wife and son died in the crash, and his daughter is lying in that hospital bed in a coma. I wanted to reach right into that television and give that man a big hug and kiss," Gretchen said.

All Victor ever wanted to do when clips came on of Murphy Kearns was to reach in that television screen and punch him in his face. "Yeah, I felt bad for him. I have a lot of those feelings running through my head. It has been so hard for me, and I try to avoid reliving it, so I don't turn on the news much these days."

Man, did Victor want to change the subject. "I feel the same way as he feels. I just want to make sure my brother and sister-in-law are remembered," he said. How about that they even existed in the first place? "Also, I want to make sure that their three kids are taken care of. I am doing as much as I can to help them out, but a college fund would ensure me that they would make it to college one day."

She reached over and held his hand. Jackpot. Maybe the conversation was not so bad after all. "It has been so hard on my mom also, losing her son. When I go see her every week, we just sit and hold each other for hours," he continued to pour it on. He made a mental note that when he needed to go see The Colonel and Leah, he would tell

Gretchen that he was going to his mother's or to see his brother's children.

"You are just too darling! I want to hold you right now." She finally did hold him that night, and plenty more. He typically was satisfied with a woman after one romp in the sack, but after a night in bed with Gretchen, Victor only wanted more.

Chapter 19

Murphy Kearns

Not much had changed with Isabella's condition. Murph brought her a box turtle that Pete picked up for him at a small pet store in Nags Head. He set the box turtle in its terrarium right beside her hospital bed. Murph was amazed with how much support he received after his interview. Isabella's lack of progress had given Murph a sense of stagnation, and the sudden motion after two long weeks in response to the Brokaw piece felt overwhelming at first and then invigorating. He took calls from a lot of the other families affected by the collision expressing their gratitude for his interview. Murph had messages from the mayor of Pittsburgh, the governor of Pennsylvania, and several other celebrities from his hometown. He was surprised to find out that Andrew McCutchen, their favorite Pittsburgh Pirate baseball player, was wearing Isabella's initials on his glove to show his support. He had seen Murph's interview, and in one part Murph talked about some of their favorite things to do as a family, which included Steelers and Pirates games. Happy to talk about Isabella's joy, Murph also mentioned that Isabella really loved the young center-fielder's hair. McCutchen immediately put the initials on his ball glove.

Murph's brother informed him that there was money coming in the mail from people all over the world who were touched by his interview and the family's story. It encouraged Murph to find out all of these people were supportive, but the hole in his heart was not getting any smaller and he didn't know if it ever would. Murph's goal of getting apologies from everybody involved started immediately, but not from the people he really wanted to hear from, those individuals who were directly involved. Instead, he received a call from one of the higher-ups at Atlantic Airlines expressing an apology.

Murph kept hearing the same three names from the Williamsburg airport. He had not heard anything from any of them yet. Apparently, Michelle Bowen was the supervisor and was absent at the time of the crash, as well as Steve Rodriguez, who was supposed to be working, but apparently left the facility to find his sick wife. The third person involved was a man named Victor Dancy. Murph had not been given any more of a description of their involvement yet, but he planned to find out more. The NTSB reports would not be disclosed for some time, but the press was building a pretty comprehensive story. Murph knew with some effort he would be sure to fill in the gaps himself.

A memorial service was planned in Vitaly at the crash site for the one-month anniversary of the accident. Murph was hesitant to go back to the site, but he knew that he was now the spokesman for the victims, so he needed to be there to demonstrate his support and continue to work toward his goals. Plus, President Jackson Reeves was going to be visiting the site and making a speech during the memorial. Johnny had been coming up a lot to sit with Isabella, so he stayed with her while Murph went to the ceremony. It was only open to the families and a couple pool photographers and reporters. It was a perfect May morning. Each family carried a dozen white roses and placed them on the site where the main portion of the Atlantic Airlines fuselage came to rest. The gouge in the earth it left was right next to the stage that was set up. President Reeves spoke for about twenty minutes and reiterated his deepest sympathies to all of the families. He emphasized that he was making sure that the NTSB and the FAA were doing everything in their power to find solutions so a collision of this nature never happened again. Murph was happy to see Sandy at the service. It was the first time he had seen her in person for a couple of weeks, though they talked regularly on the phone. She looked almost fully recovered.

After the service was over, Murph wandered out into the woods. The eeriness of the scene from the month before came back to him with complete clarity. He had only been there once, but he knew the exact path he needed to take to get to where Patrick and Maria died. Details he didn't even remember noticing were obvious as he retraced his steps. Murph found the spot between the scorched trees and barren ground where the plane bench stopped and where he found Maria and Patrick. Murph immediately fell to his knees and let out a gut-wrenching howl from the deepest part of his insides. He pictured them there with him, and all Murph wanted was a message from them letting him know that they were in a better place. He lay down on that spot and cried like he had never cried before. He was back in the woods for a long time, but he eventually heard footsteps as two men in suits approached him.

"Mr. Kearns, we have been looking for you. President Reeves would like to have a word with you before he heads on. Do you think you are up to coming with us to talk to him? He is waiting in Marine One, if you feel you can talk to him," said one of the two men.

Murph nodded his head and followed them, trying to compose himself before he met the President of the United States, without a clue as to what the man wanted to say to him.

While the inside of Marine One was very comfortable and Murph wouldn't mind flying around the country on it, the helicopter was still smaller than he imagined it would be. President Reeves was one of the country's tallest presidents standing at close to 6'4". When he stood to shake Murph's hand, he had to scrunch his neck and shoulders a little bit so his head didn't hit the ceiling of the helicopter.

"Thank you for coming to see me, Mr. Kearns. I just wanted a brief minute of your time," said President Reeves.

"You're welcome, Mr. President. Thank you for taking the time out of your busy schedule to come and speak at the service today," Murph said.

"I wouldn't have missed this for anything else. This accident has been the worst disaster of my presidency. I honestly want to do all that is possible to make sure something like this never happens again, and I want to help the victims' families in any way I can. I feel horrible about your situation, and I have been getting constant updates on how your daughter is holding up. There are two reasons I needed to briefly speak to you," he said.

"Yes, sir, I am all ears."

"The First Lady was impressed with your interview, and this was actually her idea. We realize that you have your own landscape design company, and I have spoken with the town of Vitaly, and they agreed to hire you to be in charge of designing a memorial park here where the crash occurred. Would you be interested in taking on this project as soon as you are mentally ready?" said President Reeves.

"You bet, sir," said Murph still taken aback by where he was. "Please thank your wife for thinking of me."

"Great, I am sure you will be contacted shortly about how to proceed. Sometimes these memorials are so sad. I realize that typically memorials are at places where something bad happened, but I feel like with all of this land that we should build something to celebrate the lives of the victims, not another place to mourn them."

"I completely agree," Murph responded.

"The second reason I asked to see you was to give you this." The President handed him a stuffed yellow Labrador that did not look brand new. "As I am sure you know we have two yellow labs at the White House, Molly and Abby. Our daughter, Martha, who is now ten, wanted me to ask if you could give this to Isabella. She typically doesn't bring up much to do with my presidency, but like her mother, she is very upset about all of this. This stuffed animal is named Mr. Beans, and Martha carried it around for a long time, and it means quite a bit to her. I honestly am surprised that she is giving it away, but she has a big heart, and I think she knows it is going to a better place if your daughter gets it," he said.

Stunned, Murph took the stuffed animal from the president who handled it with as much care and attention as he might the nuclear "football" that was never far from an American president. Murph didn't know why he said what he said next, but it just slipped out and were his last words to President Reeves. "I just feel really badly because Maria and I didn't vote for you."

Collisions

President Reeves laughed. "Don't worry! You were joined by close to fifty percent of the rest of the country. Good luck to your daughter, and please don't hesitate to get in touch with my office if you need anything else."

• • •

Some of the families were getting together to eat at Apple Alice's after the memorial, and Murph was invited to come. There really was not much else to pick from, and Murph thought it would be good to meet some of the others. Apple Alice's was on a side alley off of the main road in Vitaly. It was in an old home, and as soon as you walked in the door it felt like walking into Mayberry from the *Andy Griffith Show*. There was a little bakery with cakes and pies, and the cooks could easily be seen at the grill preparing the meals. The decor was somewhere between Cracker Barrel and Murph's great-grandmother's house.

There were five different families eating in the restaurant, who were all related to victims of the Atlantic Airlines flight. Three of the couples had sons or daughters from Duquesne on the flight, and the other two families had loved ones on their way back to the Virginia Beach area from business in Pittsburgh. A man with curly hair wrapped around his bald head sat at one end, and seemed to be the ringleader. Murph was the last one to join the group.

"Mr. Kearns, it is a pleasure to have you join us. My name is Chris Littlefield. We all want to express our condolences to you and our prayers for your daughter," the bald man said as Murph went around the table and shook hands with everyone.

"Nice to meet you all. Thanks for inviting me to eat with you. My sympathies to each of you for your losses,"

Murph said. His heart raced a little. He wasn't sure how it would be different to be with this group, but he knew it would. He settled into stride with each hand he shook.

Everybody else introduced themselves and told him a little about their loved ones lost. "We have all been talking through email over the last couple weeks, and we want to make sure that we are all heard, and we feel like you are the man to get our word out and be the spokesperson for all the victims," Chris said. "Just like you said in your interview with Tom Brokaw, we want our family members to be remembered. We don't want anything like this to ever happen again, either."

"I completely understand and agree with you all," Murph said. He went on to inform them of his brief meeting with President Reeves. After Murph was done telling them about their meeting he said, "I want to put a playground in the memorial park as a tribute to my son, Patrick. One that I think he would have really enjoyed. I am not sure what kind of budget I will have when designing the memorial, but why don't I get an idea from everybody at this table of something that was special to their family member. Hopefully we will be able to spread the idea around to all of the family members from both flights, and we will be able to incorporate a little bit of everybody who died on those planes into the memorial park. We want to make it a place where we can come to celebrate our lost loved ones' lives."

All of the members of the table nodded in agreement over club sandwiches and tomato soup. They spent the rest of the lunch telling a little bit about each of their family members. There were some tears shed, but for the most part everybody sitting at the table just told stories of happier times and there was actually some laughter. Murph left Apple Alice's realizing that the cheeseburger and homemade coconut cream pie were the first dishes he'd actually tasted in weeks.

Victor Dancy

Apparently Michelle was in a severe depression since the collision. The Colonel told Victor she had spent some time in a psych ward in Virginia Beach, and that she had not been eating. She was blaming herself for not being at WRA when she was supposed to. His lawyers had been in and out of meetings, and they were fairly confident at this point that he would not face any charges. The Colonel's crew of ambulance chasers indicated that Victor might not even be included on any of the civil suits that were expected.

Murphy Kearns was a major point of contention between Leah and Victor the last time he was up at The Colonel's house. Maddie was off at her new school, and The Colonel had stepped outside to take a phone call.

"Do you even care at all about your daughter? Not once have you even asked how she is adjusting to her new school. You know that she had to go through a lot because of all this," Leah said.

"Here we go again," Victor rolled his eyes.

"She cries every night because she misses her friends in Williamsburg. She also misses her daddy. God only knows why. Do you miss her at all? Because I know you don't miss me," Leah said raising her voice and rubbing her brow.

"You are damned right about not missing you," Victor said not answering her question about Maddie. "This past month has been the most relaxing month of my life."

"What, do you spend your time getting wasted and sleeping around?" she asked.

"Ouch, that hurt," he said sarcastically. "You are one to talk about sleeping around, you hooker."

"I sent one hundred dollars to all three funds started for Murphy Kearns' family in our name," she said.

"You did what? You idiot, that is the last fucking thing you should have done. I know that jackass is looking for apologies, but he will never, and I mean never, get one from me," Victor said angrily.

"Why not? Is it too hard for you to fess up to anything?" she asked. "I would give anything if you were a tenth of the man or father that Murphy Kearns is."

This struck a major nerve with Victor. He slammed down the magazine he was glancing at, and swept across the room to get in her face. "You better take that back, you bitch!" he shouted.

Trying to back away from Victor but having some confidence, Leah said, "It's true. The only reason I am glad I met you is because I got Maddie out of it, but you are the most disgusting human being I have ever met."

Victor spat right in her face. She was smarter than the last time they had an encounter in their garage, and she backed up and tried to throw one of The Colonel's vases at him. It glanced off Victor's shoulder, and he chased her down as she ran off. Victor tackled Leah from behind and pressed her face into the marble floor. "You are nothing but a worthless hooker!" he shouted as he grinded her face into the floor and she let out loud cries.

Collisions

"Enough!" The Colonel said. Victor jumped up off of Leah as his father quickly entered the room from outside.

• • •

Victor's relationship with Gretchen continued to intensify, and they went on a get-away together to Bristol, right on the Tennessee and Virginia borders, because Gretchen wanted to show Victor the "real birthplace of country music." She also showed him a little bit more of her skin, which made the trip much more bearable, since he could have gone without learning all the facts about country music. They wined and dined along State Street, and they even caught a modified stock car race at Bristol Motor Speedway. Not traditionally a racing fan, Victor carried a new fervor for the violence and intensity of the short-oval into an increasingly physical relationship with Gretchen that weekend.

If he thought that Gretchen looked country-western before, nothing was like the outfits she wore in Bristol. The funny thing was that she fit in with some of the other people they saw out in the bars. It wasn't a novelty costume in that part of the country. She constantly had a cowgirl hat on, and Victor insisted she keep it on during sex. Gretchen bought him a tan cowboy hat, which he quickly grew to like. He had never experienced anything like Gretchen, and the more he was around her, the more he wanted to stay with her. Even though she was taking him way out of his comfort zone, he enjoyed himself more than he had for as long as he could remember. At one point, she found and asked Victor about his Papa George's military trench knife that he always carried around. Victor told her all about Papa George, and for once he did not lie to her. It felt surprisingly good to tell the truth.

The last night of their weekend excursion, they ate at a bar and grill on State Street. The two got into a discussion about family while sitting out at a sidewalk table on the nice breezy evening.

"When Ricky was killed in his motorcycle accident," Gretchen said while holding Victor's hands, "I thought that my chance to ever start a family was finished. Then you came along, and I'm having second thoughts about whether maybe I did find the right person."

Victor swallowed hard. He hated his family. His wife was worthless to him, and his daughter got on his last nerves. But there was something completely different about Gretchen. Could he realistically start a family with her? "You have been tremendous, too, honey. I don't know how I would have made it through my brother's death without meeting you." First he had to figure out how to stop lying so much to her, and then how to cover up the lies he had already told her.

"Well let's just keep things going like they are, and we can move on from here accordingly," she said.

After they finished dinner, they went back to their hotel and had one last epic night in the bed, on the floor, and in the shower. When they woke up the next morning, they ate breakfast at Denny's. Victor almost got caught in one of his lies. He had originally told her that he grew up and always lived in Virginia Beach. He lied and told her that his father worked on ships, and that was one of the reason's his brother and he were always obsessed with fishing. When Victor went to see Leah, he told Gretchen he was headed back home to Virginia Beach to see his mother. Victor caught himself, when he accidentally started talking about how he moved around a lot and lived in Colorado and Oklahoma when he was young which, in fact, was all true. He didn't know if it was all of the liquor he drank the night before or the lack of sleep from the whole trip, but he started telling her a true story about what really happened to him growing up.

"What do you mean you moved around a lot? I thought you said you grew up and always lived on the coast?" she questioned.

Victor choked on his coffee a little bit, but she was not too sympathetic. "You must have misunderstood me. I thought I told you about my father's five years in the Navy. He got fired from working on the docks, so he decided to join the Navy when my brother and I were little boys, and we moved around during those five years." He believed that he had done a pretty good job of covering up the mistake.

"But aren't members of the Navy usually stationed near water? Isn't that what the Navy is all about, ships and stuff?" Gretchen asked. She had obviously been lied to by men before.

She caught him again. "Oh yeah, but there are Naval bases all over the place, just like the Army and Marines. They are meant to protect the whole country, not just our waterways. My old man was more into the technical aspect of the Navy, so that is what he did for those five years."

"So your dad worked on boats his whole life, and he joins the Navy for five years and works on the mainland? That is strange."

"What can I say? He was a well-rounded guy," Victor responded and immediately changed the subject. Gretchen was not as talkative as normal on the way back to Lake Anna.

Chapter 20

Murphy Kearns

The idea at Apple Alice's to incorporate everybody who died in the crash into Murph's design of the memorial park spread like wildfire within the victims' families. He had already heard back from close to seventy percent of the families with ideas about the way they'd like to include their loved ones in the park. There was a dog-loving veterinarian, Shelby Denison, who owned five-dogs of her own. Her husband and kids wanted an area of the park where people could bring their dogs, so Murph planned to design a small fenced off portion of the park to be just for dogs. Alice Davidson, a sculptor, was heading home to eastern Virginia after visiting the Carnegie Mellon Museum for the first time, and her family wanted one of her sculptures in the park. Her husband, Mark, was also on the Atlantic Airlines plane, and he loved rock climbing, so they thought a climbing wall would be great in his honor. Murph had been getting all kinds of great requests.

The mental and emotional movement of working on the park helped pass the time at Isabella's bedside. She was still hanging on, and if there was progress it moved slower than Murph or the doctors could measure. Before the project, Murph had fallen into a habit in Isabella's room of staring at the turtle and losing time. He was so sure that if he looked away he'd miss its deliberate progress moving across the tank. He was certain some days that he'd lost hours that way. Though he still found himself measuring time with occasional glances at the motionless turtle, now there was this distraction, this purpose.

Isabella and Murph finally had their first visit from one of the Williamsburg air traffic controllers on duty the morning of the collision. Steve Rodriguez came in with his beautiful wife, Mary, and their grown son. Steve and his wife must have been in their late sixties or early seventies, and they both had gray hair. Murph went out into the lobby and met the family, and then Steve asked if he could come in and meet Isabella, while his wife and son waited out in the waiting area. Murph hesitantly walked Steve back into the room, and as soon as the man laid eyes on Isabella he broke down. Murph let him cry, not really feeling any sympathy at all for him, and then he asked the somber man why he was there.

"I'm sorry I didn't come earlier. I've been trying to build up the courage. I know you wanted an apology from all those involved, and I wanted to not only apologize to you, but also to your daughter," Steve said. "I was a local controller working at Williamsburg the day of the collision, and I wanted to let you know that I'm so sorry. I will never forgive myself, and I know an apology will never do nearly enough." Steve's face looked gaunt and his hair greyer.

"I asked for an apology, and I appreciate you coming in, but what happened in there?" Murph asked.

"I actually was not there during the crash. Mary is sick with Alzheimer's. She ran away from the babysitter, and I left my post to a co-worker, Victor Dancy. Unfortunately, Michelle Bowen was also away from the facility with her son. Victor assured me that he could handle it," Steve said.

"You mean to tell me that there were supposed to be three of you there, but there was only one of you at the time of the crash?" Murph asked trying to remain calm.

"Yes, I can't make any excuses, but that is something that happened a lot unfortunately at our facility. I had just come back from retirement to work there, and in my old, much busier, air-traffic tower, we would have never gotten away with some of the stuff that happened at Williamsburg Regional."

"It sounds like it should not have happened anywhere. You people are in charge of keeping a lot of lives safe, and you failed," Murph told him as he tried not to raise his voice in front of Isabella.

"I completely agree, Mr. Kearns. I'm sorry. It wasn't right, and we should have never left anybody there by themselves. The NTSB agrees, too, and depending on how things shake out the FBI might as well. I probably shouldn't even be talking to you about this but..." He paused for a time before starting again. "Personally, I should have probably never gone back to work with Mary in the condition she is in. It was a stupid idea, but I had to figure out a way to pay for her care. For some reason Victor Dancy has been lying to investigators about what really happened. He specifically told me that I could take a quick leave and be back before our supervisor, Michelle, returned. Now he's telling everyone that I demanded to leave, and there was nothing he could do to stop me. Even with Victor working alone that morning, there is no way this should have happened. There were only a couple flights during that time period, something each of us individually handles every day at work. Nobody seems to be able to find out what really happened. Victor's dad is some former big-wig with the FAA, and Victor always got preferential treatment. There was also a rumor that he drinks on the job. I'm not trying to point fingers, but Victor had more to do with this horrible accident than anybody else involved, and he is getting off scot-free," Steve said becoming agitated. "I shouldn't be saying all of this to you. I'm so sorry."

He was waving his arms frantically while telling Murph all about Victor Dancy. This would not be the last time Murph heard Victor's name as the one to blame for the accident. Steve told Murph about what it was like for him to return to find out what happened, and apologized repeatedly. All of a sudden Mary walked in. She walked over to Isabella, and you could tell just by how she carried herself that the Alzheimer's was pretty far along. Mary went over to Isabella without saying a word and kissed her on the forehead. "Such a pretty little girl," she said to no one in particular.

Steve and Mary walked out of the room holding hands, and even with her condition Murph could tell that they had been together a long time and truly loved each other. As they walked out of the door to Isabella's room, Murph said to Steve, "I don't know if this will do much, but we forgive you." Steve turned to him and appreciatively nodded, and the couple walked out. As they walked down the hall and out of sight, Murph could only think about never being able to grow old with Maria.

Murph heard Mary say to Steve as they walked down the hall, "Did you see that turtle walking across its cage? Marvelous." Murph looked at the terrarium noting the turtle's new perspective.

Victor Dancy

Victor didn't hear from Gretchen for several days after they got back from Bristol. He waited a day and tried to call her with no luck. He went to The Rusted Spoon for three straight nights, and she did not show up once. He must have driven by her house thirty times, and she was never there. If she met somebody else he was going to find out, and it would be hard for him not to kick the guy's ass. Finally on the fourth day after Victor last spoke to Gretchen, she called him back. She told him that she had to go take care of a couple of things in Nashville, and she had accidentally forgotten her cell phone with his number back at home when she left for the trip. He wasn't buying it, a liar can always spot a liar, but he was glad that she agreed to go to dinner with him that night.

At dinner things seemed to be going very smoothly. Gretchen appeared to be back to her old self. She joked a lot, and they each had several beers. After dessert, they each ordered a Guinness as a dessert beer, which at the time he thought was a great idea. Gretchen was becoming drunk very quickly. The drunker she got the redder her face turned.

"So, did you see what Murphy Kearns is doing now?" she asked.

"Do we have to talk about that guy again? He is kind of getting on my nerves," Victor said.

"Well I would think that you would want to talk some more about your brother and the crash. That guy just happens to be designing a memorial park for all of the victims at the crash site. The victims' families are all giving him something related to their loved one to add to the park. I read about it in Time Magazine this week. You said you came here to help recover, but you are very vague about your personal life, besides the stories you tell me about your mom," she said. "I'm surprised that somebody has not been in contact with you or your mom about what or how you want your brother memorialized."

"I'm sorry. It's just hard for me to talk about him," Victor responded becoming more and more irritated both with this discussion and with Murphy Kearns. "My medicine for recovery has been you."

"Thanks, but you keep ducking my questions," she said, looking straight at him. "In fact, I don't think you have ever even told me your brother's name."

Victor swallowed hard. "Sure I have. I really don't feel like talking about this right now; we were having such a great time."

"Victor, just tell me your brother's name."

"It was Samuel," he said glancing at the bottle of Sam Adams on the table next to theirs.

"Ok, thanks." She went back to acting like she did during the ride home from Bristol. It was a total buzz kill, and make-up sex that night was totally out of the question. Victor was starting to get tired of Gretchen, but he was not ready to give up on her yet.

Chapter 21

Murphy Kearns

"I know the guy is old and all, and that all you asked for was an apology, but I have no idea how you didn't erupt and choke that guy?" said Sweet Pete, who might not have always brought calm, but always delivered on cool.

Conflicting emotions after meeting with Steve left Murph in need of some stability. Pity for Steve and his wife seemed counterbalanced by a growing anger at an image of Victor Dancy. Lunch with Pete was just the cure.

"Trust me, I wasn't happy, and I actually came close a couple times. Especially when he told me that they left only one person in the flight control room," Murph said. "But two things stopped me. I was always taught to stick by my word, and I said I just needed an apology. And we were in Isabella's room, and there is no way I could ever be violent in front of her."

"True. Still, you are a better man than me, dude," Pete said as he chugged his beer.

"I really don't think that Steve is a bad guy, just in the wrong place at the wrong time."

Pete said, "Sounds more like the worst time."

"I'm really concerned about the other two. Why would a supervisor leave such an important place as an air traffic control facility? Also, this Victor Dancy guy sounds really fishy," said Murph.

"Who is Victor Dancy?"

"He was the only guy working at the time of the crash. Supposedly, his dad is some hot-shot with the FAA who helped him get the job in the first place. From what Steve said, Victor Dancy also has a drinking problem. I hate to blame him for anything, since he was working by himself, but something sure doesn't seem right with him. I'm just hoping that at some point I can speak to both Victor and the supervisor." Murph felt his face flush slightly and thought to himself that it must be the mid-day beer.

Murph received a call from Sandy Hatch asking to meet with him. Sandy was very vague during the phone call, but said that somebody really needed to talk to Murph, and they wanted Sandy to be present at the meeting. Sandy would not tell Murph exactly who it was that wanted to meet with him, but said that it was very important. They decided to meet at Murph's rarely used apartment since there would be a guarantee of privacy.

Murph really didn't know what to expect, but Sandy seemed pretty insistent on the meeting. Murph watched from the front window as Sandy and another woman walked up the front walkway to his small apartment door. Sandy looked fantastic as they walked up. Confident and always poised, he could hardly tell that she was recently one of only two survivors from the plane wreck. The other woman, by contrast, didn't look very good. She was very skinny and disheveled. Murph opened the door and met the two women on the front steps.

"Hey, Murphy, it is so great to see you!" said Sandy as the two gave each other a hug.

"It's nice to see you too, Sandy. You look great!"

"How is that little princess of yours doing? I can't wait to get to the hospital to see her," said Sandy.

"She's still hanging in there. Not much has changed."

"Murphy, this is Michelle Bowen; she was a supervisor at the Williamsburg Regional Airport," Sandy told Murph. He knew immediately who the woman was just by the name.

"Yeah, I know who she is, she is the supervisor who was supposed to be in the flight tower the day of the crash, but wasn't," Murph said, staring at the woman hiding behind Sandy's right shoulder.

"That's correct. She has come here to apologize to you. Ever since you gave your interview with Tom Brokaw, Michelle and I have been communicating back and forth. She is ready to talk to you now," Sandy said.

"I'm glad that she is finally ready to see me," Murph said in a sarcastic tone. "It has only been a month and a half. It is great that she can make time for me now!" Murph wasn't sure he was ready to talk to Michelle.

Collisions

"I completely understand your frustration. Trust me, it was hard for me to talk to her at first, but please hear her out. Remember, you were the one who said that all you wanted was an apology from those involved, and Michelle is here to do just that and explain. This has been very hard on her," Sandy said, wincing at her word choice.

Murph retaliated with, "I'm sorry this has been so hard on her. I will make sure to tell that to my four-year-old daughter who is in a coma." He never took his eyes off of Michelle, who was looking down at the ground during this whole conversation. She was crying, but in a way that made it seem like she didn't have many tears left.

"Please, just let us come in," Sandy said. Murph moved out of the way with some hesitation and let the two into the small apartment. There was little furniture that came with the place, so the two women sat on the old brown couch while Murph pulled up a fold-out metal chair.

"Go ahead," Murph said in a less than friendly tone after they sat quietly for a few moments.

Michelle looked up at Murph for the first time. Her face was ghostly and haunting. Her eyes were sunken, and she looked weary. "I have prepared for this moment for a month, and I'm still not ready. It is harder than I could ever imagine."

"I'm sorry it is so hard on you, I truly am," Murph said. He was even a little surprised how condescending he was towards Michelle.

"It's okay for you to hate me. I would hate me, too, if I were you. I hate myself right now," Michelle said in a shaky voice.

Murph really looked hard at Michelle for the first time and could tell that she was a broken woman. He decided then

214

that he needed to ease up on Michelle and make it easier on her to talk. So he just sat back and listened.

"I could apologize a million times to you, and it would not make me feel any better, but I know that is what you are asking." She said as she looked right at him. Her demeanor changed from scared to determined. "I'm so sorry for the pain I have caused you and everybody else involved in the accident. So many people have been devastated because I wasn't there to do my job that day. I will never be able to repair what I have done. When I left work it was a horrible mistake, but sometimes as a parent our love for our kids clouds our better judgment. My son means so much to me. He is not much older than Isabella. Every night we pray for your daughter together. I want to be able to look my son in the eyes," said Michelle.

Murph said, "I will accept your apology, and I thank you for coming here to do so."

Michelle grabbed a hold of Murph's hand with her other hand. She began to cry then, along with Murph and Sandy. The three held hands and cried for a while. Michelle spent the next thirty minutes explaining her part in what happened at the Williamsburg airport.

"Steve has already come to meet and apologize to me, and he seemed like an honorable man," Murph said after Michelle was done.

"He is a very good and gentle man. I have seen him a couple times since early April, and I can tell how hurt he is, just like me," said Michelle.

"I still have not heard a word from Victor Dancy."

"I don't think you'll ever hear from that man," Michelle said as her face returned to a defeated look. "He is a very arrogant man. He should have been fired several times, and if it wasn't for his dad and their relationship with Sam Sheets, the head of WRA, I'm sure he would have been. If it were my decision, Victor would have been fired years ago. He was lackadaisical with his work, and I swear that he came to work drunk or hung-over frequently. We told Sam, but he never did anything about it. I should have been there that day, and it was not right for me to take advantage of Sam's leniency like I did. If I had any inkling of the possibility that Steve was going to have an emergency, there is absolutely no way that I would have left Victor there by himself. Steve's main fault in the whole thing is that he is too trustworthy of a man."

"That is the second time somebody has told me that Victor would show up drunk to work," said Murph.

"I don't know what happened in that flight room when the collision happened, but I can guarantee you that Victor Dancy had more to do with it than anybody else involved," said Michelle.

Murph decided that since it didn't sound like Victor was going to reach out to him. Maybe it was time for him to try to make the initial contact.

Victor Dancy

Victor didn't hear from Gretchen for the next several days. He finally decided to go to her house to see why she was avoiding him. He threw back a six-pack of Miller Lite first, which he did rather quickly. She was at home and only cracked the door instead of inviting Victor inside.

"What do you want, Victor?" she asked, cowering behind the wooden door.

"I want to see you. What in the hell is going on?" he replied.

"Victor, please just leave. This wasn't a good idea."

"What wasn't a good idea?"

"Us."

"What the fuck are you talking about? Just let me in so we can talk!" Victor demanded.

"Please, just leave, Victor. We're through."

"No! I'm not leaving this fucking place until you tell me why."

"I know there was no Samuel Dancy on that flight. And I know who you are now. You were working that day at the airport where this all happened. It was completely sick of you to tell me what you did," Gretchen said as she tried to close the door. Victor was too quick for her, though, as he kicked the bottom of the door. The force sent Gretchen flying backwards. Victor pounced on his victim, and grabbed her by her left ear with his right hand and pulled very hard. Gretchen squealed in pain.

"Please let go, you are really hurting me."

He smacked her with his open hand as he continued to twist her ear. "Shut the fuck up you piece of shit. Shut your fucking face. I better not hear another goddamn word like that from you. You just keep your mouth shut about the whole thing, or I will be back."

"Okay, just leave please. I won't say anything to anybody, I promise."

"Damn right, and here is a preview of what will happen if you do," he said, and then he stomped on her stomach twice with his left boot. He slammed the door on his way out.

Victor went out to get some chicken wings and some more beers and was gone for several hours. When he returned home, a Sherriff's car was waiting out front of his rented lake house.

"Are you Victor Dancy?" A tall, black deputy asked him as Victor stepped out of his car.

"I sure am. What do you need?" Victor asked.

"I have a report that you abused a woman this morning, and I need you to come with me."

"The fuck I did," Victor said, but he cooperated and got in the deputy's vehicle.

At the station, Victor met with two other deputies. They pulled out three pictures and showed them to Victor. One picture was of Gretchen's red ear, the second of a swollen eye, and the last picture was of a black and blue stomach. They told him that Gretchen wanted to press assault charges. Victor just said that he wanted to see his lawyer. Seven hours later, The Colonel showed up with a lawyer.

The next day Victor had an arraignment, a court date was set, and he was released. The news that one of the flight controllers from the Atlantic Airlines collision was involved in an assault and battery charge spread rapidly. Victor went back to his lake house with his father and the lawyer left town, promising to be back in touch soon.

Victor didn't realize that this would be the last time he ever encountered his father. The Colonel said, "You are a sick, sick man, and I am done with you. I don't want anything to ever do with you again." He pulled out a checkbook and wrote out a check for twenty-five thousand dollars. "I will send you a check in this amount each year, and I am going to make it a part of my will that once I die, you will continue to receive this amount yearly until my money runs out or you die."

Victor laughed at his dad. "You know what old man? You did this to me. You were never there for me. You belittled me every opportunity you had, and you made my life hell growing up. You were never a father to me!" Victor shouted.

"Leah asks that you leave her alone as well. She doesn't want anything to do with you ever again. I will let you use my lawyer to get out of this recent mess, but then my lawyers are off-limits as well."

"If I go down for anything, you will go down with me!" Victor continued to shout.

"I have made the necessary precautions to make sure that doesn't happen. I strongly suggest you get as far away from here as possible because people will be watching what you do now."

Victor's anger spilled over. He charged at his dad and tackled the old man to the ground. Victor, Sr. was once a strong fighter, but he didn't have the strength anymore to fight back against his much stronger son. Victor pulled out Papa George's knife. "You remember this? I wish Papa George was my father and not you!" Victor put the knife up against his dad's throat. For the first time in all of Victor's life, he saw fear in his father's face. He relished in this fear, and it stopped him from slicing his father's throat. Instead, he smashed the wooden end of the knife against his father's face with one hand and choked him with his other. Eventually he released the grip on his father's throat, and Victor, Sr. let out a loud gasp. He slowly got up and walked out of the house, without ever looking back at his son.

Chapter 22

Murphy Kearns and Victor Dancy

The first call placed from Murph Kearns to Victor Dancy went out on May 24th, over a month and a half after the collision. Murph stood outside of the hospital pacing back and forth. He liked to listen to music to get pumped up for big athletic games when he was younger. When he would go for runs, he'd listen to the Avett Brothers and Delta Spirit. He was listening to "Trashcan," by Delta Spirit, on his phone and air-drumming along to get himself pumped for the call, just like he did before a road race.

Since The Colonel left, Victor was at his lake house when he received the call. He had not left except to go to a local liquor store and to get food. Victor was pretty wasted by the time Murph called him.

Victor: Hello.

Murph: Yes, is this Victor Dancy?

Collisions

Victor: Yeah, who the hell is this?

Murph: This is Murphy Kearns. My wife and son were on…

Victor (interrupting): I know who you are. Go fuck yourself!

Victor hung up his cell phone, and Murph was too mad to call right back.

The second phone call took place two days later. This time Murph had to get away to make the call. He drove into Colonial Williamsburg, trying to compose himself on the way so that he didn't call yelling. He started the conversation just outside the Governor's Palace in Williamsburg. Murph liked to walk around when he made important calls; it was hard for him to sit still. Victor was in the car on his way to see Leah, drunk as usual.

Victor: Hello.

Murph: This is Murphy Kearns. Don't hang up again!

Victor: Who the fuck do you think you are talking to? Don't ever call me and tell me what to do! What do you want?

Murph: I have talked to Michelle Bowen and Steve Rodriguez. All I am asking for is a conversation with you to give you a chance to tell your side.

Victor: I don't really give a rat's ass what those two idiots did. Stop fucking calling me!

The third and last call happened later that evening, but this time Victor placed the call to Murph. Victor had just left his father's house where it appeared that everybody was out of town. He knew because every time they left on vacation they would leave the hall light on both downstairs and upstairs, and a backlight on that was only used when they were gone for a while. Victor tried his keys, and to his dismay the locks were changed. He went to the normal hiding place for the spare key under their large deck in the back, but there wasn't one. He went to a local bar and got even drunker than he already was. Murph was sitting beside Isabella when the call came in. He immediately recognized the number and quickly stepped out into the hallway. He made his way to the stairs in the hospital to try to get some privacy.

Murph: Are you calling to set up a meeting?

Victor: No. If I ever met you, I would beat your scrawny ass to a pulp.

Murph: If that is what you had to say, then why in the world are you calling me?

Victor: You called me. I am just ready to put you in your place. You will never receive an apology from me as long as I walk this earth. It doesn't matter what involvement I had. I really don't care about you or your family. It is obvious to me that you are just in it for the fame and money now. Bud, your fame will run out quickly, and you will go back to your pathetic little life, you tiny piece of shit.

Murph: Why are you doing this?

Victor: Because I am sick of seeing your face plastered everywhere trying to be the dad of the year. I am sick of seeing your daughter's picture in that princess dress. I can't watch anything on television or read any newspaper without seeing something about your pathetic story. Then you think you can call me and have me apologize to you? You should be grateful to me, plain and simple.

Murph: Is that all you want?

Victor: No, it sure as hell is not. Don't think you are the only one that suffered from this shit. I lost my family, too. There were other people on those planes affected, but you want all the attention for yourself.

Murph: Okay, I've had enough; I am getting off now. It doesn't seem like this will ever work.

Victor: That is the first thing you have ever said that I agree with. Rot in hell.

Victor swelled with the final word, making his head spin with alcohol and his perceived power. Murph was more furious than he had ever been in his life. Victor pulled into a rest area about ten miles further down the road and passed out.

What Victor did not know was that Murph decided to record every conversation he had with Victor. Murph had talked to Pete about his plan to call Victor. Pete told him about an article he read about a kid that was getting bullied by a teacher and used a device on his phone to record some of the bullying. Murph bought the recording device at Best Buy, and he would save that conversation for good use later on.

Chapter 23

Murphy Kearns

Murph wasn't expecting his call with Victor to go the way it did. He wasn't exactly expecting a humble apology. He wasn't expecting to be bullied, either. Victor was really the only person he wanted an apology from after the successful visits he had with Michelle and Steve. The more he learned about Victor, the more he despised him, and the more he wanted to do something about it. He felt that he should try to find out some more about the guy, especially after a quick search revealed Victor was recently arrested for assault in the middle of Virginia. He was not impressed by what he was finding out about how Victor's dad helped push him up the ranks at the Williamsburg Regional Airport, so he figured the father would just be more frustration.

Murph originally thought that Victor was a part of the flowers that Isabella received from Leah Dancy, but after speaking to him, he thought otherwise and realized it was most likely only Leah who had sent them. Murph saved all of the cards that Isabella received for her to read if and when she woke up. Luckily, Johnny was up for a visit, and he helped sort through the cards to find the one from Leah. While they were looking, Murph told Johnny about his calls with Victor.

"There is something not right with that guy," Johnny said. "He sounds a little sick in the head."

"The more I learn about him, the more he disturbs me," Murph said.

"When I was in the Navy, there was this crazy guy named Frank. The guy was a really cocky son of a gun that was on a major power trip. He would get wasted and take it out on people like me who were ranked beneath him. I am not a violent guy, but I wanted to kill that guy. Luckily, he was caught and kicked out of the Navy. Victor sounds like Frank," Johnny said.

"Sounds like a real bad guy."

"You bet he was. What are you going to do about Victor?" Johnny asked.

"I am hoping to talk to his wife and find out more about him, but I really don't know beyond that."

About thirty minutes into their search, Johnny found the card from Leah. Murph opened it up. It read "Isabella-We are thinking about you and your family, and we pray for you each day." The card was signed by Leah and Maddie Dancy, who must be their child, but there was no mention of Victor. Sandy Hatch had been in visiting Isabella and looking at her cards, when she told Murph who Leah Dancy was related to. She had received a card from a Leah Dancy, too, and had mentioned to Murph that it was, in fact, Victor's wife. Sandy said she had decided to reach out to Leah in much the same way she had done with Michelle Bowen. Murph knew that

Sandy had a huge heart and that she was curious to find out more about the people behind the accident. Murph found Leah's address on the back of the card, and decided he was going to make the two hour drive to Alexandria, Virginia, to have a talk with Leah about her husband.

When Murph arrived in Alexandria, it took him about twenty minutes to find the house. It was a huge colonial house, and the name "Victor Dancy" was on the mailbox. Murph figured that the house must belong to Victor's father. He went to the door, but nobody answered after ringing the doorbell a couple of times. There was one truck parked in the expansive driveway, but it didn't appear that anyone was home. A tall chubby man in coveralls came around from the back of the house.

"Can I help you?" the man asked.

"Are you Victor Dancy?" Murph asked, thinking there was no way that this man looked very powerful.

"No, sir, I am just his gardener. He went out of town for a couple of weeks."

"Is Leah Dancy with him by any chance?" Murph asked.

"Yes, both Leah and little Miss Maddie went along. I can give you her cell number if you want, it's in my truck. She asked me to call her if she had any visitors. Can I tell her who you are?"

"My name is Murphy Kearns, and I just wanted to talk to her for a minute if possible."

The gardener went to his truck and got on his cell phone. A minute later he came over and handed Murph the phone. "She wishes to speak to you," he said.

Collisions

"Hello, this is Murphy Kearns."

"Hello, Mr. Kearns, this is Leah Dancy. I understand you are looking for me?" Leah asked.

"Yes. I was hoping that I could talk to you about your husband," Murph said. "Are you nearby?"

"Actually we are a little closer to you and Isabella. We rented a beach house on the Chesapeake Bay. Could I meet you in Williamsburg?"

"Sure, I will head back now. Can you meet me at the Williamsburg Regional Hospital tonight?"

"Yes, I can. Do you mind if I bring my daughter, Maddie," she hesitated. "She really wants to meet Isabella?"

"That's fine, see you tonight." The two exchanged phone numbers, and Murph felt some relief.

Murph didn't realize that Victor Dancy was sobering up in his car on the street and watching Murph talk to the gardener.

Leah Dancy

Leah wasn't expecting the call from Murphy Kearns, but she was glad to receive it. She wanted the poor man to know just who her husband really was. He deserved to find out all about Victor. Leah had spoken to both Michelle and Steve recently, and found out that they both met with and apologized to Murphy Kearns. She knew that Victor would not, so she wanted to do it in person herself.

After Victor was arrested for beating up that woman in Lake Anna, and after what he did to his father, they all

228

decided that it would be best to get out of Alexandria for a couple weeks to let Victor cool off and move on. They decided to find a nice, relaxing beach house on the eastern shore of Virginia, a place that Maddie would enjoy. Leah made the two hour trip from the coast to Williamsburg to meet with Murph without knowing what to expect.

Maddie had been asking Leah a lot of questions lately about why her father wasn't around. It was beyond her four-year-old mental capacity to understand that it was her father's choice not to be there. Even though he never, ever played the part, Victor was still "Daddy" in Maddie's eyes. She would still ask to see him frequently and thought he was just working and would visit soon. On the drive down to Williamsburg, Maddie seemed subdued and upset about something. She wasn't her usual cheerful self in the back seat, reading books or singing along to her favorite songs. Maddie just stared out the window the entire time.

"What's the matter, honey?" Leah finally asked her after about an hour into the trip.

Tears began to form in Maddie's eyes as Leah watched her from the rearview mirror. "Why does Daddy hate me?" she said.

"What are you talking about? Where on Earth did you get that idea?" Leah asked.

"I heard you and Granddaddy talking and you said it," Maddie said. Leah's heart sank into her stomach. She knew exactly what Maddie was talking about. Leah and Victor, Sr. had been talking about Victor at the beach house. She thought Maddie was napping, but apparently she was awake and listening to their conversation. While describing all the awful things about her husband, Leah punctuated the description rhetorically, "How can a man be so despicable that he hates his own four-year-old daughter?"

"Maddie, I was just angry. Your daddy doesn't hate you, I promise."

"Then why does he never want to see me?"

"He does want to see you; he is just a very busy man with work." Leah had been making sure that Maddie never came close to seeing anything on the news about her dad. She also asked parents of Maddie's friends to try to keep their kids away from it all so they didn't say anything to hurt Maddie accidentally.

"I don't think so, Mommy. I don't think he loves me. I don't think he loves you," Maddie said as tears began to flow. Though she no longer loved the man, it was hard enough on Leah that everybody was learning exactly what kind of a man Victor Dancy was, but the most painful realization was his daughter getting the picture too.

Leah and Maddie walked into the hospital holding hands. Leah was very tentative to meet Murph and see Isabella. She knew that she was not responsible for the horrible deed done to their family, but she still felt a pang of guilt for even being associated with her husband. Maddie was very eager to see Isabella. Leah knew she had done a great job of keeping Victor's involvement in the collision from Maddie, but Maddie did know some of the stories about Isabella. Leah was sure that she did not understand what a coma was, but that Maddie did understand that Isabella was very sick. Maddie wanted to bring Isabella a present, and they stopped at Target to get Isabella a Dora the Explorer doll. Leah read Maddie an article that was in USA Today about some of Isabella's interests. A month and a half after the accident,

Isabella had become a media darling, and people nationwide were still actively following her progress.

Leah and Maddie were allowed into the room, and Leah shook Murph's hand. There was another man sitting in the room with a ponytail that Murph introduced as Pete. It was strange for Leah to meet Murph because she felt like she already knew him from everything she had seen on television or the news about his family. Leah had been glued to all of the coverage since it happened, unable to take herself away despite her husband's involvement. She wanted to know everything that was going on. Maddie took the doll over to Isabella's bed and stuck it beside the "sleeping girl." Maddie just sat and stared intently at Isabella. Leah asked her if she would be okay sitting for a while with Isabella to keep an eye on her with some help from Pete. Murph and Leah went to go talk down in the cafeteria.

"Do you think Maddie will be alright with your friend?" Leah asked on their walk down.

"Oh yeah, sure. Pete is about as loveable a guy as I have ever met. He comes up here from the Outer Banks at least twice a week to be with Isabella, even though he never met her before the accident. I'm sure he will be telling your daughter stories about all of the hospital equipment and playing games with her in no time," Murph assured her.

She had rehearsed in the car and knew she needed to say something before she clammed up. "Your daughter sure is pretty," Leah told Murph. She was unsure whether or not to ask him about Isabella's progress, and she decided not to.

They got down to the cafeteria and each ordered a coffee. They sat down in a corner protected from the rest of the cafeteria goers by some plants. People in the hospital knew who Murph was, and he had become a sort of celebrity there. Leah could see people looking and pointing at Murph, but for the most part they were respectful.

"Thank you for seeing me," Leah breathed deeply once they were settled.

"Thank you for coming, I was hoping it would be your husband."

"Trust me, he won't be my husband for much longer, and I wouldn't expect an apology from him," Leah said.

"Yeah, I figured that after our phone conversations if you can call them that," Murph said. He told Leah about the three calls.

"I'm not surprised at all. That sounds just like Victor. He was probably drunk." She told him about the incident between Victor and his father.

"That's terrible. It sounds like a case of Victor's dad letting him get away with too much his whole life, and now he is finally regretting it, unfortunately way too late."

"You don't know the half of it." For the next two hours Leah told Murph everything. She told him about how they met, even her life as an escort. Murph seemed somewhat surprised, but not nearly as much as Leah thought somebody might be. He was the first person that she had told about her former occupation since she stopped being an escort. She told him about some of the verbal and physical abuse she suffered from Victor. She told him about Victor's drinking. "I am positive that he was drunk that morning of the crash. I saw him drinking the night before at Chili's. He was out all night, and he smelled horrible when he came to the house that morning. Victor is a horrible person and a drunk, but he is also very smart. I don't know how he got out of any responsibility. I'm sure his father played a part, but if anybody in this world could get out of something that huge it would be Victor."

Murph was outraged. His entire demeanor changed. "We have to do something about Victor!" he said.

"I don't know," said Leah. "Victor always knows how to get out of things, and I'm scared he might retaliate if he feels threatened."

"We will make sure that we get enough information before we do anything," Murph said to reassure her.

They agreed to meet again after Leah was able to get Maddie back and settled in Chesapeake. They decided to start by gathering as much information about Victor's current situation as possible. Their first stop would be Lake Anna and the woman who was charging him with assault.

Chapter 24

Murphy Kearns

Given the frustration over his conversation with Victor, Murph was in disbelief about how different his experience with Leah Dancy had been. She was a very attractive woman and seemed compassionate and smart. He was shocked to find out about her previous employment and about all of the abuse she had endured. He didn't understand what compelled her to be an escort or to marry such an asshole. She seemed to be the type of woman who could get any man she chose. Murph guessed that some women really were just attracted to that type of man, but for Leah's sake, he hoped she could find somebody better the next time around.

The day after they met at the hospital, Leah was back for the drive over to Lake Anna to find the woman who Victor had recently roughed up. Sympathy, pity, and disgust were tempered by a realization that Victor would never change. The population of the small country town was only a little over one thousand people, so they figured they could find out who the woman was pretty easily. Murph's mother was back in town, so she stayed with Isabella for the day. Rooney was also up visiting, but Murph decided to take him for the ride since he missed the big guy, and Leah didn't seem to mind dogs, even big ones.

The three took the hour and forty-five minute drive in Murph's Jeep, and they had plenty to talk about the whole way. They talked about the similarities between their two daughters, and Murph told her a lot about Maria and Patrick. Once they passed through Richmond, they hit some beautiful Virginia countryside on Interstate 64. Rooney rested his huge head on the console between the two front seats, panting the entire ride.

"Victor absolutely hates dogs," Leah told Murph.

"That doesn't surprise me at all; it seems like there is not much that Victor actually *does* like."

"You're spot on about that," she said chuckling. "But when I say hate, I mean more because he is scared of them. It is actually kind of funny how much of a wimp he is about dogs. It could be a big dog like Rooney or a little prissy rat dog. He won't be in the same room as them, and if one comes near him he does whatever he can to avoid it."

"Now that does surprise me," said Murph. "A tough guy like Victor is scared of little dogs. Why is that?"

"Apparently it happened when he was in middle school, and he was being himself with a neighbor's dog. He was just a minor league asshole then, but if he was gonna make the big leagues, Victor really needed to prove himself, you know?" Murph shot her a glance to make sure he was just behind the timing. Humor had been out of reach to him for a while, and he was out of practice. Leaning back in her seat she continued, "His dad said that he always tortured any pets they had up until that point, and in this particular instance he was shooting a pellet gun at the neighbor's yellow Labrador. Knowing Labs, it was probably a really good dog, but nothing was going to put up with Victor. After a week of the dog being Victor's target practice, the dog struck back. Victor was walking up the alley that afternoon behind his house and the dog spotted him without his gun. It jumped the fence and chased Victor a couple blocks. He tried to climb a metal fence to get away, but the dog caught up to him halfway up and took a big chunk out of Victor's jeans and his butt."

Murph was taking a swig of his sweet iced tea when Leah said this. He was mid-swallow and a little bit of it came out of his nose as he choked on the tea. "The dog bit him in the ass?"

"Yeah, it took a chunk out. He still has a scar there, and he is very self-conscious about it. He wouldn't let me see his behind for the first two years I knew him."

They both cracked up. Murph felt good as it was the first time he remembered laughing like that since the accident.

"A real ass chewing... I will make sure if I ever get the chance to meet Victor to introduce him to this big guy," Murph said as he patted Rooney on the head. He breathed more deeply as momentum towards whatever the new normal would be built around him.

Driving up Main Street in Louisa wasn't much different than Vitaly. The street was pretty empty with only a few businesses in the landscape. There were a couple banks, restaurants, and on the block behind an old-fashioned water tower that said, "Louisa" in faded letters. Murph agreed with Leah that their best bet to find out any information would be to check out The Rusted Spoon, the small bar they passed on their way into town. It was only noon when they arrived, but luckily the bar was open. If anybody was going to tell them the town gossip, they figured it had to be at the lone watering hole.

There were three older men sitting at the otherwise empty bar and only one woman working. Murph and Leah ordered a beer. In no time, Leah struck up a conversation with one of the men, a black guy with a gray beard and a fishing hat. Murph figured that anybody with Leah's looks probably didn't have much trouble talking to men. The man was retired and had moved with his wife to the lake so he could spend his days fishing and she could spend hers painting. He told them that Lake Anna was one of the top bass fishing destinations in Virginia. He was very friendly and liked to talk, and Leah soon found the opportunity to ask about crime in the area.

"Oh, yeah, not much crime around here, let me tell ya," the man said. "There might be a fight here or there, but not much else. Until recently when this out-of-towner came in here and beat up on my girl Gretchen Sanders, one of the nicest people I have met since I have been here."

"What happened?" Murph asked playing dumb. The man told them all about what they already knew, without many new details.

"It's a shame, too," the man said after telling them the story of the assault and how it was such big news for the small town. "In fact, we even had CNN down here. Can you believe that? CNN in the little town of Louisa, I'll be damned. I don't watch much on television besides football, so I didn't see it. But I saw their van down here, parked right here on Main Street."

"So you know the woman?" Leah asked.

Collisions

"Yeah, she is one heck of a pool player. She kicked my tail every time I tried to play her."

"So she comes to the Rusted Spoon?" Murph asked.

"Yeah, she used to be up here all the time, but I haven't seen her since that guy beat her up. In fact, they met up here one night from what I understand. They would come here together pretty regularly for a couple of weeks then. I didn't know why she was with him. I guess she just was lonely. Besides me and the fish, there ain't much catch around here for the ladies," he said snickering.

Murph said, "That's too bad. I hope she didn't leave town because of it."

"No, I heard she's still around. She had her own place. She moved in with her sick mom over on Winston Way to help out, but I think she's out there so she can stay away from that man. I have seen that guy around here, too, afterwards. Everybody wishes he would just pack up and leave. Did I already tell you that he was working at that airport in Williamsburg when the really bad plane crash happened?"

Murph and Leah both shook their heads no, but they both knew far too well. They talked a little while longer and then left. Murph told Leah that it couldn't be too hard to find Sanders on Winston Way in such a small town. He plugged Winston Way into his GPS and the machine routed them the ten, short miles.

With only two houses on the tiny street, it wasn't hard to find the mailbox labeled Sanders. The house couldn't have been more than one thousand square feet. It was a tiny, brick, one-story ranch with white shutters that needed a new paint job. The house was on ample land with a large wooded area behind it.

Murph and Leah went up and knocked on the door. An older woman in her bathrobe gingerly shuffled to the door with a walker. They asked if this was the house where Gretchen lived. She told them it was but that Gretchen was out at the grocery store and would be back shortly. Ms. Sanders asked them to come in and wait, and she gave them both a glass of sweet tea, which took her about ten minutes to fix. About twenty minutes later, Murph heard a car pull into the gravel driveway. He was surprised when he saw Gretchen walk into the door. She wasn't exactly what Murph expected. She was very attractive, but in a different way than Leah. Leah was beautiful in a Katie Holmes, "girl next door" way. Gretchen was more sexy than beautiful, the quintessential country western bar girl, big hair and all. Murph felt that if he met the two of them together for the first time and somebody said to pick the one that used to be an escort, he would pick Gretchen nine times out of ten. She, however, knew immediately who Murph was.

"Baby, you got some visitors. This is Murphy and his friend Leah," Ms. Sanders said to her daughter in her shaky voice.

"Hello, I know who you are Murphy, I have seen you on television quite a few times," Gretchen said as she set down a bag of groceries and shook both of their hands.

"We were hoping that we could have a little bit of your time?" Murph asked. "Leah is Leah Dancy, Victor Dancy's wife."

Gretchen looked at Leah and said, "Oh my, I am so sorry. I had no idea that Victor had a wife, no idea at all," a little breathlessly.

Collisions

"It's okay, I understand. I feel like I should apologize to you, too," Leah said lowering her eyes. "We just want to find out what happened, if you don't mind sharing with us. I'm sure it was hard. I know…" she hesitated and started again, "We know…" but couldn't finish.

Gretchen said, "Sure, just let me get the rest of the groceries in so the milk doesn't go bad, then we can go sit on the back porch and talk as much as you would like." Murph helped her bring her groceries in, and he let Rooney outside to wander around the woods in the back.

The three sat on a screened-in porch facing the backyard. Part of the screen had a big hole in it, and it really needed a good paint job. Rooney chased the scent of some rodent in the woods as they talked. Gretchen told the two a little about her background. Murph wasn't surprised at all to find out that she spent time in Nashville trying to make it as a country singer. It made perfect sense. She told them the sad story of her husband's motorcycle accident and how she moved back to Louisa to be with her mother. Gretchen told them how she met Victor and about their brief affair.

"The sick son of a bitch told me that he had a brother on the Atlantic Airline flight, and I ate it up," she said.

Murph felt sick when Gretchen recounted all of Victor's lies. She seemed as angry at herself as at Victor. Murph began to seethe. He wondered how a man could be so deranged that he would lie about a plane crash and say he had family on it when, in truth, he had a large part to do with the collision in the first place. Murph clenched his teeth as Gretchen talked, his jaw aching.

"I'm usually really tough, I take no shit, but I am scared of that man," Gretchen continued. "I really thought he was going to kill me. I have never seen eyes like that. He looked insane." Murph looked over at Leah, and it was clear to him that Leah had seen those same eyes. Gretchen told them that her lawyer was confident that Victor would face some consequence for the assault, but he highly doubted Victor would see any jail time.

"He was able to get me a restraining order, so Victor can't come within one-thousand feet of me," Gretchen said. "I just want him gone for good. I won't trust anything about that man until I know he is out of my life for good."

That was a mutual feeling all three of them felt. They chatted a little bit more, and then Murph and Leah thanked Gretchen and Ms. Sanders and headed on their way. Murph was more frustrated and shaken on the way back to Williamsburg than he imagined he could ever be.

Leah Dancy

Daughter of a negligent father and an alcoholic, pill popping mother, Leah didn't think despising somebody as much as she was beginning to despise Victor was possible. She didn't think he could shock her any more than he already had, but what Gretchen told her definitely was a new depth of depravity. She decided that she needed to have a serious heart to heart with her father-in-law. He had always been very upfront with her. He was very strict and set in his ways, but he was the father she never had. She definitely didn't believe in everything he did or all of his beliefs, but she knew he cared deeply for her and for Maddie. She took Maddie into Williamsburg to visit with an old friend of hers, and she met Victor, Sr. at Bray Bistro, where they both loved the scallops and the view overlooking the James River.

Collisions

Two shocking revelations came out during their meal, one for each of them. Leah told her father-in-law about her life as an escort. She went into detail about her life growing up, and how she met Victor. He told Leah that he knew that she had a tough upbringing, but he was stunned to find out about her being an escort. He then told her about his bribe of an escort that Victor had used the night before the plane collision, and how he had helped Victor out of some serious potential jail time by using his connections with the government. Leah could not believe what he was telling her. She could not believe that the father-in-law that took her in as a real daughter had done so much to cover up and protect a prodigal son. It was disturbing to her, and she left the restaurant with Victor, Sr. sitting there by himself.

She called him later and told him that he meant too much to her for her to completely shut him out of her life, but that she would need some serious time to forgive him. He was very remorseful for what he had done, and he told her that no matter how bad Victor was, it was not in his blood to give up on his son. He had never been able to quell the instinct to protect his son from the consequences of his actions in the past and that momentum propelled him to keep helping him. Leah's reaction, more than Victor's violence, helped him recognize he was done with Victor once and for all. He had already disowned a son. He didn't want to lose a daughter and granddaughter too. Leah knew that Maddie meant more to her grandfather than anything else in the world, and Maddie loved him the same way.

Leah told Victor, Sr. to give her some time and space, but she was hopeful that things could get better between them. She told him the first step to mending the relationship was for Victor, Sr. to give her the escort's contact information and to promise to leave her alone. He was hesitant to do so, but he eventually relinquished her address.

He told her that he would go back to Alexandria and let Maddie and Leah stay at the house they were renting on the eastern shore for as long as Leah needed. Victor, Sr. said, "I love you" at the end of the call, but Leah could not bring herself to say it back.

She immediately called Murph and said, "There is somebody we need to talk to!"

Leah and Murph met the next day. She told Murph everything her father-in-law had told her. Murph seemed beyond the point of disbelief. They drove to Norfolk to talk to Laticia, the escort Victor used the night before the collision. Leah told Murph to let her take charge when talking to the woman, since they shared a common background.

Laticia lived on the top floor of a ten-story brick apartment building near downtown Norfolk. Murph was surprised the apartment building was in such a good part of town, and was so well kept. They rode the elevator up and found her door. A little boy answered in a Mickey Mouse t-shirt.

"Mommy, there are two people here I don't know," he shouted back. A couple seconds later, a tall and attractive woman came to the door.

"Can I help you?" she said.

"Yes, we would like to talk to you about Victor Dancy."

"I don't know that man."

"We know you do, Laticia," Leah said.

"Derrick, go to your room and play with your toys," she told the boy.

Collisions

"But Mommy, you said we could go out to McDonald's for a cheeseburger," the boy whined.

"We will, baby, but please go to your room so I can talk to these people for a quick minute," she said. "If you are good and quiet, I'll get you a sundae while we're there."

The boy rushed to his room. "Are you two the cops?" Laticia asked as she turned to them.

"No, I am Victor's wife," Leah said. Laticia slammed the door in their face.

Leah wasn't going to leave without talking to the woman, so she banged on the door. "Listen, we just want to talk," Leah said.

"Go away now," Laticia said through the door.

"We aren't going anywhere," Leah said back through the door. "We know everything, and I am pretty sure you aren't going to get the police involved. We aren't mad. We just want to talk to you. We will just sit here until you let us in," she demanded.

After a minute or two, Laticia opened the door. "Come in," she said in an unhappy tone.

They sat down on a worn-out, brown sofa, and Laticia pulled up a kitchen chair. The place was tiny, and it was obvious that it was just Laticia and Derrick living there because all of the pictures were just of the two of them. Leah told her about what she knew.

"Listen, I am not a bad person. I am sure you come in here and think I'm just some crazy hooker. I have done some bad things that I wish I had not done, but I have a good heart. Some people have it tougher than others. I want my

244

boy to live a good life, and I'm trying to move on. That man and his crazy father were a blessing, of sorts. I quit the business."

"Laticia, we aren't here to demean you, and we aren't mad at you," Leah said. "You won't believe this, but I once was an escort myself."

Leah noticed that Laticia looked her up and down again and then Laticia said, "You're shittin' me."

"No, I'm not." Leah went on to tell Laticia all about her past.

"Well I'll be damned," Laticia said. Leah noticed her relax.

"We just want to know what happened the night before the collision," Murph said, opening his mouth for the first time since they entered the apartment.

Leah looked at Murph and then to Laticia before adding, "You know there was an accident, don't you?"

Laticia looked at the floor and said, "Yes" before continuing. She told them that she got a call to meet a man at the Hilton. It was later in the night than she usually took calls, but she was way behind on the rent, and she needed the money. She told them about the night, including some of the stuff Victor wanted to do in bed. It all rang true to Leah; she had experienced it all. Laticia told them about the drug use and that Victor appeared drunk when she arrived and that he continued to drink in her presence.

"So what time did you leave?" Murph asked. Leah could tell that Murph was struggling to contain himself. She saw that the more Laticia told them, the harder Murph clenched his fists. She had noticed him doing the same thing when they talked to Gretchen Sanders.

"We were up until at least five," Laticia said.

"And you were drinking and doing drugs the whole time?" Leah asked.

"Yes, we were. We might have slept for a couple of hours before his alarm went off. I'm so sorry," Laticia said, finally apologizing.

Murph looked to Leah, "There is no way that he sobered up by the time the collision happened. He was stoned and drunk in that flight tower!" Murph got up and stormed out of the apartment. Leah stayed on the couch. She felt that she needed to give Murph some time to cool off.

"You must know how it is," Laticia said to Leah. "I'm just trying to get a better life for me and my son. I got a job at a dry-cleaners. The pay is shit, but I'm getting by with that money that wretched man gave me. I saved some of it for Derrick, and I am going to put a little towards taking some classes at Norfolk State to try to finish up my nursing degree. I started there and then I had Derrick, and I couldn't afford it any more. Please don't tell on me, I can't be taken away from my baby."

Leah thought about it for a minute. She had come from the same place and wanted to give the woman a chance. "We won't say anything, and I will make sure you get the rest of your money. But you better promise me that you will stay clean and keep a respectable job. Don't make the mistake I made and settle for a loser. Find yourself a good man because Derrick needs a father," she said as she thought the same thing about Maddie.

"I promise." The two sat for a time, the stale air of a stuffy apartment hung around them and sounds of televisions echoed softly through the walls before Laticia said, "Must be nice to have a brother to stand up for you like that."

Leah's confusion lasted only a moment before she said, "Oh, he's not my brother."

Before Leah could explain, Laticia followed, asking evenly, "Who is he?"

"That's Murphy Kearns."

Laticia's eyes looked swollen and red-rimmed as Derrick pattered back into the room asking, "Now, Mom?"

Leah reached out to squeeze Laticia's hand and stroked Derrick's head as she left. She found Murph down by his Jeep.

"We have to go to the authorities about Victor. I've had enough!" he said as she got in the passenger door. Shaken by the sight of his red-rimmed eyes, Leah agreed that something had to be done. She just didn't know what.

Chapter 25

Murphy Kearns

It took Murph a couple days to recover from the shock of confirming that Victor had been heavily impaired just hours before the collision. Details seemed to point towards that conclusion, but Murph wanted to believe that nobody could be such an asshole. He could not understand how the investigators didn't uncover this during their investigation. He was furious not only with Victor, but also with Victor's father, Laticia, and the FBI and NTSB. He didn't know whether to unleash his fury to the media and let them know everything or if he should go to the FBI and NTSB with the information. He still had the recordings from the three phone conversations he had with Victor, and he knew that he was still a media darling. He was leaning towards going to the media when circumstances dictated a different course.

Murph received a call from the hospital insisting he come in as quickly as possible. He had been spending the past week staying at the apartment he was renting to try and get some regular sleep. He rushed from his spartan quarters to the intensive care unit. The nurses at the desk paged Dr. Griffin as soon as Murph arrived at the hospital. Griffin was one of the many doctors who watched over Isabella. He was very matter of fact, but Murph liked him.

"I'm sorry Mr. Kearns, but Isabella has developed a pretty severe case of pneumonia," Dr. Griffin told Murph.

"What does that mean?" Murph responded.

"It's possible for a person in a coma to get pneumonia. It can be caused by a lack of movement. We do turn Isabella every few hours, but she has been in her coma for close to two months now, which is a long time to go without moving around. Or she could have contracted it from one of her visitors. Unfortunately even though we have done as much as we can to keep Isabella healthy, she is still exposed to viruses. In her reclined position, she can't expel any extra fluid that builds up in her lungs," he told Murph.

"What do you do now? Is she going to be alright?" Murph asked.

"It's serious when anyone contracts pneumonia and even more so for Isabella in her fragile state. She has been strong so far, but this is a pretty severe case. We will have to monitor her closely, and she will be given a new round of antibiotics. We are hoping to get it cleared up," the doctor answered.

"You are hoping?"

"We just don't know right now. She has a very high fever, and we need to get that down first. The next two days will be critical. We are going to ask that there be no more visitors for at least a week."

Collisions

"I can't be in there with her? She needs me," Murph said.

"We will let you be with her again once we get the fever down. We need to take every precaution. I am sorry, but that is all we can do," Dr. Griffin said as he patted Murph on the shoulder, then turned and walked away.

Murph's mind reeled. He had been thinking about what to do about Victor before he found out about Isabella's pneumonia. The time for apologies and public opinion had passed. He called Leah, and when she didn't answer he left her a message telling her he was on his way to her rental and for her to meet him there.

Leah Dancy

It had taken Leah a couple days to recover from everything she had learned and to begin thinking clearly again. She knew that she would never forgive her husband, but her father-in-law's fate was still up in the air. It was hard to discuss how important Victor, Sr. was to Maddie. Could she really take both Maddie's father and grandfather away from her at the same time? What would she do as a single mother? With her credentials, she knew it would be a struggle.

Maddie was still staying with her friend's family. Leah was sitting at the kitchen table of the small rental, trying to find distraction in a book when somebody banged on the front door. She went to the door and was surprised to find Victor hammering the door with his fist.

"Get out of here!" she yelled to him, not opening the door. She saw that he had that look in his eye, the one that she had come to fear and that Gretchen had also seen.

"Let me in this fucking door right now!" Victor shouted as he began to thump louder.

"Leave now, or I will call the police!" she replied. Victor started banging against the door with his entire body.

Leah turned and ran back to the kitchen to find her cell phone. Of course, it wasn't there when she needed it. She quickly remembered that she'd left it in the car to charge when she returned from getting some groceries. There was no landline phone in the rental either.

Before she could do anything else, Victor was at the backdoor, which was unlocked, and he barged in. "Shit" was all she could muster as she prepared herself for what she knew was coming. This would not be an argument. She tried to find a weapon to help her and grabbed the closest thing, a pair of scissors.

"Get away, Victor!" she screamed at the top of her lungs hoping that somebody would hear. Unfortunately she realized that neither of the two houses next to her were being rented or occupied at the time. A couple on their honeymoon had just left one of the houses the day before.

"Where the fuck is he?" Victor asked. Throwing the table out of the way and inching closer to Leah.

"Where is who?" she asked.

"Where the fuck is Murphy Kearns?"

"What are you talking about, Victor?"

"You are sleeping with that prick! I saw him at the house in Alexandria, and I found out that he was with you in Lake Anna. What, were you trying to show him off to me by coming there?"

Collisions

"Victor I promise, I'm not sleeping with him! He just wants an apology from you."

"An apology that he'll never get! So you admit that you were with him, you whore. I'm sure you two are sleeping together."

"No, Victor." It was too late. He threw the last chair out of the way. Leah held the scissors out in a feeble attempt to hold him off or scare him. He slapped her wrist and in doing so cut his arm with the scissors, but it was a hard enough blow to knock the scissors out of Leah's hands. She realized too late that she had made a mistake cornering herself between the table and the kitchen cabinets. There was nowhere for her to go. She tried swinging at him, but he kicked her as hard as he could in the knee. She immediately felt an excruciating pain as the force of his strike translated to her body. Her knee buckled, and she fell to the ground. He had done something really bad to her knee. Before she could do anything else, he was on top of her. "Victor, please!" she cried.

"It is time for you to die!" he said as he slammed her head against the tile floor. She felt her head collide against the floor twice before she was knocked out. The last thoughts she had before she blacked out were of Maddie.

Chapter 26

Murphy Kearns

Murph left an envelope beside Isabella's bed with a letter addressed to her that he wrote a couple weeks after the collision, soon after his episode on the skiff. The doctors let him go in the room with a mask on so he didn't spread any more germs. He was hoping that he could give it to her when she woke up, but when he left to head to Leah's, he wasn't so sure anymore that would happen with the pneumonia setting in.

Dear Isabella-

I didn't have a chance to give your mommy or little brother a real goodbye. You are in a coma right now, and I hope that I get to watch you grow into the beautiful woman that I know you will be. I'd like more than anything for you to wake up so that I can hide this letter away until you are a grown woman with a family of your own. I needed to get these thoughts down on paper though. It's helping me carry on.

Collisions

I want to make sure that you realize that I loved your mother very much, and I was privileged to get to spend the years I did with her. She was an amazing wife and mother, and it saddens me that you had such a short time with her. You were a great big sister to your brother, and he loved you so much. I know it will be hard for you to remember them when you are older, but I will do my best to always keep them in our thoughts and remind you how much they loved us.

When your mom was pregnant with you, I made a list of things that I wanted to make sure we did together. We have already done some of these together. I tell you how pretty you are all the time. I play hide and seek with you. You ride on my shoulders, I hold you upside down, and we swing at the park.

There are still plenty of things left on our list. I'm going to make sure we do the following, and I want you to check off that we did them when you read this eventually:

1. *I want to play baseball with you. I'm not going to force you to play in any leagues, but I want to teach you the simple joy of catch.*
2. *I want to get you your first puppy.*
3. *I want to take you on fishing and camping trips.*
4. *I want to take you on a roller coaster ride.*
5. *I want to catch you when you take your first jump off a diving board.*
6. *I never want to miss any of your birthdays.*
7. *When you get older, I want to teach you to drive both an automatic and manual car.*
8. *I want to go on your college visits with you, and I promise it will be your choice, but GO PITT PANTHERS!*
9. *If you need to come back home for a while after college, my door will be open.*
10. *I want to walk you down the aisle for your wedding, but I won't mind if it's when you are 40!*

Most of all I want you to know that I will always love you. I can't wait to spend the rest of my life watching you become the amazing woman you are destined to be.

Love,
Daddy

As Murph placed the envelope on the table by her bed he noticed the turtle bob its fully extended head. Murph paused, pinched a bit of food for the turtle, and turned to leave.

• • •

Leah had never returned Murph's call, and nobody answered the door when Murph got to her rental house. Her van was parked in the driveway, and some lights were on. He decided he should call her again, and as the phone was ringing, he walked around the side of the house towards the back. The back door was wide open, so he walked up to it. Murph suspected immediately that something was wrong because the kitchen table was flipped over. He shouted out her name, and she yelled, "Help, Murph, I'm over here."

He darted over to where her voice was and found her leaning up against the kitchen cabinets. She looked terrible. She was holding her knee in pain, and there was blood on the floor. "What happened?" he asked.

"Victor," she managed to get out. "I feel woozy, and there is something really wrong with my knee."

"Okay, stay still. I'll call an ambulance," Murph said. As he dialed, he grabbed some kitchen towels and ice for her to put on the back of her head and on her knee. He was definitely not a doctor, but he could tell Leah needed to see somebody soon. Her eyes were glazing over, and she was very dazed. He got off the phone with 911, and held the ice pack on the back of her head. Leah's head slumped as sleep pulled at her, but Murph knew he better keep her awake until some help arrived. A fire truck pulled up first, and a couple minutes later the ambulance arrived. The EMTs secured her on a gurney because she was complaining about neck pain and she couldn't walk. Murph followed the ambulance to the county hospital.

When he arrived, Murph rushed in to see what was going on with Leah. It took about thirty minutes before the staff allowed Murph to go back. Leah was hooked up to an I.V., a far too familiar sight for Murph. He was sick of hospitals. He was sick of their smell. He was sick of how clean they were. He was sick of their food. He never wanted to be in a hospital again.

"I have a concussion, a neck sprain, and they think I have a bunch of ligaments torn in my knee, but the doctors won't know for sure until I have an MRI," Leah told Murph as he sat down. Her color was back. Murph noticed that she was still out of it, but he figured it was partially because of the concussion and partially because of the pain medicine.

"I was worried it would be a lot worse. I'm so sorry this happened to you," he said.

"He wanted to kill me," Leah said as she burst into tears. Murph comforted her for a couple minutes. "He really wanted to kill me," she said when she was composed. "I don't know what stopped him. I really thought I was going to die."

"Well, you are here, and it's going to take some time, but it sounds like you will be fine," Murph said. His anger had reached a crescendo, but he was surprised that he was able to remain so calm. All he wanted to do was find Victor, but he wanted to be smart about it. "What happened?" he asked.

"He just came barging in the back door. He actually thought we are a couple," she said.

"Who's a couple?"

"The two of us," Leah answered.

"What? That's crazy. The guy's absolutely crazy!" Murph exclaimed.

Leah said, "He's not going to stop until I'm dead."

"That's not going to happen," Murph replied.

"You have to do something, Murph. He has to be stopped."

They looked into each other's eyes in silent agreement. There was a knock on the door to her room on the emergency floor. It was a local police detective coming to question Leah about what happened.

"I will be back," he said. "You'll be okay, I promise." He turned to leave, and Leah called him back.

She put up her hands for a hug and when he bent over, she pulled his ear towards her. "He always carries a knife, be careful!" They looked in each other's eyes one more time, and Murph left.

He called to check in on Isabella as he walked out of the front doors of the hospital. Then he called Pete. He told Pete he would text him a location, but he needed to meet him immediately. Pete could tell just by his voice that this was an emergency. Murph told Pete to bring Rooney and Johnny if he could find him.

Collisions

Since the phone calls with Victor, Murph was constantly churning over how to respond. His emotions dictated the reactions, but now he allowed his mind to plan the details. He never thought he would do anything about them, but things had changed and now he knew he had to.

Leah Dancy

Leah's knee was feeling considerably better, but her head was killing her. All she could think about was what Murph was going to do to Victor. She knew that Murph understood what she wanted him to do, but she immediately had second thoughts after he left. She couldn't let him throw his life away. He had a young daughter who might or might not recover, and if she did she would definitely need her father. The poor girl had already lost her mother and brother, and now her father was off to find Victor, and who knew what Victor was capable of. He tried to kill her, and he had gone completely off the cliff. Leah recognized that Murph's anger was driven by Victor's insanity. In the short weeks she had known Murph, Leah watched Victor's actions turn a gentle man looking for an apology into an angry man seeking revenge. She felt horrible for sending Murph off to find Victor on his own. What Leah wasn't able to see because she'd never known it in her own life was a man compelled by loyalty.

Leah was unable to focus on the detective who questioned her. He told her that he could tell she was tired and that he would come back later when she was up to it. She figured that he chalked it up to her medications or concussion. She knew that she could easily get Victor arrested this time. Without Victor, Sr.'s help and the pending assault charge from Gretchen Sanders, Leah was somewhat confident that Victor might actually go to jail. She

258

contemplated calling Murph and asking him to stop, but she thought he might be beyond that, that he would not listen to her, that he could not stop. She also considered getting the detective back into her room to tell him what was going on. Maybe the cops might be able to get to Victor before Murph did.

The problem that Leah couldn't let go of was that in her heart she really wanted a confrontation between Murph and Victor. Murph deserved to get his revenge, let alone his apology. Victor was an evil man, and Leah knew she would always live in fear knowing that Victor was out there. With his track record, he would figure a way out of serving time in jail or a very minimal stay in some white-collar facility, and then he would be back out. She thought she might be able to deal with it if it was only her, but she had Maddie to consider, and she could never live if anything happened to Maddie because of Victor. Leah wanted Victor gone for good. She was exhausted, but she knew that there would be no sleep for her until she heard from Murph.

Chapter 27

Murphy Kearns

Murph met Pete at a coffee shop in Glen Allen, Virginia. He had Johnny and Rooney with him. Rooney waited in the car as Murph told Pete and Johnny everything that had happened concerning Victor. He told them all about Victor's abrasive phone calls. He told them about his meetings with Laticia, Gretchen, Michelle, and Steve. He told them that Victor had been drinking heavily and doing cocaine just before the collision and that he was sure that Victor was the cause of his wife and son's deaths, along with all the others on the planes. Murph told them about Victor's father always protecting his son from the consequences of his actions. He also told them about what Victor had just done to Leah.

Murph told them that he was going to demand an apology from Victor and then make sure the man was arrested. Murph told them he needed help ensuring that Victor didn't run. He trusted them and felt that they were the best two people to help. They devised a plan as they drank coffee, and Murph readied himself to go after a man that he hated completely, in a way he had never felt before. Leah had shown Murph where Victor was staying on Lake Anna when they were there to see Gretchen. The three men jumped in Pete's Range Rover with Rooney and drove the fifty miles to find Victor.

On the drive to Victor's lake house, Murph readied himself by thinking about Maria, Isabella, and Patrick. He thought about Maria's beauty, her sarcasm, and how great a teacher and mother she was. He thought about how smart Isabella was for her age, and how much the two of them loved each other's company. Murph reflected on Patrick's comical laugh, louder than anything he had ever heard, and how much his son looked like his beautiful mother. He contemplated all of that and then he thought about how one man, Victor Dancy, had taken away two of those loved ones, and left one hanging on by a thread.

As Pete's Range Rover turned the corners of the winding gravel road leading up to Victor's house, the three men sat quietly. The only sound in the car was Rooney's panting in the back. Pete and Johnny didn't know what to expect, but Murph knew he could count on them. As they pulled up to the house, Murph sensed that he had undergone a change. He gathered strength from all of those that had been wronged by this man he was about to meet. Murph looked at Johnny and Pete one last time, and with a nod he was out of the car and walking towards the house.

The crackle and crunch of the pine cones, dead leaves, and gravel under his feet on the walk from the car to the front door reminded Murph of running through the woods of Vitaly. Victor Dancy set in motion the events of the last two months. Murph accelerated towards the door. The blinds were all pulled down on the front windows, but Murph sensed that Victor was inside. He banged on the front door. Victor opened the door with a smile, like he had been expecting a visit from Murph and was excited to see him. Murph walked through the door, bumping Victor on his way.

Now in the foyer of the house, Victor closed the door behind them. The two men stared at each other for what felt like minutes to Murph, but were really only a few seconds. Victor had a smirk on his face that Murph immediately wanted to wipe away with his fist, but he steadied himself. He needed to talk to Victor first.

"So we finally meet," Victor said. "You're even smaller in person than you appear on television," he said as he looked Murph up and down. "I don't know what Leah was thinking, screwing you."

"Is that why you beat her up? Because you thought we were sleeping together?" Murph asked.

"I was in Alexandria when you went to my dad's house. I found out that you've been with her a lot. She's a hooker, of course you were sleeping with her," Victor said.

"I didn't sleep with her. I just lost my wife, the only woman I ever loved," Murph responded. He'd been in the house less than a minute, but Murph felt he was on his heels already. "And I think you had something to do with that!"

Victor laughed and said, "By now, my wife might be dead, too."

"No, she's not. I found her, and she'll be okay," Murph said leaning forward. He thought that Victor looked a little surprised to find out that Leah was going to be alright. He must have thought that he killed her.

After Victor composed himself he said, "That damn mailman coming to the door freaked me out. I thought that I had done enough to kill her, but I guess I'll have to finish her off later."

"You won't get that chance," said Murph.

Victor laughed again. "You're one cocky son of a bitch. I've thought that all along, from your interviews to your phone calls. That's why I knew you would eventually come looking for me."

"I'm only going to give you one chance to apologize for everything you have done," said Murph, squaring his shoulders.

"Apologize for what?" Victor spat out.

"For beating up Gretchen Sanders and for going after Laticia." Murph noticed that Victor looked very surprised when he brought up Laticia. "And for blaming something that was your fault on Michelle Bowen and Steve Rodriguez."

"Those two idiots had just as much to do with it as I did!"

"No, they didn't, and you know they didn't. You used your dad to get away with it all. You were drunk and high when those planes collided. You damn well know whose fault it was." Murph said as he gained control.

"Don't cry on me, little girl," said Victor. "There's no proof to any of that, and there never will be. It's too late!"

"I'm sick of listening to you. I want an apology now. You took my family!" Murph said as he pulled out his wallet. He grabbed a photo of Maria, Isabella, and Patrick that he always carried with him and showed it to Victor.

Collisions

"I'm not apologizing for anything."

"Then I will make sure everybody knows what you did, even if you don't get into trouble for it. You will be the most hated man in this country by the time I get through with you."

"I'm not scared!"

Murph turned back to the door to go back outside and regroup.

Victor saw this but wasn't ready for Murph to go. "I won't apologize for anything, but I will admit that, yes, it was my fault," Victor said. Murph, with his back to Victor, smiled for the first time because he finally had Victor where he wanted him, admitting to what he had done. "I messed up in that flight tower. It was my fault, and I am glad your wife and son are dead!" Victor said mercilessly trying to goad Murph.

With speed he didn't know he had, Murph turned and dashed at Victor, sticking out his right arm and close-lining him. Murph sent the bigger man flying back into the staircase of the front hall. Murph jumped on top of him and hit him twice in the face with his right fist with everything he had. Victor grabbed Murph and bear hugged his much stronger arms around Murph. Victor lifted Murph off the ground. Surprised by Victor's strength, Murph felt his breath going as Victor squeezed harder. Victor looked Murph in the eyes and whispered, "You are dead now, too. You can go join your wife and kid, you piece of shit," and the picture fell from Murph's grasp.

With the little energy and breath he had left, Murph cocked back his head and smashed it into Victor's face, squarely striking his nose with a loud crunching noise as Murph's forehead crushed the cartilage. Victor released his grip on Murph dropping him to the ground and staggering back a bit. Murph saw Victor's eyes fill with water as his nose gushed dark red blood. He pounced on Victor like a tiger on a wounded gazelle. Murph began to wildly throw his fists at Victor as the rage of the last two months coursed through his body. He connected as many punches as he missed, but he could feel each connecting punch dig into Victor's face. Victor eventually fell back to the ground. Murph jumped on top of him again, but with all of his adrenaline, he didn't remember what happened last time he made that mistake. Victor once again wrapped his arms around Murph effectively stopping the fists. Victor was able to roll over on top of Murph and pin him to the ground. He released his left arm from Murph, and Victor grabbed his knife with his left hand. He was unable to get it from its case without letting go of Murph with his right arm as well, and when he did Murph capitalized. Out of breath and seeing that Victor had a knife, Murph did all he could to stay alive. As Victor pulled up off of him in an attempt to get the knife, Murph sent his knee pounding into Victor's groin. The blow of Murph's knee sent Victor back and the knife flying across the hall. Murph jumped up and kicked Victor in the stomach three times. He then went and retrieved the knife, but Victor was up and was slowly running through the dining room towards the kitchen in the back of the house.

He heard Victor opening the back door and then a childish yelp just like Leah predicted. Johnny waited at the back door with Rooney. When Victor opened the door, Rooney was there waiting for him and jumped up onto him, knocking Victor back into the kitchen. Victor turned to run back through the house in fear of the big dog. What he probably didn't realize was that for all of his master's fury, Rooney was probably just chasing Victor through the house because he thought they were playing. Murph stood panting and trying to collect himself in the hall. Murph held the knife in his left hand as Victor ran into the room. Victor stopped in his tracks when he saw Murph. Rooney barged into the room and ran straight into Victor's back, knocking him forward and into Murph. Murph's body tensed in anticipation of the collision, giving the knife a foundation to meet the other body's weight. His grandfather's trench knife ripped through his ribs and sank deep into Victor's chest. Victor slumped on top of Murph, and they each looked into the other's eyes. Murph didn't think he saw fear, but relief in the man's eyes as he passed away.

Murph pushed Victor off of him, and Papa George's knife remained wedged in Victor's chest. Murph gagged and wiped Victor's blood from his hands onto his chest and pant legs, looking in disbelief at Rooney. "Or pull me out of a ditch if I should ever fall into one. I can find a Newfoundland that will do as much," Murph said to himself. He quickly stopped thinking about Victor and had visions of Maria, Isabella, and Patrick as he lay there hurting and tired.

Pete and Johnny ran into the hall following Rooney. Rooney ran over and immediately began licking the mixture of Murph's own blood and Victor's off of Murph's face. Murph heard Pete say, "Whoa, dude," as he entered the hall. Murph pushed Rooney off of him, and Johnny came over to help him up.

"Are you okay?" Johnny asked as he pulled Murph up to his feet.

"Yeah," Murph said. "I think I'm okay."

Pete looked at Murph and snapped out of his shock, remembering something important. "Murph, while you were in here the Williamsburg hospital called. It was about Isabella!"

Before they rushed out of the lake house, Murph looked down at Victor one last time, not really sure what happened. He scanned the floor and found the dropped picture. He picked it up and put it back in his wallet, before walking out the front door.

Leah Dancy

After sitting and worrying about Murph for a couple hours, Leah was finally able to fall asleep. She figured that the pain killers and concussion must have trumped her stewing over Murph. Maddie woke Leah from her sleep when she entered the room. Unsure of how long she had been out, Leah tried to get her bearings. Maddie ran over to her mother, and gave her a big hug. It was physically painful for Leah to bear the hug, but having Maddie there warmed her heart. The two held each other for several minutes without saying anything. Leah was very happy to have her daughter with her, the person whom she cared about more than anything else in the world.

Eventually Maddie looked at her mother, "Are you okay, Mommy?"

"I'll be fine soon, honey, but I feel so much better with you here now!" Leah said.

"I was so scared when Granddaddy picked me up and said he was bringing me to the hospital to see you," Maddie said beginning to cry.

"You don't have to worry anymore, I am fine, honey. We're fine."

"It was him, wasn't it? Why is he such a bad man, Mommy?" Maddie asked. Leah presumed that although

Maddie was young, she was finally able to understand what kind of man her father was.

"Yes, it was, but I have a feeling we won't have to worry about him anymore," Leah said.

"Good, Mommy. He scares me."

Leah hurt for her daughter. She was too young to go through this and to lose her father, but Leah also knew that Victor needed to be out of Maddie's life. The two hugged for a while longer, and Maddie eventually fell asleep in her mother's arms. "We're fine," Leah repeated to her daughter.

When the detective knocked and entered her room a while later, Leah had no emotion left for the news he delivered from the Lake Anna Sheriff's Department. Instead she kissed Maddie's hair and said again, "We're fine."

Chapter 28

Murphy Kearns

After Pete told him that the hospital had called, Murph and Pete sprinted to the Range Rover with Rooney closely following. Johnny waited at the house for the sheriff, who Pete had already called. Murph knew that they weren't going to be happy with him leaving the crime scene, but there was no way he wasn't going to see his daughter. On the drive back to Williamsburg, Murph sent a file from his phone containing the recorded phone messages between him and Victor plus the encounter that they just had, which he was also recording on his phone, to Carmen Paul at the Williamsburg Daily Express. Murph didn't know what would happen to him now that Victor was dead, but he did know one thing, he needed to use his public appeal to help him out.

On the drive, Murph switched his bloody shirt with Pete, and he wiped Victor's blood from his body with a towel. Pete made it back to Williamsburg in no time going well over the speed limit. Murph thought it was a good thing that Pete had a high-tech radar detector in his car. Murph wasn't sure that Pete would have stopped if a cop tried to pull him over. Pete was on a mission to get Murph to his daughter.

When they got to the hospital, Pete pulled right up front, and Murph jumped out and ran through the hospital to Isabella's room in the ICU. As he got to her floor, he noticed a lot of the nurses looking at him with smiles on their faces. He got to the doorway and took a deep breath. Murph entered the room to find his daughter awake. Murph ran over to her and gave her the biggest hug he could possibly give her.

"I love you so much, Bella!"

She looked at her father and said, "I love you too, Daddy."

Murph leaned over and held Isabella for a long time. She was obviously groggy. The doctors told him that it would take her a while to completely come out of the coma. It had been a couple hours at that point though, so Isabella was able to focus a little more than she was when she first snapped out of it. The doctors said that they had never seen anything like it, but they guessed that her high fever due to the pneumonia must have had an influence on Isabella waking up.

Murph stayed with Isabella for the next several hours. They talked some, and she slept some. She was still a sick little girl with the pneumonia, and the doctors and nurses were constantly coming into the room to monitor her. Isabella didn't remember anything about the crash. She asked about her mommy and her little brother, but Murph wasn't ready to tell her anything about that yet. To get her mind off of where they were, Murph sent to have Rooney brought up. Isabella's eyes lit up when Rooney galloped into the room just like they had done when Murph came in earlier. Rooney ran over to Isabella and gave her a big lick on the face, and she laughed for the first time in months.

Murph spent the next two nights with Isabella. He did not know it yet, but the sheriff's department in Lake Anna and the FBI decided to give him two days with his daughter before they brought him in for questioning about the death of Victor Dancy.

Leah Dancy

Leah cried when she found out about Victor. She was not sure if the tears were coming because she was glad he was finally out of her life, or if they were because there was a part of her that was sad. She hated the man, and he had tried to kill her, but he was the father of her child. She spent close to the last decade with him.

Leah was released from the hospital into a throng of reporters shouting questions. When she saw the swarm, she asked a hospital representative to take Maddie to the car separately in anticipation of the questions. Leah didn't answer too many questions, but she did recognize Carmen Paul who she knew from the Junior League of Williamsburg. She stopped by Carmen and asked for her card, telling her that she would be in contact soon.

Leah and Maddie went back alone to the rental house on the eastern shore. When she wasn't playing with Maddie, she watched the news. She was ecstatic to see that Isabella had come out of her coma. Leah was also surprised to see two days later that Murphy was taken back to Lake Anna for questioning about Victor's death. The media reaction outside of the Williamsburg hospital as Murph was escorted to the sheriff's vehicle made the swarm of reporters that she had encountered seem tiny in comparison.

Leah called and invited Carmen Paul to her house to do an exclusive interview because Leah felt that she needed to get her story out to the public in support of Murph. The interview started with Leah telling Carmen about the abuse she had endured from Victor throughout their relationship. She went on to describe the beating she took in the same house where the interview was taking place, and how Victor left her for dead.

Carmen: I understand that you were spending time with Murphy Kearns before his encounter with your husband. Did you know what Murphy was planning to do?

Leah: No, and he didn't either. He didn't go to Victor's house for a physical confrontation. He went there for an apology. Murphy was forced to fight for himself, because Victor just snapped.

Carmen: How do you feel about Victor's death?

Leah (after a pause): Murphy, nor the other survivors of the victims of that horrible crash, will ever get completely over it. As for me, I don't think that Victor would have ever left me or Maddie alone. It wasn't in him to give up on anything. He was an evil, evil man.

Carmen: What do you think should happen to Murphy Kearns now? Apparently there is the belief that he won't be charged with murder, but something more like involuntary manslaughter.

Leah (looking right into the camera): Murphy Kearns should not be charged with anything! He did nothing wrong. The man has had enough taken away from him. He should be allowed to go home and be with his beautiful daughter.

Chapter 29

Posted: June 05, 2009, 9:17 am

Carmen Paul/Williamsburg Daily Express

Louisa, VA-The Louisa district attorney indicates that Murphy Kearns will be charged with involuntary manslaughter in the June first death of Victor Dancy later today. In a case that has sparked a major debate on whether or not the death was vigilante justice by Kearns or if he was protecting himself from a man that had caused his family major harm.

Prior to his questioning and subsequent arrest, Kearns released three phone calls that he recorded between himself and Dancy. Dancy's three calls are confrontational and laced with extreme profanity. He threatens to beat Kearns up and tells him to "rot in hell" during the calls.

Kearns also released the tape of his encounter with Dancy at the Lake Anna, VA lake house that Dancy was living in at the time of his death. In the tape Dancy once again threatens to kill both Kearns and his own wife, Leah Dancy. In a shocking development, Dancy also appears to take responsibility for the Atlantic Airlines and US Couriers collision above Vitaly, VA, on April 10th, which killed one hundred and forty-one passengers on the two flights. A flight attendant, Sandy Hatch, and Kearns' daughter, Isabella, were the only two survivors from either plane.

In his hometown of Pittsburgh, PA, groups of protestors have come out in support of Kearns being released without charge. Murphy Kearns is currently incarcerated in Louisa, VA, while his daughter recovers in Vitaly, VA, from injuries sustained during the accident. Kearns' daughter is currently recovering from a coma, which she awoke from on the same day as the death of Dancy. Leah Dancy has come out in full support of Kearns' release, calling her husband an "evil man."

Debate about what should happen to Kearns has raged across the world. His supporters, who strongly out-number his opponents, believe that he went to the house looking for an apology and was attacked by Dancy. Some also believe that he was warranted to kill Dancy in response to Victor Dancy's apparent criminal negligence, now speculated to be the primary contributing factor that lead to the death of Kearns' wife and son, in addition to another 139 passengers and crew. Kearns' detractors feel that he is a vigilante and that he didn't have the right to attack Dancy, no matter what the circumstances.

Members of Congress have weighed in on the debate on talk shows across the country. Senator Penn O'Neill of Oregon said, "Murphy Kearns and more importantly, his daughter Isabella, have been through enough. The man should be set free without consequence."

Murphy Kearns

Murph was taken aback to see the crowd of supporters outside of the courthouse for his arraignment in the death of Victor Dancy. He found out that there were supporters from Pittsburgh to Nags Head in the hundreds standing outside of the courthouse, picketing for his release. He saw some familiar faces like Pete, Johnny, Michelle Bowen, Steve Rodriguez, Sandy Hatch, victims' families of the collision, and Leah as he walked up to the Louisa courthouse door. But he was more surprised by the countless faces he didn't recognize. Some of the unknown faces had signs saying things like "Free Murphy Kearns" and "Justice is ALREADY done!" The roar of the crowd was thunderous as Murph was escorted past the crowd by a couple sheriffs' deputies. Murph appreciated the support, but he would have easily given it up to just be free and back by Isabella's side.

Murph's parents were in constant contact with him as he awaited his arraignment in the tiny jailhouse in Louisa. Everyday Isabella was doing better and remembering more. She was up and out of the bed, which took a little work. Murph could only imagine how hard it was for her to get her muscles moving after being in bed for so long, only turned occasionally with the aide of nurses. Isabella was very upset about not having her mother or father with her, but Murph was allowed to Skype with her several times a day. The sheriff's department was very accommodating as Murph sat in his holding cell and waited. They brought him comfortable pillows and blankets. They gave him access to the internet through a laptop, and they even brought him meals cooked by people in the area who supported him. One deputy went as far as to tell Murph that they were all supporting him, but that they had to do their jobs. Since the county prosecutor charged Murph with involuntary manslaughter, he had to stay with them until his arraignment, but the deputies were going to make that stay as pleasant as possible.

No matter how much support Murph received from his friends and supporters, he still couldn't get comfortable. His daughter needed him with her, and it killed him to be away from her. What was even worse for Murph was the fear of not knowing what was next for him. His lawyer told him that if he was convicted of involuntary manslaughter that he could spend up to eight years in jail, but the average time could be as short as five years. The lawyer figured that with good behavior, the most time Murph would spend in jail would be three years. Murph still felt that any time away from Isabella would be too much for her.

As Murph walked into the tiny courthouse in Louisa, he took a deep breath and took it all in. The antique courtroom with wooden benches, tables, and decor made him feel like he was stepping back into time to a courtroom more familiar to Harper Lee's in *To Kill a Mockingbird*. Though he hoped his lawyers had the same passion and control as Atticus Finch, he needed a better outcome than Tom Robinson's. It certainly seemed that he would have a friendlier courtroom of spectators.

Murph was so accustomed to the swarm of media around him that it became an afterthought to him. He was comforted by the quiet of a public space that the media weren't allowed into, except for one pool reporter and one pool photographer. He didn't want Isabella to ever see pictures of him in court.

Murph had to sit through a couple hearings that were on the judge's docket before they got to his arraignment. One hearing was about a man that vandalized his neighbor's John Deere tractor out of frustration about the neighbor's morning habit of five o'clock mowing. The second hearing was about a woman that was charged for stealing prescription medications from the drug store she worked at in Louisa. The woman looked to be in her seventies to Murph, and looked more like one of the Golden Girls than a pill-head. Midway through her hearing, the bailiff brought a stack of paper to the judge. The judge quickly looked at it and set it aside. It appeared that he had a second thought and looked at it again. He raised his glasses to his forehead to look through the packet, and Murph could tell that he was astonished by what he was reading. It took the old woman's hearing about fifteen more minutes to wrap up. As the judge kept staring towards the area where Murph was sitting, Murph could tell that the judge was itching to get through and get on with his hearing.

Judge Armstrong was younger than most judges, and he had a Deep South drawl. He spoke very slowly and made sure to annunciate all of his words. Murph could tell that he was enjoying the attention that Murph's case was getting, and he was eating up the pool reporter's presence in his courtroom. Murph doubted that reporters spent much time covering courtroom cases about vandalized tractors. Murph also doubted that this day's conduct was ever documented in any courtroom.

Leah Dancy

Leah decided to go to Louisa on the day of Murph's arraignment to show her support. The past couple days had been strangely filled with stresses, but also a release from her past. She found out that when Victor kicked her in the leg he completely tore her anterior cruciate ligament. She would require surgery to have it fixed, but the doctors wanted to wait until the swelling was completely gone. She was recovering quickly from the concussion, and she was glad to find out that her neck was fine and she wouldn't have to wear the brace.

The family had a very small funeral for Victor the day before Murph's hearing. The Louisa sheriff's department was able to get the autopsy done in three days, and the family wanted to immediately bury Victor as soon as his body was released. They kept the location of the service and burial quiet so the media would not invade their privacy. Leah decided not to bring Maddie to the funeral. There were no good memories her daughter would have as a legacy, and Leah didn't want the funeral to prolong her relationship with a dysfunctional and abusive father any longer. She wished she could wipe Victor from Maddie's consciousness of men and fathers. At the funeral, Leah didn't shed any tears. As the dirt was thrown on his casket, she felt a huge burden slowly lifting from her body. She didn't speak to Victor's father, who was noticeably upset, but she did give him a brief hug before she left. He had lost a son. She was still undecided about the future of her relationship with Victor, Sr., but she knew that she wanted a complete break from the entire Dancy family for at least a while.

Standing outside of the courthouse in Louisa, Leah was thrilled to meet Johnny Johnson and see Pete. She knew they were at the lake house when Victor died. Neither man was charged with anything since Murph told the authorities that they were outside and had no idea what was going on in the house. After watching Murph enter the courtroom, the three headed together to The Rusted Spoon to wait for the hearing to conclude. They spoke mainly about Murph, and never about Victor.

"I have spoken to him several times since he was arrested," said Pete. "They are treating him exceptionally well, but all he cares about is being with Isabella."

"They can't really charge him, can they?" Johnny asked, unsure of his question.

"There is a push, it's a small one, but there is a push from this crowd that says Murph is a vigilante. They say that if Murph doesn't get in trouble for this crime that people across the country will feel that they can take justice into their own hands," Pete answered.

Johnny said, "That's complete bullshit!" surprised at his own response. "It was an accident."

"How many people will ever suffer everything that Murph suffered at Victor's hands?" Leah asked. "Nobody ever will. Victor being gone is better for everybody involved!"

"It's great to hear that Isabella is recovering faster than anybody ever thought," Pete said. "Murph is relieved, but he wants to get her home to let them both try to move on with as normal of a life as they can."

"I don't know how easy that'll be with their celebrity. I don't think this will just be fifteen minutes of fame. Murph and Isabella are both familiar faces now across the country. I saw a poll that said Murph is more important than LeBron James, Taylor Swift, Harry Potter and even the president right now. He's a national hero!" Leah said.

In a vintage Johnny, he asked, "Who in the hell are LeBron James and Taylor Swift?"

"Dude," said Sweet Pete.

Leah spent the next several minutes explaining the Taylor Swift and Harry Potter phenomena to Johnny. As the hours passed, the three became silent waiting for news from the courtroom. When the reporter outside of the courtroom came on CNN, they were all dumbfounded to find out what she said.

Chapter 30

Murphy Kearns

Heavy air sat in a room with air conditioning ill-suited for the number of people in the courtroom that hazy morning. The bailiffs all sweated, and people fanned themselves with newspapers, docket pages, and hats. Upon closing with what would otherwise be the normal business of a day in this county courthouse, the judge mopped his brow and straightened his hair.

"I have a very surprising packet here in front of me from none other than the White House of the United States of America," Judge Armstrong said dramatically though his tone didn't display surprise at all.

Murph sat up straight in his seat in shock not expecting to hear those as the judge's first words. Everybody in the courtroom stopped completely. Judge Armstrong actually stood up to deliver the next part of what was now an impromptu performance. Murph wondered if the guy was auditioning for a television show, and this was his real chance to stand in the spotlight.

"President Jackson Reeves wrote a letter to the courthouse, along with some official paperwork that he has signed. I will present the contents of said letter to the courtroom now," Armstrong read, letting the ultimate syllables in "courthouse" and "signed" hang in the back of his throat before being projected from his diaphragm out into the tepid air. His pitch rose slightly as he finished.

"After considering the issues complicating the pending charge of involuntary manslaughter in the case of Victor Dancy and Murphy Kearns by the Louisa, Virginia, prosecuting office, I have come to the decision that it is appropriate for me to take what some may consider unprecedented action. I have been briefed completely of all of the circumstances of the death of Victor Dancy on June the first. My legal counsel has also thoroughly reviewed all documents of this very rare and unusual case. Let me first say that in no way do I support the killing of another human being or a vigilante murder. I do not find this to be the case in this particular death. Murphy Kearns appears to have protected himself from Victor Dancy, the same man who admitted to playing a major part in the collision of the Atlantic Airline and US Courier flights in April of this year. A man who had recently beaten two different women nearly to death, a man as addicted to drug and drink as he was to himself, a man who said he would never admit to having done wrong, to the public or himself.

The tragic collision over Vitaly, Virginia, two months ago prompted us to take action as a nation, passing sweeping legislation to ensure that those 141 Americans did not die in vain and to protect the millions of Americans that fly daily from that same fate. Congress and I truly believe that these laws will make flight control towers more capable, more responsive in the future, and we are putting a great deal of time and effort into making sure airlines and flight towers are able to work together in a more efficient way.

I had the chance to speak to Murphy Kearns in Vitaly. He is a good man, who deserves to be with his daughter, Isabella. The family has been through more in the past two months than anyone should have to deal with in a lifetime. He is not a vigilante killer. He is a hero that fought for his family. Therefore, I'm issuing a full presidential pardon and ordering that Murphy Kearns be released immediately with all charges in this instance removed from his permanent record. The enclosed documents grant the full pardon. Sincerely, Jackson Reeves, President of the United States of America." Judge Armstrong finished, leaving his mouth open as to let the "a" in "America" resonate while he watched his performance's effect on the crowd.

Murph sunk back into his chair, and the courtroom exhaled. Unsure whether he breathed as the judge read the letter from the president, Murph's breaths started shallow and then filled his chest. There was plenty of noise around him as he took in the judge's announcement. Murphy Kearns felt this force granted delivery and a certainty that his passage, Isabella's passage, was granted. He didn't hear the noises of astonishment around him. He didn't feel the pats on his back. He didn't notice the photographer rapidly snapping shots of him. Tears flowed freely, and he was in his own world. The judge's announcement, "Murphy Kearns, it looks like you are free to go. Congratulations and good luck!" went in one ear and out the other. The rest of his life with his daughter started immediately. It wasn't an easy passage, one without a wife and son, mother and brother, but it was assured. They were going to have to carry on with just the two of them. Murph really did not feel like he would ever be able to love another woman, and if so, never like he loved Maria. Murph sat for several minutes and breathed deeply as the tears turned to a smile.

"We are fine," Murph said to himself. "We will be fine."

Leah Dancy

Leah sat in amazement as the reporter informed the public that Murphy Kearns was going to be released on accord of clemency granted by President Jackson Reeves. The crowd behind the reporter outside of the courthouse a few blocks away was crazy with excitement. Leah looked at Pete and Johnny who both smiled as they watched the reporter. As the reporter finished, all three jumped up and gave each other a hug. They headed outside and jogged up Main Street Louisa to the courthouse. Eventually, Murph came out of the courthouse, avoided the reporters, spotted the three unlikely friends, and headed right their way. Leah hugged Murph without concern for what people might think about Victor Dancy's wife hugging the man that killed him. She felt Pete and Johnny join the hug.

Murph released their embrace and looked at the three of them. "Thank you for everything! Now take me to my daughter."

The four got in Pete's Range Rover and headed back through central Virginia to Williamsburg.

Chapter 31

Posted: June 06, 2009, 7:30 am

Carmen Paul/Williamsburg Daily Express

Williamsburg, VA - Yesterday afternoon, President Jackson Reeves sent a packet to the small courthouse in Louisa, VA, granting a presidential pardon for Murphy Kearns, which effectively frees him from any prosecution in the death of Victor Dancy.

The pardon grants clemency to Kearns, who was expected to be charged with involuntary manslaughter for the June first death of Dancy. Dancy was stabbed by Kearns at his lake house rental home on Lake Anna in Virginia. Kearns claims that he acted in self-defense. There are several recordings that have been released to the media of phone calls between Kearns and Dancy in addition to a recording of the fight between the two men at the lake house.

Members of the courtroom sat in silence as Judge Garrett Armstrong read the letter that President Reeves sent attached to the pardon. Similar to President Gerald Ford's pardon of President Richard Nixon, President Reeves granted this clemency before Kearns had been convicted of a crime. Kearns sat in the courtroom for several minutes after the letter was read in tears and apparent disbelief.

The news spread rapidly across the country, and there was minimal backlash against the president for his decision. The small faction that was concerned about it being a vigilante killing became quickly drowned out by the large majority that supported Kearns.

Kearns headed to the hospital in Williamsburg where another large crowd greeted him. He spent the rest of the day with his daughter in her hospital room. There has been word this morning that Kearns will give a brief statement to the media.

Murphy Kearns

Murph sat staring at Isabella for the entire night on the pullout couch in her hospital room. He sat in astonishment at everything they had been through. He was relieved to know that she was now able to make her way around the hospital. She spent a lot of her time playing with Trevin, who was still in the hospital, but not for long. Murph knew that it would be a hard road in front of the two, but the fact that he at least had Isabella with him made him feel much more optimistic about the future. He thought about Maria and Patrick a lot. He decided that he wanted to live a life that would honor the two. He wanted to continue doing volunteer work every week. He wanted to continue pursuing a career as a landscape architect and to establish his firm. Murph considered that advertising would be a little easier now that he was a household name. More than anything, Murph wanted to spend the rest of his life watching Isabella grow and cherish the time he had with her.

After dinner, Murph decided that it was time for a quick press statement. He made a few calls, including one to Carmen Paul from the Williamsburg Daily Express. He wanted to do it in Vitaly, so he rode with Pete to the projected memorial site and the place where he lost so much. There were hordes of media waiting for him, and a makeshift podium was already set up.

The sun set beautifully behind the trees outside of the old Campioni Chocolate Factory in Vitaly. Murph walked straight up to the podium from the car and began his statement.

"First off, I want to ask that there be no questions when I am done, and thank you all for coming. As you can imagine, the past two months have been incredibly trying for me. It's going to take my family a long time to recover from this. I ask that our privacy be respected as we try to repair our lives.

There is a long list of people I would like to thank for their help. It gives me such pleasure and relief knowing that I didn't have to endure any more separation from my daughter, Isabella. I would like to thank my parents and my brother for helping out with Isabella during the past two months. I appreciate the apologies from Michelle Bowen, Steve Rodriguez and the FAA for their parts in the collision. I have been very excited to follow the changes that are being made by the FAA and the federal government, because we all know that something like this can never happen again.

I would like to thank Gretchen Sanders and Sandy Hatch for being such strong women. Once again, I want to express my condolences to every family member of everyone that perished in the collision of the Atlantic Airlines and US Courier flights. These family members are heroes to their loved ones in their own right, and should be to the American people as well, as they, too, attempt to mend their families in the wake of all that has happened. It is the will to carry on in spite of the circumstances that should be regarded as heroic.

I would like to extend a huge thank you to three very close friends, who I hope I can call good friends for the rest of my life. Leah Dancy helped me out so much, and she is a wonderful woman who was put through way too much at the hands of Victor Dancy. Please respect her as she tries to carry on her life with her precious daughter. Pete Mitchell and Johnny Johnson, who I barely knew before this, have been at my side this whole time. I can't thank them enough for everything they have done.

Most of all, I would like to thank my family. Our dog, Rooney, who probably wants to get on with his life more than anybody, was a huge help. The big guy has been shuffled around everywhere for the past two months and has done more for me than most will ever know. I want to thank Maria for being the best wife a man could ask for. She was gorgeous both inside and out, and I will never find another woman like her because there aren't any out there. My son, Patrick, who was on this earth for far too short a time, was always a joy to be around. I will profoundly miss getting to see him grow. And lastly, I would like to thank the strongest and most beautiful human being I have ever met, my daughter Isabella."

As Murph spoke Pete opened the backdoor and let Isabella out of her car seat. She walked slowly over to Murph and gave him a big hug. He picked her up and turned back to the microphone. He could see the surprise on the faces of the members of the media. "Isabella would like to thank some people as well," Murph said.

"I wanna thank the doctors and nurses that helped me," Isabella said quietly as she leaned over to the microphone. "And I wanna thank my daddy," Isabella improvised, which both surprised and overjoyed Murph. The cameras flashed continuously at this unexpected guest. Murph leaned over and said the last things he would say to the reporters, "Lastly, I would like to thank everybody out there for all of the support! You all have been a huge part in helping me believe in the importance of standing up for what is right. Now my daughter and I are going to move on with our lives."

Murph turned and walked back to Pete's car ignoring the handful of questions shouted by eager reporters. He turned one more time holding Isabella in his arms, not to look at the reporters, but to look back at the site where so much wrong had happened. As the orange sky sat in the background, he didn't think of the horror he saw there on April tenth, but he thought about what a beautiful memorial site he was going to make it.

Chapter 32

Over the next year, Murph will take Isabella to a Pirates game and cross the Clemente Bridge in Pittsburgh. He will teach her about Roberto Clemente's character, his volunteer efforts, and his untimely death in an airplane on his way to help earthquake victims in Nicaragua. Murph will tell Isabella as they sit on the massive yellow bridge that her mother and younger brother also died as heroes. He will tell her how both her mommy and Patrick went to Heaven together, and that she shall see them again one day. He will take Isabella to the memorial service that they are finally able to have for Patrick and Maria.

Murph will take Isabella to meet Maddie, and they will enjoy spending time playing together and talking about Dora like there are no cares in the world. He will be glad to find out that Leah has moved on with her life by going back to school, something she always wanted to do. Leah will not have forgiven Victor, Sr. yet, but she will tell him that she may one day.

Murph and Isabella will invite Johnny Johnson to Pittsburgh for Christmas. The three of them will go to a Steelers game to see their new favorite quarterback, Big Ben Roethlisberger, carry his team to an easy win against the hated purple-people eating Baltimore Ravens. Johnny will bring a Santa Claus suit with him, and surprise Isabella on Christmas morning. Murph will think that Johnny looks funny with four stuffed pillows in the outfit, but Isabella won't notice them or won't care. She will be thrilled to know that Santa Claus actually visited her house on Christmas morning. They will not fill the void that Patrick and Maria leave that day, but the healing will have started. Johnny will get to meet Ms. Linker, and Murph will be very surprised to see how quickly the two older people hit it off.

In April, Isabella and Murph will go to the one year anniversary of the crash. Murph will be glad to know that Isabella still doesn't and probably never will remember the crash. The memorial will be close to completion incorporating all of the requests families of the victims want to memorialize their loved ones. He will join the same families that he ate with at Apple Alice's, but this time Isabella will be with him. She will love the cheeseburger, home fries, and chocolate pie in a way that most cannot enjoy such mundane pleasures.

Murph will see President Reeves and his family at the memorial dedication. It will be the first chance Murph gets to thank the president in person. The president's daughter will enjoy meeting Isabella. They will continue to write letters to each other throughout the year.

Murph will find great satisfaction and purpose in the playground that he designs for the memorial park. He will watch Isabella go up and down the winding and curving slides. Watching Isabella enjoy the slides will give Murph a sense of relief knowing that every time a kid uses the slides, Patrick will be off watching them from some cloud and smiling. Murph will walk by a volunteer center built at the park and named after Maria. The center will focus on keeping the park well-maintained and clean as well as offering outreach projects for kids in the community. It will be completely run by volunteers just like Maria would have loved.

Despite intent to let momentum carry him forward, Murph will be unable to avoid noting the lives of others impacted by the force of the collision. Michelle Bowen will go back and forth between states of depression, taking her own life nine months after the collision. Steve Rodriguez's wife will pass away, and, now alone, he will remain shaken by the crash. Sandy Hatch will survive a car wreck three months after the plane collision. She will write a *New York Times* bestselling book about surviving two near-death catastrophes in such a short time. Its message will be of the importance of connection to the people whose lives you intersect. There will be little more mention of them in the press, minor footnotes at best, and the Dancy's will fade into obscurity for most.

Murph will sometimes find himself washing his hands late at night or when he is alone with a vigor that he can't understand. His heart will race, and he will scrub, sometimes until his knuckles bleed, leaving dry cracked hands that he will be able to explain away as a consequence of his trade.

Duquesne will honor its sixty-one students by donating a large amount of money to the creation of the memorial. The Duquesne funds along with Congressional funding supported by President Reeves and the local representative for the memorial and other donations will be enough to make it a place for people of all ages to visit for generations. The park will bring joy.

J. McLain Callahan

Kearns Design will get so many business opportunities that Murph will have to turn some down, even after he hires several new employees, including Johnny. Isabella's college fund will far and away exceed what she will ever need to pay for college, so Murph will donate to scholarships for less-privileged students and to the effort to find a cure for leukemia.

Isabella and Murph will be thrilled to find Trevin in remission. They will visit Trevin and give him the Plasma Car that was meant for Patrick. Murph will enjoy watching Isabella and Trevin drive their new cars around the street in front of Trevin's house. Trevin will move on from Ironman to dressing up like Teenage Mutant Ninja Turtles, which Isabella will really like. Isabella will have moved on from Alice in Wonderland to Rapunzel. Isabella will move a little closer towards a normal life.

The FAA will close down the Williamsburg Regional Airport, and the government will introduce several new laws in an effort to prevent a collision from ever happening again on United States soil. The FAA will rewrite its policies on hiring practices and promotion.

After the funeral, Murph will take Isabella and Rooney to the Outer Banks, where Pete will have opened the newly finished Duck Resort. Murph and Isabella will stay at the resort for a week, and Rooney will enjoy the dog hotel named *Rooney's*. Pete will sweeten with age. Murph will see Pete sneak off with a younger woman one night when they are at the resort, and he will catch him smoking a joint another night. Pete will wake up late and go surfing every morning, or what he considers surfing. "Dude," Sweet Pete will say, "Dude."

Murph will finally take Isabella turtle egg hunting. They will go out to the shores of the Outer Banks to look for loggerhead eggs. They will get to see some actual turtle nests. After being out all night, they will witness the slow determination of a loggerhead turtle crawling through the sand. Murph will marvel at the odds a turtle overcomes to move forward, let alone protect the legacy of its species. Rooney will chase the turtle, while Murph and Isabella laugh at their companion. As Murph and Isabella scurry to corral the big guy in the early morning sun, a woman and her child will walk up laughing, too, and want to pet Rooney.

Murph will keep the spa and bed & breakfast gift receipts that were to be gifts for Maria, and he will begin to hope that maybe one day he will find somebody to give them to. He knows that he will never find anybody to replace Maria, nor will he want to, but he will hope to find happiness like theirs again someday.

Murph will be content to be with Isabella for the time being, though. Once again, Murph will say, "We will be fine!"